D0427083

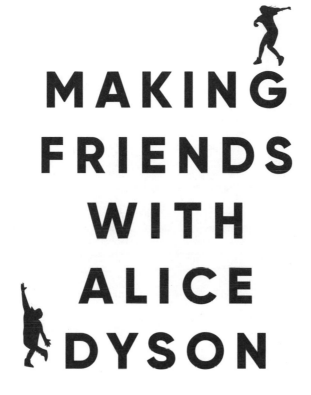

MAKING FRIENDS WITH ALICE DYSON

POPPY NWOSU

WALKER BOOKS

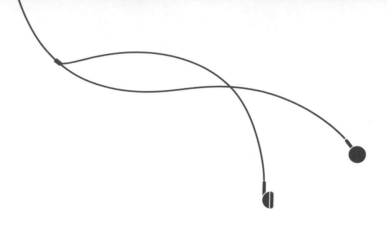

Copyright © 2018 by Poppy Nwosu

First US edition 2020
First published by Wakefield Press (Australia) 2018

Library of Congress Catalog Card Number pending
ISBN 978-1-5362-1478-9

20 21 22 23 24 25 LBM 10 9 8 7 6 5 4 3 2 1

Printed in Melrose Park, IL, USA

This book was typeset in Amasis MT Pro.

Walker Books US
a division of
Candlewick Press
99 Dover Street
Somerville, Massachusetts 02144

www.walkerbooksus.com

MIX
From responsible
sources
FSC® C103098

For my lovely Gus. You are my favorite.
And for my parents, the best in this world.
And the next.

chapter 1

ANYWHERE BUT HERE

Even before I reach the gate, it's obvious something is different.

A group of girls outside the school turns to stare, whispering as I walk inside. I glance over my shoulder as I slowly climb the building steps. What was that about?

Inside the hallway it's cool and dark, opposite to the burning sunshine outside. Our school is near the ocean, so even in the long, dark hallways, the scent of salt is strong. It invades everything, eating the gutters on the roof, biting into the teachers' cars outside. I swear even the tap water here tastes of salt.

Hushed whispers murmur from the lockers ahead.

"All she cares about is studying. It couldn't be her."

"It definitely was."

I step around the corner and the two girls shush each other, giggling. Soon they've scurried away to class, leaving me with an odd sensation blooming inside my chest.

It's not me. They weren't talking about me.

Still, I'm wary now as I unload my books into my locker. I keep glancing over my shoulder, but the hallway is empty. The bell has already rung, and suddenly it's as if I'm alone at school, the only person here. A strange feeling for me because I'm not normally late. I'm a really good student. I am usually on time and get good grades and no one ever has to reprimand me.

Except today is an odd day, nothing going as planned. Even with all the stress of rushing, though, I don't mind this feeling of being alone at school. Maybe that's why all those other kids are perpetually late. Maybe they're chasing this feeling, too.

I shrug it off and hurry to my first class, except when I open the door, a hurricane of noise drops into utter silence, a sea of faces all drawn to where I stand in the doorway.

Staring at me.

"What are you all doing?"

Startled, I jump at the irritated voice behind me.

"Stop blocking the doorway, Alice. Hurry up and sit down."

I do as Mr. Jenner says, sliding into my empty desk in the second row. I hang my head low and don't glance right or left. I don't look at anybody but still feel all of them looking at me.

Mr. Jenner starts the lesson on the history of our area, a topic I'd normally be absorbed by, but right now I'm barely listening. My cheeks burn, my gaze locked on my clasped hands on the desk. Because something is very wrong.

It *is* me.

Everyone is whispering about me.

My skin prickles, blood pounding in my ears harder and harder until I think I'll explode. A hand reaches across the aisle to stuff a small square of folded paper between my clenched fingers.

When I glance at May, she's already sitting straight and attentive at her desk again, eyes forward like nothing happened. I unfold the crumpled paper, reading the scrawled writing inside.

I need to tell you something. It's about you and Teddy Taualai.

I look at her sharply.

Teddy Taualai?

She knows what happened?

Stupid, stupid, stupid!

I glance around the room at the snickering faces and knowing smiles. Even Sophia is watching with a smirk. Sophia, who until this morning probably didn't even know I existed. Our eyes lock and she smiles even wider, until I swing back to face Mr. Jenner again, my cheeks burning hot.

I can't believe this is happening.

I didn't even do anything.

I sit agitated, feet tapping and hands clenching until finally—*finally*—the bell rings. It's chaos as everyone tries to leave, grabbing their books and yelling.

Mr. Jenner raises his voice over the mayhem. "Alice, can you stay a minute? I need to have a word with you."

I freeze while laughter and catcalls flood the room. A few

boys even slap my back as they walk past my desk on their way out.

Soon the classroom is empty, with only May still hovering in the open doorway, her face pale and pinched. Mr. Jenner sighs and waves her away. "I'm not going to bite her, May. I just want a word. You can wait outside. Go on; hurry up."

"Yes, Mr. Jenner."

May glances at me again, and then she is gone with a swish of her short dark hair, the door swinging shut behind her.

I sit still and awkward as Mr. Jenner clears his throat.

"Alice. I hope you understand, I'm not trying to embarrass you, but as your teacher and, I hope, a sort of mentor, I think it's my duty to speak with you about this."

He pauses to clear his throat again. It's pretty obvious he's feeling just as awkward as I am.

"You're consistently top of my class, and you never cause trouble. You clearly have a bright future ahead of you. This might not be my place, but I feel I should offer some guidance. And, well, you're normally so levelheaded."

He pauses and I hang my head, pulling off my glasses to rub my eyes. Hard. I can't believe I'm having this conversation with my teacher.

"I don't know what happened yesterday, and I don't want to know, but I'm aware the other kids are gossiping, and I think you should be mindful that students like Teddy Taualai are . . ."

I stiffen, waiting, but now Mr. Jenner doesn't seem to know what to say.

4

He coughs. "Well, I think it's very important you surround yourself with only good influences. Especially during such an important year. Don't you think?"

My voice is barely a whisper, skin hot and flushed. "Yes, Mr. Jenner."

He nods. "Okay. Good chat."

Yeah.

Great chat.

"Yes, Mr. Jenner."

He waves his hand. "Well, I suppose you can go now. If you want."

"Yes, Mr. Jenner." I shove my glasses back onto my face so quickly they hang crooked over one ear. I want to tell him I didn't actually do anything, but I also want to leave the room. Right now.

I choose the second option, and before he can say another word, I've grabbed my bag and am almost flying toward the door, throwing myself into the hall so quick I swear my feet don't even hit the ground.

I smack right into May. Hard. Clearly she was listening at the door. Both of us fall to the floor in an ungraceful jumble of arms and legs. May squeals as pens and books spill into the hallway right in front of a stampede of students migrating between classes.

I'm so embarrassed I don't know where to look. Everyone in the hall is staring at us. And whispering. About me.

I'm about to hyperventilate. I should be invisible. I don't

talk to anyone other than May. I don't have other friends. No one gossips about me because I never do anything worth gossiping about.

And that's exactly how I like it.

"Alice. Alice?" May is helping me collect my pens, scraping them into a big pile. "I need to talk to you . . ."

Her words trail off, and my hand, which is following a stray pencil rolling across the floor, stops dead right in front of two ratty green sneakers.

My gaze follows the shoes up over long legs to a towering figure.

I stand abruptly.

Tall, black eyes, messy hair, a permanent scowl on a permanently angry face. Our school's delinquent, a waster, the kind of boy who always sits at the back of class.

The kind of boy even popular people like Sophia are afraid of.

Teddy Taualai.

I move close to hiss at him beneath my breath. "This is all your fault." I resist the urge to stab my finger into his chest. "I can't believe you told everyone about yesterday."

Sudden silence stretches over everything. I turn slowly. A small crowd has gathered around us now, milling students all listening with bated breath, desperate to hear whatever it is I'm about to say to Teddy Taualai. I look around at them all, and finally I get it.

The nerd and the delinquent. The teacher's pet and the most violent boy in school.

I explode.

"What are you all looking at? Nothing even *happened*!"

I'm so shocked at myself that for a moment I can't do anything except stand there staring. But then the moment breaks, and I turn tail and run as fast as I can down the hall, leaving my bag behind. Leaving May calling after me.

And leaving stupid Teddy Taualai.

chapter 2

SEEDS

I'm out of breath by the time I find a quiet corner in one of the library cubicles, collapsing with my head in my hands. No matter how hard I try, I can't understand how everyone found out.

Not that there's anything to find out. Because nothing happened.

The idea of going back out there terrifies me. The idea of not being invisible anymore terrifies me.

I take a deep breath. Just stay calm.

"It's Alice, right?"

The voice startles me. Sophia is sitting on the desk next to mine, appearing like a ghost out of thin air. Two other girls from her group hang back near the doorway, waiting like guards.

Sophia is clearly here to see me. Which is ridiculous.

"Y-yeah. Y-yes. That's right." I stammer like an anxious little girl. Sophia's smile only grows wider.

"You should hear the rumors about you." She raises her brows. "What are you trying to do?"

I blink. "What do you mean?"

She holds her phone toward me as a blurry video begins to play. Two people wearing our school uniform, walking together along a boring suburban street. Completely normal. Ordinary. Except then . . . except . . .

"Dancing?" Sophia breathes. "Really?" She scrolls down the page to the comments, rolling her eyes at the sheer, mind-boggling number of them. "It's not even that cute. Look at all these people, acting like it's the most adorable thing ever. What a complete bunch of . . . Oh, wait—"

Her lips curl into a satisfied smile.

"Look at *this* comment. They said 'It was probably staged by an attention-seeking schoolgirl.'" She laughs and then lifts her eyes to mine. "You know, having everyone talk about you on the internet is different from actually being popular. I'm just warning you so you know."

She pulls the phone away, leaving me gaping.

"You should be careful." Sophia straightens her school skirt across long legs. "I'm not trying to be a bitch. I just want to help you. You shouldn't pretend to be something you're not. That's all I'm saying."

She smiles sweetly and hops off the desk, leaving me reeling at the absurdity of it all. Her two friends follow her from the library until I'm alone. The door swings shut with a loud click.

In seconds I'm on the internet, searching for it. And it's there. It's everywhere.

The video.

I watch it with my mouth hanging open. Read the comments with my hands in my hair.

How did this happen? Who filmed it?

The sheer number of people watching and sharing makes my throat squeeze tight. Their reactions range from weirdly infatuated to downright vicious. Even though I know what happens, I still watch to the end, watch as two idiotic school kids trade goofy awkward dance moves on an empty street.

A spur of the moment impulse. An anomaly in my structured, planned-out life.

A ridiculously enormous mistake.

The video finishes with me tearing away toward the train like an absolute lunatic, leaving Teddy Taualai standing on the road outside our school, staring after me.

I decide right then and there I'm going to find the person who filmed this. I'm going to find them and then I'll . . . I'll . . .

I'll figure that out when I get there. First things first.

Teddy Taualai.

I find him lounging outside the library, leaning over the railing of the second floor as if he doesn't have a care in the world. As soon as he sees me, he straightens with a rare smile.

"Alice—"

I cut him off, grabbing his arm to drag him through the library doors to the cool darkness within. No one's inside because class is about to start, but still I propel him toward the back, dragging him into the stacks so no one coming through the front door will see us.

"Everything okay?" he splutters. "You seem a bit . . ."

His voice trails off as I whirl around to face him. This time I don't resist the urge to wave an accusing finger at his wide-eyed face.

"No, I am not okay, *Teddy Taualai*! Have you heard what people are saying?"

He just shrugs. "Yeah, so?"

I flinch. "So? *So?* Everyone in the entire school has seen that stupid video, and they won't leave me alone."

He grins. "Yeah, I heard it even got on one of those news pages. You know, the homepages? Like it's actually news or something." He laughs as if he finds it all hilarious. "Harry told me it's gone viral overseas, too."

"What?"

I can't breathe. Overseas?

Everyone will harass me about this forever. I will never live it down. I think of Mr. Jenner. Will he tell my parents? The thought makes my insides twist.

"Hey, are you okay? You look kind of sick."

"This is all your fault, Teddy Taualai!" This time I really do stab him in the chest with my finger. Hard.

He rubs his hand over his collarbone where I hit him. "How is this my fault? And my name's just Teddy. You sound like a teacher."

"It *is* your fault. You probably took the video, too. You're trying to ruin my reputation."

He snorts. "I didn't take the stupid video. And also, what reputation? All you ever do is study. No one in this school even knows who you are."

"And you have no idea how hard I worked for it to be like that, Teddy *Taualai*. And now everyone is gossiping. About me. Even the teachers are hearing it."

"I think you're overreacting. Besides, as soon as something more exciting happens, everyone'll forget about it. You'll see."

"Don't patronize me! You have no idea what you're talking about. My parents will *kill* me if they find out about this." I put my hands over my mouth as that realization slowly sinks in.

He leans against a book cart, frowning. "Really?"

Taking deep breaths, I shrug. "Well, they're a bit intense about school stuff."

Teddy Taualai nods wisely. "Yeah, I'm getting that."

He pauses, watching me. Finally he shrugs. "Listen, like you said, nothing even happened, so who cares what people think? Everyone'll forget about it by the end of the week. And no one is gonna tell your parents. Unless, you know, they actually use the internet." He laughs as if he made a joke.

I scowl. "That's easy for you to say. You're a . . . a loser. A bad student. This isn't going to cause any problems for you."

"Hey, why am I a loser?" He looks offended. "And how do you know I'm a bad student?"

"Oh, come on," I say. "Everyone knows about you. You're practically famous for being scary."

"Excuse me? Scary?"

He seems surprised. Like maybe he didn't know this about himself. I frown at him, reassessing. Surely he must realize everyone at school is terrified of him. He walks around the hallways like he's inside a storm, all dark glares and angry eyebrows. No one wants to catch his eye in case he kills them.

I pause. "You really didn't know?"

Teddy Taualai makes a face that turns truly fierce and demands, "When did I ever do anything scary?"

I open my mouth to answer, but he holds up a hand to stop me.

"Not rumors. Tell me, when did *you* ever see me do anything scary?"

I shut my mouth again, thinking.

He *is* kind of loud at the back of class sometimes. And when he plays sports he can be a bit rough, but then so can a lot of the guys. And he swears a lot, but then everyone does that. Except for me. My father says swearing shows a lack of intelligence and a limited vocabulary.

"Oh! I know," I say suddenly, making him jump a little. "You gave Mr. Oliver the finger that time. When he said you'd never amount to anything. And you left class in the middle and slammed the door."

I'm triumphant, my point proved.

"Seriously?" Teddy Taualai stands straight, looking mad as hell, and actually he is quite terrifying. "That was nearly *three years ago*." He gestures furiously as he speaks. "And only that one time. I can't believe *that's* your evidence. Weak."

He scowls as he leans back. "Besides, that teacher was an absolute prick. What a dumb thing to say to a fourteen-year-old."

After a long moment I lean against the book cart beside him.

Well, that's true.

"He was a bit of a . . . prick." I blush a little, not accustomed to calling my teachers bad names.

Teddy Taualai grins at me. Leaning over, he gently nudges me with his elbow. "Actually, just so you know, I get really good grades."

I make a face at him. "You do not, Teddy Taualai. Don't lie to me. Everyone knows you're totally failing."

He shrugs, still smiling. "I'm not, though, but whatever."

I lean my head to the side, watching him. "Do you really not care what everyone thinks? I mean, because of the video."

"Nah, not really."

I bite my lip.

Interesting.

"And you really didn't take the video, then?" I ask again, just to be sure.

"Seriously, I said I didn't. Anyway, I'm *in* the video. How could I have filmed it?"

I shrug. "I don't know, one of your loud friends could have done it."

He laughs. "Yeah, I asked one of my *loud* friends to hide in the bushes and film me after school, just in case I happened to come across Alice the nerd and invite her into a freaking danceoff. Yup. That's what happened."

Alice the nerd?

"Hey, Teddy Taualai," I say, offended. "I don't know what you and your friends do for fun."

He raises his eyebrows. "Definitely not that."

I huff at him and start to stalk away.

"Hey, hey." He jogs after me, grabbing my arm to stop me. "Sorry, sorry. It was a joke." He grins, not letting go of my arm. "So what are you gonna do now?"

For a moment I just stare at him, because I have absolutely no idea. Except then I remember my resolution from earlier. "I'm going to find the person who filmed this, and I'm going to make them pay."

Teddy Taualai rolls his eyes. "I'm sorry I asked."

"And you're going to help me," I inform him, walking out the library door.

"What?"

chapter 3

QUEST

I feel a lot better after talking to Teddy Taualai. Maybe it's because I have direction now, a focus for my mortification, namely the finding and shaming of my video stalker.

With a clearer mind, I head off to my next class, not even feeling guilty about spending Chemistry hiding in the library with Teddy Taualai.

Well, not overly guilty, anyway.

I sit next to May in English. She's picked up all the stuff I left behind in the hallway because that's what best friends do. She hands me my bag, and I spread my books across the desk in readiness for class, glancing at her. I'm so grateful to have a friend like May. She's tiny and pale, with chin-length dark hair and a cute toothy smile. Not that she's smiling right now, of course. Instead she's gazing back with big haunted eyes, obviously still worried about me, and I nod to let her know I'm okay. Leaning across the space between our desks, I whisper, "Don't worry. I know what to do now."

She squeaks. "What do you mean, 'what to do?'"

"I just have to find the video stalker." I rest my hand reassuringly on her shoulder. "The one who filmed it. Once I've revealed who they are, everyone will be way too busy talking about them to even remember the whole"—I wave my hand dismissively—"dancing thing."

"Video *stalker*?" She gapes. "But there's something I—"

Our teacher walks in and cuts her off, and I sit attentively for the next hour while May fidgets beside me. I concentrate on keeping my head held high to prove to the teacher, and every other whispering, gossipy student in class, that no stupid rumor is going to derail my focus. I am on fire, a learning machine. And mostly I'm able to concentrate on the work at hand. And I hardly ever think of Teddy Taualai at all.

As soon as the bell rings, I sweep out of class. May tries to follow, but I don't want her dragged down by my problems, so I lose her among the whispering kids in the hallway and head outside onto the sunny oval. The fields reach right to the line of towering pine trees separating the grounds from the beach and the green, sparkling sea. It's beneath those big, shady pines that Sophia's group eats their lunch.

Sophia's rosebud mouth twists down when I walk toward them, but her boyfriend, Finn, smiles. I ignore him, though, and head toward one of Sophia's friends instead, one of the girls who stood guard in the library. She's small and sweet-looking, with round cheeks and curly hair. She goes home by train, too, and might have seen something. My hands are sweaty, chest tight and nervous. I force myself to smile. "Hi, Julie," I say.

"Um, hi, Alice." Julie glances at Sophia as if to ask for permission but receives nothing. Sophia turns her head away as I sit down beside Julie on the grass. Normally walking into this group would feel like approaching a pride of lions ready to devour me, yet somehow today I'm uncharacteristically brave. I mean, I'm still scared out of my mind, but I'm forcing myself through it.

So even though everyone is gossiping about me and apparently I'm known as "Alice the nerd," my voice still only shakes the smallest bit when I say, "You go home on the train usually, right?"

Julie bites her lip until Sophia rolls her eyes and makes a "whatever" kind of noise, which I guess means Julie is allowed to talk to me, because then she's really nice and tells me everything I want to know about what she might have seen, though it's not much. Just when we're done with our conversation, I spot Teddy Taualai way across the oval, jogging toward us. I wave at him and climb to my feet. Just as I'm about to leave, a laugh erupts, loud and derisive behind me.

Sophia. She's lounging on the grass like a cat, her long legs tanning in the sun. "You're not seriously hanging out with him now, are you? I thought you wanted to be popular."

All her friends slowly turn, one by one, to watch this new game unfold. One of the other girls even joins in the giggling, as if the idea of me being popular is hilarious. She manages to squeeze words out between her giggles. "You'll never be popular if you hang around with Teddy. He's a total freak."

I blink. "Freak?"

Finn nods. Unlike the others, he isn't smiling. "You know he nearly hit me when he first transferred here, right?"

I didn't know that.

Sophia leans back on the grass. "Such a freak."

Finn scowls. "I was just talking to him and then, bam, he pushed me against a locker and was about to punch my face. I'm lucky Lucas and Jamie Gorecki were there to pull him off."

The other giggling girl I don't know chimes in. "What a loser. They should've expelled him from *this* school, too."

I stand there staring at them as Teddy bounds up, coming to a halt beside me. He glances from me to Finn, who's smiling now like we share a secret. Teddy's eyebrows draw close and his face turns dark. "Come on. Let's go."

I let him pull me away as Sophia whispers something that has the others erupting into laughter behind us.

"What was that about?" Teddy glances back at the row of pine trees.

I don't answer at first, waiting until we're out of earshot, until we're nearly at the school building again. "I think Finn really hates you."

Teddy smirks. "Yeah, well, I know that."

I glance up at him. How can he be so calm about it? Finn

is really well liked at school, and everyone follows his lead. If he hates Teddy, everyone else will, too.

"Yeah, but *why* does he?" I probe. I'm curious now.

Teddy grins wide and shrugs. "He's just jealous of me for being too cool."

I stare at him. "That's the dumbest thing I ever heard, Teddy Taualai."

"I know, right? He's such an idiot."

"You're the idiot," I mutter, rolling my eyes. But I give up asking about it. I have way more important things to worry about right now anyway.

On the video stalker front, at least, I am getting somewhere. Teddy Taualai has a friend named Harry who, he tells me, apparently also takes the train home, though I've never noticed him on the platform. Harry is kind of excitable. He keeps asking questions about my investigation instead of actually answering any of mine about what he may or may not have seen from the train platform at precisely 3:25 p.m. yesterday afternoon.

It turns out Harry is a little obsessed with detective shows. My situation doesn't have much in common with any *CSI* episode I've ever seen though, so I'm glad when Teddy Taualai finally draws me away. The day is wearing on and I still have a lot more people to interrogate.

"Interrogate," scoffs Teddy Taualai when I tell him. And then he just goes ahead and drapes his arm over my shoulder as he says, "You're acting like this is serious or something."

"Get *off* me, Teddy Taualai!" I push his arm away. "It *is* serious. This is the only way to throw everyone's attention off me and get them to focus on something new."

"I told you already: by the end of the week everyone's gonna forget about it. Bet you ten bucks and an ice cream from the kiosk down the beach."

"What?"

But he's already pointing down the hall at Stacey Green. She's tall and pretty with long dark hair and one of the worst reputations in school. Or at least that's what all the boys like to whisper about her. She's also one of the students I asked Teddy to question for me.

"Hey, Stacey!" He tears off down the hallway toward her. "Stacey, wait!"

The poor girl is terrified, standing frozen in her tracks as Teddy Taualai hurtles toward her. I smother my laugh.

Nothing about this situation is funny, after all.

Later, I climb the stairs to the school's upper building and lug my heavy bag into an empty classroom. Teddy Taualai is already waiting inside, as arranged.

Hot afternoon sun burns bright through wide windows, yellow light flickering across the desks and floor. Teddy Taualai grins at me. "Hey, Sherlock. Whatcha find out this time?"

I drop my bag onto the floor with a thump.

"So Julie, Amy, and Theresa were all at the train platform

at 3:25 p.m. and none of them noticed anything out of the ordinary, though they all said they saw me nearly miss the train at 3:33 p.m."

Teddy Taualai raises his eyebrows. "Pretty specific, Sherlock."

"Stop calling me that. Anyway, your weird friend Harry and also Rhiannon reckon some girl was near the station who was maybe holding a phone, but neither remembers anything else about her, like if she was from this school or not, 'cause she wasn't wearing a uniform."

"Interesting." Teddy Taualai stands and rubs his chin with a flourish. He paces back and forth like a detective from a cartoon, one arm folded behind his back. I think he looks ridiculous.

"I spoke to a few people, too, like Stacey, for instance, but she knows nothing." He straightens. "Seriously, though, she was really unhelpful! She seems kind of . . ."

"Don't be mean!" I cut him off before he can say it. I know what everyone thinks of her.

Slutty. Stupid. Vapid.

People have a lot of nasty things to say about Stacey Green, though I've never heard her say anything nasty about anyone else. I glare at him, but he just seems confused.

"I didn't say anything, though."

True. But beside the point.

He shrugs, pacing again. Getting into the spirit of things. He clears his throat. "But I did go back and talk to Harry about the girl he saw, and he reckons she had short dark hair."

"Oh!" I'm getting excited now. "And?"

"And nothing. That's it. She had short dark hair."

I make a face at him. "Yeah, but was it like chin-length dark hair, or was it a pixie cut? What kind of dark was it? Black or brown?"

Teddy Taualai just stares at me. "Pixie-what? I don't know. It was dark and short." He gestures around his head in a completely useless way. "Oh, and Harry said she was wearing like a dress thing with a big design on the front that said *GS*. Like this." He waves his hand in front of his chest, presumably drawing a big *GS*.

Which is weird.

Until a thought pops into my head, like a giant flashing neon sign.

"Teddy Taualai—"

"Please stop calling me that. It's so weird."

I wave dismissively, deep in thought. "Tell me, what color did Harry say the girl's dress was? Was it yellow?"

Teddy Taualai snorts. "I'm not sure he noticed."

"Well, he should have. How can he be into detective stuff if he doesn't even notice details?"

Teddy Taualai tries to protest, but I hold my hand up to silence him. I'm onto something now; I can feel it.

"I think it *was* a yellow dress," I say. "If that's right, then the *GS* Harry saw probably stands for *goal shooter*, which would make it a netball uniform. And I happen to know that after school on Wednesdays, the Peninsula under-eighteen girls' team trains on our court. I think the mystery girl with the phone was a netball player."

Teddy Taualai is suitably impressed, but already a seed of doubt is unfurling within my mind.

I know someone who plays netball every Wednesday afternoon.

And the description: Short brown hair? On the netball team? A goal shooter?

I think it actually must be—

Right on cue, the classroom door bursts open and May throws herself into the room, a whirlwind of energy and stumbling steps. Her cheeks are wet with tears. "Alice! Where have you been? I've been looking everywhere for you!"

"May! I was . . . are you okay?"

She shakes her head, short dark hair tumbled and wild. "I've been trying to talk to you all day."

She hiccups, breathing heavily as she uses the heel of her hand to wipe at her eyes. She dissolves into a bout of heaving sobs and I wrap my arms around her shoulders. It only makes her cry harder. Teddy Taualai backs away toward the far wall of the classroom, as if May is a bomb about to explode.

"I'm sorry. I'm so, *so* sorry." May buries her face in my neck. Wet. "I didn't mean for it to be like this. I didn't know everyone would laugh at you. I never would've uploaded it if I'd known. I'm so sorry, Alice. I'm sorry. Please don't hate me."

She looks up at me with big, watery eyes and I hesitate. It's just the sort of thing May would do, act first without thinking of consequences. She's always been like that, ever since we were kids. But her face is scrunched up and her lashes are dripping, tears streaming down her cheeks. I hug her tighter. "It's okay. I'm not going to hate you."

At my words, May's sobs subside and she grows quieter, hands loosening their grip on my school shirt.

"Really?"

I nod, drawing her close again.

Soon Teddy Taualai is brave enough to venture back from the other side of the room, hovering nearby and fidgeting. I gesture at him from behind May's back, pointing from my sniffling friend to him and then back again. It takes ages for him to catch on, and by the time he does I've been waving my arm in the air and making faces at him like a lunatic.

"Oh! Yeah. It's um . . . totally fine. No harm or whatever." His face breaks into a grin. "Actually, it was funny. I ended up having a totally interesting day."

I scowl at him as May wipes her face.

She sniffs. "Neither of you is angry?"

Maybe I should be. Everyone was laughing at me, after all.

And it's not like I'm exactly excited at having gone viral, but . . . May's been my best friend forever. Me and her. Her and me. And when a best friend makes a mistake, you forgive them.

That's how you stay best friends.

I glance at Teddy and we both shake our heads.

May's relief is palpable.

"It's fine," I say. "I'm okay. I promise."

I am a little surprised to realize it's true. I *am* okay. And I don't say it aloud because Teddy Taualai would hear, but actually it *was* kind of funny. I suppose I had an interesting day, too. A break from my normal life.

Teddy Taualai asks, "Not that it matters, but how come you put it online? I'm just curious."

May pauses, cheeks flushing pink. She glances from me to Teddy, chewing on her lip. "Well, I was coming to find Alice before practice, just to say bye, but then you started dancing, and it was . . ." She trails off, face burning. "Well, actually I thought it was really cute. And I uploaded it on my Finsta, but I didn't know that Mia follows my Finsta, and she must have shared it and then everyone was sharing it and then . . . well, you know." She glances at Teddy Taualai shyly. "But it was cute."

"May!"

"It was!"

I want to say more because Teddy Taualai and I are most definitely *not* cute, but a car horn blares from the parking lot. May launches toward the door. "My mum! She's picking me up! I forgot. Oh man, oh man . . ."

The door slams behind her, and I see two of her books still lying on the floor. I sigh, reaching down to collect them, and tuck them into my own bag for safekeeping. I swing the whole heavy thing over my shoulder and step toward the door, turning to raise my eyebrows at Teddy Taualai before I go. "Well, see ya."

A flash of surprise runs across his face but then he bounds over and falls into step beside me. "What will you do now? There's no culprit for you to shame publicly."

I nod. That's true.

There's no way I'm going to make May feel any worse. And besides, I'm not that upset anymore.

I glance across at Teddy. Will tomorrow be just as bad? After all, I spent the entire day with Teddy Taualai and everyone saw. Even the teachers. Maybe that was a mistake, asking him to help. Maybe I've just made things worse.

I frown. He's a bit different from what I expected, though. Different from the rumors.

"Besides," Teddy Taualai is saying, "it was only dancing. Not exactly a big deal. Oh, and you know that Sophia is having some big party at her house this weekend, right?"

I look at him in surprise. "Were you invited to that?"

He snorts. "Of course not. I just mean, next week after her party there'll be a bunch of new gossip for everyone to talk about. This thing won't even be a blip on their radar by Monday." He grins. "Promise."

I watch him for a moment, thinking he might be right. He's kind of knowledgeable about these things, I suppose. Though *his* rumors have stuck around for nearly three years.

I shrug anyway.

"Okay, Teddy Taualai," I concede. "I'll trust you just this once. You may not be book smart like I am, but you seem to know a thing or two about school scandals, having had so many yourself and all."

He rolls his eyes. "I told you, I *am* book smart. I'm going to bring my report card in tomorrow and you're going to read it."

I scoff. "Whatever."

Late afternoon light spills through the empty hallways as we arrive at the main entrance of the school. Outside the clouds are tinted orange and the air carries the scent of salt. As we walk toward the train platform, Teddy smiles. "Today was fun. What do you want to do tomorrow?"

I turn and frown at him.

Maybe I do feel a tiny bit interested in Teddy Taualai and his rumors and his angry face, but tomorrow things are going back to normal. That is one thing I know for certain. I'll go to class and study hard, and slowly I'll become invisible again. I don't have time for anything else.

Even if it was a very interesting day.

chapter 4

AFTERWARD, ADAPTING

Teddy Taualai is everywhere.

I don't know how he does it, but I mean literally *everywhere*.

Obviously I always knew who he was. I must have passed him in the hallways a million times since he transferred here. We've probably been on the same teams for PE, and I know I share some of my classes with him. After all, we're both in the same year.

What I didn't know is that his locker is only two over from mine, that he shares my homeroom and art classes, that he likes to arrive at school at the exact same time I do, and that I sit right next to him in math class. Literally, *right next to him.* I'm not sure how I possibly could have not noticed before.

It distracts me, him fidgeting beside me. Am I really so unobservant? Is that the kind of person I am? Or maybe, just maybe, Teddy Taualai has started following me around since yesterday. It's possible he swapped desks, swapped lockers, swapped classes . . .

Nope.

May stands in front of my desk, shifting from foot to foot and complaining loudly about this flower-shaped clip that's gotten all knotted in her hair. Amid her whining, she tells me he was always there. She sits near the front of class in math, while my desk is closer to the back beside the windows. Despite how far away she is, even *she* noticed Teddy Taualai. Which makes me think I have an issue with my levels of observation.

As in, I have no levels.

Which is what May thinks. She says it in a nice way, but she still says it. And it's possibly true, but my good grades don't materialize out of thin air. They require focus.

I tell her this, but May doesn't care about school; she only cares about people.

Anyway, now I'm sitting beside Teddy Taualai in math class. The bell hasn't rung yet, and the teacher is nowhere to be seen. Every single person in class is shouting and going crazy. Two boys even shove each other in a sort of playful way, except it's not that playful because they manage to knock over a chair, which crashes loudly against the floor.

I'm trying to untangle May's flower hair clip while Teddy Taualai says, "Look, Alice, I brought my report card. See? I *told* you I have good grades."

I don't even look at him, but he keeps waving his paper in front of my face anyway. Until May shrieks because I've accidentally pulled too hard on her hair. Which is when Teddy's friend Harry decides to come hover over me, too, although I have only ever spoken to him once, yesterday. Even so, he stands close, like *really* close, invading my space and leaning all over my desk. He keeps offering advice on how to untangle May's hair clip, but really I think he's just trying to ogle down her shirt.

All of it makes me want to scream.

I don't, though.

Yet the feeling doesn't go away. Everything is just a little bit more overwhelming than my usual Friday routine, and suddenly I get this really odd feeling, like maybe I've opened a can of worms by dancing with Teddy Taualai. Maybe my life will never be the same again.

Or more specifically, my life will never be *peaceful* again.

Which is a terrifying thought.

When Ms. Breannie finally arrives, I'm relieved. She strides in the door already shouting at everyone to get back to their desks, and within moments both Harry and May have scampered off. The flower clip is still stuck in May's hair, bobbing up and down as she runs. As soon as everyone is settled, Ms. Breannie starts the lesson and I begin to feel calmer, more or less happy to be in math class where no one can bother me and I can study.

Math is pretty good. I used to find it difficult, but these

days it makes sense. I like numbers and I like the finality of it. You either learn it or you don't; you know the answer or you're wrong. It's easy in that way. Math isn't mysterious. With math, I know where I stand.

I look down at my desk, ready to write notes. Except I can't because Teddy Taualai's stupid report card is sitting on top of my textbook. I turn to him in disbelief, but he's all innocent and engrossed in Ms. Breannie's lecture.

I glance back down at his report card.

I can't believe he actually brought it in.

Ridiculous. Teddy Taualai is ridiculous.

Still, I read it.

At lunch May and I sit together on the oval, basking in the shade under one of the huge pine trees that line the wire fence of the school grounds. Beyond the fence lies a small quiet road and then some scrubby sand dunes leading toward the beach. The very tops of the frothing green waves are visible breaking across the sand, in constant motion as they lap the decaying gray wood of the jetty.

A breeze blows in, salty and cool, which helps a little with the heat. It doesn't help with the grass, though, which is burned dry and yellow on the oval, crisp beneath my fingertips. On the other side of the field, a bunch of students are playing soccer, leaving me more than a little impressed. Heat like this is best experienced from the shade, but none of them seem to care.

"Everyone's forgotten about it today," May says, sipping

juice. "I'm so glad. Yesterday was awful." Her cheeks flush a little. She's still feeling guilty.

I nod. "Yeah, it hasn't been that bad today. Maybe everyone is bored already."

None of that is strictly true. But I think May has been traumatized enough already, so I don't tell her about the two boys who shouted at me from the bus this morning. And I don't tell her about the completely inappropriate song Lucas sang at me as I walked from math to English class. I remember Lucas was one of those boys who got involved when Finn was almost in a fistfight with Teddy outside the lockers. With Lucas's floppy blond hair and goofy grin, I find it hard to imaging him doing anything as stupid as fighting. He did serenade me in the hallway, though, so maybe he's just an idiot.

I also don't tell her how odd it feels to transition overnight from a total nobody into the kind of girl boys sing to in the hallways. It's strange to suddenly be someone everyone knows—even the people I've never spoken to before.

Most of all, though, it's just plain weird to be the kind of girl that Teddy Taualai screams at from across the entire oval, "Hey Alice, I'm going to play soccer!"

Like I needed to know that.

Like I needed the entire student population on the oval to know that.

"He seems to think we're friends now," I explain to May as I open my sandwich, frowning as Teddy jogs across the field to join the game.

May giggles a bit before her face darkens. "Oh no. It's Emily."

I turn and sure enough, Emily Cooper, the school gossip, is stalking over to us.

May makes a face. "She kept asking me about the video yesterday. I bet she wants to talk to you about it, too."

"Why?" I ask blankly.

May waves her hand dismissively. "What do you mean, *why*? It's gossip, Alice. She wants to feel involved, that's all."

We both giggle a bit at that but straighten as Emily arrives, struggling to keep our faces blank. She sits down, entirely oblivious. Smiling at May, she basically ignores me. For the sake of May, I will try my best. But Emily grates my nerves. She's talented at it.

Like right now.

Catching me glance across the oval at Teddy Taualai, her eyes widen and she says, "You should be careful. He's really violent, you know. A total psycho. I know you think he's nice because he danced with you, but Alice, he only did that to get into your pants. You do know that, right?"

I frown, taking a long, calming sip of my drink.

"Seriously," she continues, her eyes bulging now, "everybody's saying the same thing. Why *else* would he hang around with someone like you?"

I grit my teeth, but she doesn't stop talking.

"Haven't you heard the rumors about him? About what he did?"

Emily stops and waits expectantly, but I just continue sipping on my water bottle.

"I don't know," May interjects, her voice flustered. "If you actually think about it, he hasn't really done anything bad since he transferred here."

I nod.

Teddy Taualai has a crazy reputation. And he's crazy. But I don't think he's a psycho.

"He *hurt* someone!" Emily's mouth twists. "He totally beat them up and sent them to the hospital." Leaning closer, she lowers her voice to a stage whisper, as if Teddy Taualai might hear her from waaaaay across the oval. "I heard it was his teacher. That's why he was expelled from his old school."

I roll my eyes.

"Emily, that was three years ago." May's still playing the mediator.

"So? He walks around looking like he wants to smack everyone. Even Finn's afraid of him. And I hear he's totally failing."

At this I do speak up.

"He isn't failing. He gets really good grades."

Emily scowls at me. "Oh, really? And you know that how? Don't tell me you're friends with that psycho now."

I glare at her, anger rising in my chest, making my throat constrict.

Five minutes ago, I probably wouldn't have said it. Five

minutes ago, I would have denied it for all I was worth. But here and now, in the face of Emily's stupid judgmental expression, I find myself nodding, like it's not a big deal to be friends with Teddy Taualai.

I lift my chin stubbornly. "So what if I *am* friends with him?"

Emily just laughs. "Do yourself a favor, Alice; don't ruin what little shred of reputation you have by hanging around with a psycho like him."

"Emily!" May's skin is flushed pink as she tries to shush Emily, clearly aware that this conversation is about to go downhill.

But it's too late.

"What's *wrong* with Teddy Taualai?" My voice rises despite myself. "You shouldn't say stuff like that. You've probably never even talked to him."

Emily looks like I've just slapped her in the face, her mouth hanging open slackly.

A surge of triumph rushes through my chest, because it serves her right.

Except . . .

Maybe she's a little *too* shocked, a bit *too* scared.

Abruptly she stumbles to her feet, her face burning bright red. She murmurs something about buying lunch and then rushes off, almost tripping over her own feet in her hurry to get away.

Slowly I turn around.

Sure enough, Teddy Taualai stands right behind me, looming like some sort of monstrous shadow, eyebrows drawn together and black eyes burning. He blocks out the sun, his face lost in shade, an impending hurricane about to break.

May and I glance at each other.

How much of our conversation has he overheard?

Just when I think he's going to explode, Teddy Taualai throws himself down on the dry grass instead, lounging back comfortably on his elbows as if he doesn't have a care in the world. May and I share another look as he begins stuffing an apple into his mouth, crunching and sweating after his soccer match, but never saying a word.

His gaze flicks to my face and then away again, over and over, until finally May breaks the horrifying silence.

She talks about some problem she had in her math home-work, her voice rambling on and on. I sit stiff and straight, commenting in all the right places, but at that moment all I want to do is hug her. She is infinitely better at dealing with people than I am; she's the type of girl who always knows what to do.

As Teddy Taualai continues to munch loudly on his stu-pid apple, I am just so thankful she's here. Because Teddy Taualai definitely heard.

Even so, he spends the rest of lunch sitting quietly beside me, so silently, in fact, that eventually May and I just for-get he's there. Soon we talk to each other like normal, as if Teddy Taualai didn't just hear Emily call him a psycho.

By the time lunch is over and we're walking back to our lockers, Teddy is back to his usual self, loudmouthed and overly familiar, as he chatters about his soccer game.

"Gross. You're sweaty and you stink." I glare at him, but he just shrugs.

"That's the price you gotta pay to be a soccer professional."

May giggles, clearly enjoying my discomfort.

"And anyway," he adds, "you're looking a bit sweaty yourself, Alice. Don't hate until you try to relate."

May's laughter explodes as I rub my hands over my face. "Shut up, Teddy Taualai. You are driving me crazy."

He grins at me, all close and in my face. "Yeah, but we're friends now, right? Isn't that what friends are for?" He turns to May, all innocence, with wide eyes. "That's right, isn't it?"

May nods eagerly like the traitor she is.

"Definitely," she declares. "Alice would waste away in the library if it wasn't for me. She'd seriously shrivel up and die. Friends are important for a girl like her."

"Excuse me?" I'm offended.

May reaches out and shakes Teddy's hand enthusiastically. "Welcome aboard, Teddy. It's a hard job, being Alice's friend, and I'm glad to have someone to share the burden with."

"Glad to be here, ma'am." Teddy's voice is ridiculously serious. He returns the handshake vigorously, and I roll my eyes at both of them.

When we reach our lockers, Teddy Taualai suddenly stiffens. "Oh man! Ms. Breannie!"

Both May and I jump from the sudden outburst, watching as he slams his locker open and drags books out in an explosion of paper and pens. Within seconds he sprints down the hallway, students throwing themselves against the walls to keep out of his way. As I watch him go, I wonder what's just happened.

Apparently now I'm friends with Teddy Taualai.

"I think it's a good thing," declares May like she's read my mind. "You need to open up to people. You can't stay locked in the library studying forever."

"It's not forever," I mumble. Here we go again. "It's just until the end of the year."

"Nuh-uh. You've been studying like crazy for three years now. You need change. This is our last year of high school!"

May's constantly saying strange stuff like this lately. It's like she's become fixated on it. She doesn't seem to get that the reason I'm working so hard at my studies is precisely *because* it's our last year of high school.

She suddenly clasps her hands against her cheeks. Very dramatic. "No, *I* need to change. High school's nearly over and I still haven't done any of the things girls are meant to do."

I stare at her blankly. "What things are we meant to do?"

She grabs my shoulders and shakes me. "Parties! Boys! I want my first kiss. I want to be popular!"

Popular?

That one is new.

"Why?" I ask, genuinely taken aback, but May just scowls.

She steps back from me. "This is all your fault, Alice Dyson. You never come shopping with me. You never want to go to parties. You never let me do your makeup."

"What about the girls you play netball with? Can't you do that stuff with them?"

She huffs at me. "No way! Those girls are really snobby." She says it in a way that makes me think it's May who's snobby. But then abruptly her mouth trembles and her pretty eyes glisten. "You know, Sophia is having a party this weekend at her house. We could go."

I am completely unmoved.

"Nope. I won't do it. And besides, high school isn't nearly over; it's still the start of the year. There's plenty of time for you to kiss some poor boy."

"You're like the Grinch," she says, the cutesy act clearly finished. "But one day you'll change your mind. You're going to ask me for help to make you look pretty, or you'll want me to go somewhere stupid with you and I'm going to remember this!"

I'm too busy to pay much attention to her.

I have big plans for next year, plans that I've been working toward for a very long time.

Nothing, and nobody, is going to get in my way.

The weekend passes by.

I spend my time working at the cinema and studying. May doesn't mention going to Sophia's party again, which, I might add, we weren't invited to anyway, but she does send some sad faces in a text on Saturday night, just to remind me that I said no. I think she's planning to wear me down with her sadness in hopes I'll go with her next time.

I won't, though.

On Monday morning, I see that Teddy Taualai was right.

When I get to school, all anyone can talk about is how Stacey Green made out with some guy at the party. There's even a photo, a big wet mess of glazed eyes and sloppy tongues, and everyone is laughing about it, whispering and pointing as Stacey walks through the halls. She hides beneath a curtain of long, dark hair, hunched over and alone, and I can't help but notice how no one seems to laugh or whisper at the boy she kissed.

No one cares that last Wednesday afternoon Teddy Taualai and I danced together after school.

No one even remembers it happened at all.

chapter 5

DISTANCE

A few weeks later, I'm in art class. I think I like it even more than math.

Which is surprising because I haven't been that interested in creative stuff over the last few years. I think it's because I don't like subjective things, yet somehow art has become one of my favorite subjects.

Maybe because it's the one subject, other than sports, that my parents don't care about me failing.

Except I'm not failing. Apparently I'm pretty good at it.

Or at least that's what Mrs. Kang says. I think she just wants to have one of those inspiring student/mentor relationships, like something out of a movie. It means I can't be sure if her encouragement is actually for me or for her to justify why she became a teacher in the first place. Because frankly, it's a pretty unforgiving job, and mostly no one listens to her at all.

Like right now.

Art class is everyone's favorite excuse to slack off. And they aren't ashamed of it, either.

Like my friends, for instance. Because apparently I have plural of those now.

We're meant to be expressing our inner selves via self-portrait, but instead Teddy Taualai's goofing around, wearing my glasses.

I don't even know how it happened, but May says Teddy looks much better in them than I do. Annoying. She also says she doesn't understand why I don't get contacts because glasses don't suit me. I glare in her general direction. I can still see her outline, her shape; it's just her features that blur. I reach toward Teddy Taualai to try to save my glasses from whatever hell he's planning next.

"Ouch! Alice, stop," he yelps. "You poked me in the eye."

I'm pretty sure I didn't.

He grabs my hand, whimpering like it's my fault he got hurt.

Infuriating.

"Give them back!"

Of course he doesn't.

He is so distracting.

It's been building up ever since the video. This feeling of almost . . .

Suffocation.

Everywhere I turn, it's always Teddy Taualai. Like there's

a *million* of him, all of them out to distract me from studying, or get me in trouble with Mr. Jenner. Or somehow make it so Sophia hates me. Two months ago, that girl didn't even know I existed, and now, because of Teddy Taualai, I think she actually wants to kill me. Me! Invisible, nerdy Alice.

It's inconceivable.

And Mr. Jenner! I remember when he told my parents I was his favorite student, but now everything is different.

And all I did was say Teddy and I are friends in front of Emily Cooper.

Which was clearly a huge mistake.

"I think you look strange when you're not wearing glasses," Teddy says in a thoughtful voice, looming with his head cocked to the side like he's assessing me.

"Give them back," I mutter. "I can't finish my picture without them. I get headaches. And class is nearly over."

But nothing I say ever gets through to him.

I sigh, annoyed that he won't give them back, annoyed that no matter what I do, I spend every single day like this, trying to fend off Teddy Taualai.

And Harry, too. Because being friends with Teddy apparently means I'm also friends with Harry Nguyen, who is currently yelling something about me being no fun. I swing around in my chair to scowl at him, too. Except when I turn back, I stiffen because Teddy has suddenly leaned really close, and whispers in a low voice, "Don't listen to him. And so you know, I don't agree with May. I think you look hot in glasses." He pushes them back on my face and the world flicks into focus as he grins widely at me.

Then he hops up and disappears to his own desk to finish his portrait.

My face burns after he's gone.

He is just so distracting. And so inappropriate.

I glance down at my drawing and begin working on it again as Teddy's voice echoes from the back of class, laughing loudly at whatever Harry just said. I swear, he never does any work. I have no idea how he gets such good grades.

I glare at him again over my shoulder for good measure.

I was always told that effort is the path to success. That's certainly what my dad believes, anyway. He uses it as his motto, and I've heard him say those words more times than I could ever count.

I try to imagine Teddy Taualai meeting my father. Or my mother.

Terrifying. Absolutely terrifying. Something that can never *ever* happen.

My parents would hate him. And I should, too, considering how much trouble he's caused me. I grit my teeth as I think back to last week, when he put a note on Sophia's back that had a big heart with SOPHIA LOVES MR. VIRK scrawled inside. Mr. Virk is our principal, so it was clearly just stupid, but I still ended up chasing her halfway down the hall trying to get it off. And by then people were giggling at her, and of course I was standing right behind her when she found it. So Sophia decided it was me who stuck the stupid thing there, and now I get the evil eye.

And then the week before that, I got in trouble with Mr. Jenner for making faces during class, even though Teddy Taualai totally started it, and I only did it that one time because he wouldn't stop. Infuriating.

And the week before *that,* Teddy recorded me humming while I was studying, and he changed his ringtone so whenever someone called him my voice would come bursting out sounding all whiny and off-key. It took me three days to convince him to change it back.

Excruciating!

"Alice. Hey, Alice."

It's May, waving her hands in front of my face to get my attention, snapping me awake.

"Hmm?"

She shoves her sketch onto my desk.

"What do you think?"

"Oh, it's . . . great." I'm trying to sound enthusiastic.

The corners of her mouth turn down. "What's wrong with it?"

I glance at the drawing, wondering if I can tell her it's basically a potato with hair. For some reason that thought has me on the verge of giggles. Quickly I choke them back. I must be hysterical, probably because of Teddy Taualai. My nerves are all over the place. Because he's driving me crazy.

I take a deep breath. "No, nothing. It looks really good. Is it finished?"

She glares at me. "That's the last time I ever show you one of my masterpieces, Alice Dyson. You're fired from being my friend!"

"I'm sorry! Really, it's just that I was surprised." I try to backtrack, but then Teddy is there, too, leaning in close to peer over my shoulder. Too close. It makes my body go all stiff and still.

"What is *that*?" He squints at the drawing.

May glares, but he snatches the picture out of my hand to examine it more closely.

"I dunno," he says seriously. "It's not bad. A bit potato-y, but not too bad, you know."

As soon as he says it I just explode with laughter, unable to suppress it. I press my head down on my desk and cover my face with my hands.

"Alice!"

"I'm sorry," I gasp. "I'm so sorry."

And of course Teddy is gone, and I'm left to deal with the aftermath alone. Which basically involves apologizing over and over again to May as she huffs about quitting art class. She does forgive me eventually, but the whole thing leaves me wondering why I spend so much of my time in weird situations these days, instead of just quietly getting through my last year of school.

Mrs. Kang calls out, trying to bring the class to order, and eventually the shouting dies down enough for her to talk. She's got a bunch of famous self-portrait examples, and she calls Teddy, of all people, up to the front to pass them around. While he's moving around the classroom, she holds up a van Gogh print and asks us what we think.

Of course no one answers, so I raise my hand and talk about his depression and the evidence left behind of what he might have been feeling when he painted it. It's not like it's anything profound. I just read it in the textbook.

But some idiots still whisper behind me.

"Nerd alert," shouts a boy from the back.

Everybody bursts into laughter. May's head is down, eyes locked on her desk, her cheeks flushed. I just sigh and ignore them, waiting for Mrs. Kang to calm them down, which she is clearly attempting to do. Except then Teddy Taualai says really loudly, "I like smart girls."

He stands there awkwardly, like he isn't quite sure what he just said. Of course everyone just explodes, jeering and taunting him. Some kid yells, "Lame!" and everyone laughs even harder, like it's the funniest thing ever.

Stupid.

Just when all the dancing gossip has finally died down, he goes and says something like that. If he thinks he's helping me, he's an idiot.

I scowl at my picture, a half-drawn outline of a head with a load of tiny shapes escaping it. It's odd, but it's a pretty accurate representation of how Teddy Taualai is driving me crazy.

Mrs. Kang likes it, too.

She says it's "expressive," and before class finishes she

holds it up for everyone else to see, saying that it clearly shows how my thoughts are trying to free themselves from the cage of my mind.

I don't know about that, but I'm glad she likes it, even if that does mean the class just whispers about me all over again. I sigh. Maybe I am a teacher's pet.

Before we leave, Mrs. Kang reminds us about the upcoming excursion to the art gallery in the city. She hands out permission slips and tells us about how fun and informative it will be.

"Both fun *and* informative?" Harry says in a fake high-pitched voice as we all pile into the hallway. "I can't even *wait!*"

"Well, I'm not going," announces May. She's still peeved about her drawing. "It's stupid. Anyway, I've been there before, last year."

"Yeah, I probably won't go either," agrees Harry straightaway. "It does sound pretty boring."

I watch the two of them from the corner of my eye as we walk down the stairs. Harry agrees with everything May says these days. I haven't figured out yet if she likes that or not, but she doesn't say no when he offers to buy her a drink from the snack bar.

Two weeks later, nothing has changed, and the suffocation feeling has only gotten worse.

Every day at school, the gossiping gets worse.

I hear from Emily Cooper that apparently Teddy and I are

dating and we sleep at each other's houses. I hear from May, who heard from Stacey Green, that Teddy's secretly cheating on me with May, and then the next day I hear that it's actually me who's cheating on him with Harry.

Every time I hear something new I grit my teeth and feel the air growing thicker, the walls getting closer together. Like I can't breathe. I haven't studied enough, haven't spent enough time preparing for exams, and some days I haven't even managed to finish my homework on time. None of which fits into my life plan at all.

I think Teddy Taualai might be ruining me.

"Are you gonna go?" Teddy falls into step beside me after math class, pulling his bag over his shoulders and juggling a water bottle in his hands like everything is totally fine.

"Go where?" I say in monotone. I am tired and worn out.

"To the art gallery. You know, for the excursion thing. You gonna go?"

I shrug. "Probably."

"You're into all that art stuff, right? What did she say, 'expressive'?" He grins at me.

"It's not hard; that's all." My voice turns defensive.

He doesn't notice, pressing his shoulder against mine and saying something about a math assignment. I'm not really listening, because suddenly I'm wary around him. Why am I encouraging this friendship when I don't want any complications in my life?

I almost stop walking.

Should I tell him to leave me alone? Is that best?

Yes, he's super distracting and annoying, but if he wasn't here, would I be better off?

Probably. Obviously.

Teddy is completely oblivious to my discomfort. He keeps rambling on about something that happened in the morning, and it's all I can do to answer in the right places.

"Did you see what Andrew was trying to mix together in Chemistry?"

"No."

"I think it might have actually exploded if Kramer hadn't been so quick to stop him." He gestures manically with his hands, almost dropping his water bottle.

"I don't think it would have."

"You should have *seen* his face! Kramer nearly had a heart attack, poor dude."

"No, it wouldn't."

Teddy glances down at me.

"Are you even listening?" He stops suddenly and grabs both my shoulders, shaking me. "Wake up, Alice! What's going on with you?"

I pull away. Hard.

"Nothing! Nothing's wrong. I'm just going to the library to study."

I take a step backward away from him, and then I just blurt it out.

"Don't follow me, all right?" I'm breathing heavily, still

backing away. "I don't need friends like you, Teddy Taualai. Just *stay away* from me!"

He stops, opens his mouth to say something but then just closes it again, his cheeks slowly turning pink and his body growing still. A swell of sickness twists in my gut as I back away down the hall, leaving him frozen there. None of it feels right, not how I thought it would. Which doesn't make any sense.

The library is empty and quiet when I arrive. Which should be a good thing; it's what I need, peace and quiet. It's what I wanted.

But I keep thinking about Teddy Taualai and his black eyes. It wasn't hurt I saw. It was some other thing.

I take a deep breath and pull out my books, glancing through the window to the sky outside. Already the weather is changing. It's still warm, and the days are hot and long, but somehow there's a new feeling in the air as winter draws nearer.

chapter 6

SAFE

The house is dark and cool when I get home from school. Empty. Cavernous. I drop my bag on a stool near our breakfast island just as my phone buzzes loudly. Fishing it from my pocket, I clear my throat. "Hi, Mum."

"You home, hon?"

"Uh-huh."

"Good. Your father and I will be a bit late tonight."

My belly clenches even though I already knew they would be. "Oh."

"We told you we have that important dinner." Her frown is almost palpable through the phone.

"I remember." I open the fridge, searching for something to cook. Sauce. Vegetables. Pasta.

Pasta it is. Pasta for one.

I sigh. But I don't let Mum hear it. "When will you come home?"

"Late, honey. Don't wait up." She sounds a little distracted, a horn honking in the distance. They're clearly driving somewhere. Stuck in traffic. "Will you be all right on your own?"

That almost elicits a giggle. "Obviously," is all I say. My parents are out. It isn't the end of the world. Besides, they're always out. "I'm used to it."

I wish I hadn't said it, because from her sharp intake of breath, I know immediately what's coming next. "Alice, you know my work is important to me. And we've got the mortgage to pay."

I glance around the empty open rooms of our house, the blush of sunset shining against the windowpanes. Big. Quiet. Deserted. I shut the fridge, giving up on my pasta mission. "I understand, Mum. Sorry."

"Good, hon. Thank you." I'm not sure if she's talking to me or my dad, but she sounds mollified, so that's good. "What will you do tonight?"

That question is definitely aimed at me. "Study, I guess."

Like I always do. A big quiet house is perfect for studying.

And studying is important, because it sucked back when my grades weren't so good. It made things really difficult.

"Excellent," Mum says. Muffled laughter comes through as she whispers to Dad, "Our daughter takes after me. Ambitious, that one."

A small smile creeps across my lips. I like it when she says that. I like it even though it isn't true. Not that I'll ever tell her that.

"You alone?"

I rummage around in the pantry, pull out bread and peanut butter. "Of course."

"Good girl." She pauses. "You should hear what Celeste's stepdaughter did. Apparently she vandalized school property with some boy and got a suspension."

I cradle my phone in the crook of my shoulder, muscles straining as I quickly spread peanut butter on my bread. "Who's Celeste again?"

Mum makes an annoyed noise, like it doesn't matter. "A colleague. That's not the point."

I know what the point is.

The point is I'm the perfect daughter. And Celeste's stepdaughter isn't.

I never do anything wrong. And Celeste's stepdaughter does.

I am particularly *not* the kind of girl who dances with a boy in a viral video and then struggles to get her homework done because he won't leave her alone.

"I better go," I breathe into the phone. "I've got loads of work to do."

"Okay. Don't stay up late. Work hard."

She tells me she loves me. And then she clicks off.

I shove the sandwich into my mouth, eat quickly. I do have a lot of work to do. A lot of catching up. My parents want me to go to university and get a good job. If I work hard, then I think I can make them happy. And that's all I want.

At least until school finishes.

I'm not sure how they'll feel after that.

That's why it's good I told Teddy Taualai to leave me alone. Really good.

And it's also good I've managed to keep him away from my house. It's still a sanctuary of peace and quiet. I tell myself that, and don't even think about Teddy once, not even about how his cheeks went pink and he stopped looking at me.

Sighing, I grab a drink from the fridge and am climbing the stairs to my bedroom when the doorbell rings. I freeze, immediately thinking it must be Teddy Taualai. But then I remember he doesn't know where I live.

And he probably wouldn't want to see me now anyway.

Balancing my math textbook and glass of juice against my chest, I open the door. May stands on the doorstep, smiling brightly at me.

"I've come to visit," she announces, even though she almost never comes to my house. Before I can say anything, she bursts inside and practically runs up the stairs to my room.

"May," I yell after her. "Come back down here!"

"No!"

"I have to study," I complain loudly, but I still close the front door and follow her up the stairs. I'm secretly glad to see her. The house feels less empty now.

Upstairs I find May already sprawled out across my bed. She smiles at me, the sea breeze from the open window ruffling her hair.

"Your parents aren't here? Are they working?"

She pushes some of my books down onto the floor to make more room for herself, and I frown as I pick them up. "Yeah."

"Oh, that's too bad." She squirms about my bed dreamily, distracted. "Although I wish *my* parents would work late. It must be nice to get the whole house to yourself all the time. Not that you would ever use it properly, though." She suddenly sits up, her eyes wide. "Alice, we should have a party!"

I gape at her and she quickly backtracks. "Oh no, I just mean a little one, like after school. We could invite Harry and Teddy and maybe Stacey and some of those other girls, like Julie and Sophia."

"That will never ever happen." I cut her off before she gets too carried away. "I mean it. I'll kill you if you ever try to bring anyone here after school. My parents don't like me bringing friends home. They say it's disruptive."

"Pssh, what do they know?" she says dismissively. "Having a social experience is part of high school, too. It teaches you how to relate to other people. How do they expect you to get a good job and network or whatever it is they do if you can't even handle talking to Stacey Green at school?"

I blink.

She does kind of have a point.

"And what about job interviews?" May continues, sliding over to the edge of my bed. "How are you gonna handle the questions and the *scrutiny* of job interviews? Huh? You always avoid people you don't know."

I'm discomfited by how much sense she's making. I wonder if my parents have ever thought of it this way. Somehow I doubt it.

I must look upset because May laughs. "Alice, calm down. I'm making it sound worse than it is."

She bounds off the bed and hugs me. "You're fine with people, really, when you try. Look at how you met Teddy. You weren't shy then, were you?"

I nod.

May's right. On that one strange day, I connected with Teddy Taualai just fine.

Which is why I haven't told her what I said to him.

May loves how different her school life is now. For her I think it's a dream come true. She loves that she has more friends, like an actual potential friend *group* instead of just me. And though her new group of friends may not be a particularly popular one, which I'm starting to believe is her *real* dream, she still credits Teddy Taualai for being the first person to draw us out of our self-imposed high school isolation.

Or that's how she puts it, anyway.

May throws herself back on the bed and gives me the side-eye.

"I think you can easily talk to other people if you want to." She shrugs. "I just don't really think that you do. *Want* to, I mean."

She says it in such a matter-of-fact way. But her words sound like I'm a terrible person who doesn't care about anyone else. I know that's not what she meant, yet I can't help but think of Teddy's expression at school.

A kind of heaviness weighs me down, and I slump on the bed beside her.

"It's not that I don't like people," I say slowly, wanting to explain. "It's just that I'm busy. There's so much I've got to do and people are . . . distracting."

May smiles. "Like Teddy?"

I nod, immediately exasperated just by thinking of him. "He's the worst! I can't get anything done when he's around."

May doesn't say anything, but she's being weird now, smiling at me in a knowing way.

"What?" I snap.

Raising her hands in mock surrender she answers, "Nothing. I didn't say anything."

She sidles closer to me, batting her eyelashes as she adds, "Look, I can help if you want. I can totally organize your social activities!"

"May." I roll my eyes. I knew this whole conversation was driving somewhere. We've come right back around to the party thing. "No. I don't want anyone coming here. I told you, my parents would kill me."

"But it's for your education, Alice! Your *social* education. You *need* this."

I can't help but burst out laughing. She is not a subtle girl.

"Nice try." I clap at her in mock admiration. "That was truly a good solid try."

She giggles now, too, and that's when it's clear she's admitting failure.

She sighs. "Well, I did my best." She flops back on the bed. "At least now I can die with no regrets."

"They can write that on your tombstone," I mutter, lifting my hands to gesture in the air like a banner. "'She did her best.'"

May giggles.

I giggle, too. Then I wrinkle my nose. "Is that actually why you came to visit me? To convince me to wreck my parents' house with a party?"

"I *told* you, it would only be small." She pouts and sits up, but then her expression abruptly turns serious. "But no, actually, I wanted to tell you something. About Harry."

"What, that you've finally decided to go out with him?"

Her eyes grow wide. "How did you know?"

I shrug. "I didn't know. I just guessed."

What else could she possibly want to tell me about Harry, after all?

May nods. "He likes me and he's funny, so I thought, why not?"

"Well, I guess that's as good a reason as any," I say carefully.

Actually, it sounds like a terrible reason to me, but who am I to tell May that? I don't know anything about feelings or boys, and even if I did, I don't think May would listen to me.

Still, I'm not sure if she really likes Harry all that much.

Sure, as a friend she likes him fine. But more than that? Maybe she just likes the way *he* likes her. She likes the fact that it's not just her and me all alone at school every day.

But of course when May sets her mind to something, there's no stopping her.

And within a week my best friend has experienced her first boyfriend, her first kiss, and then immediately after, her first break-up.

chapter 7

ON MY MIND

I don't talk to Teddy Taualai that week.

He doesn't come find me during lunch, he doesn't sit near me in PE, and he doesn't turn up suddenly at the library to annoy me while I study.

Whenever I pass him in the hallway he acts just fine. Normal. He laughs with Harry in class and shouts loudly on the oval playing soccer. Just like he always does.

But it doesn't feel normal.

Which just makes me annoyed at myself. Because when did having loud and infuriating Teddy Taualai around become my normal? I should be relieved he's taken the hint and backed off because that's exactly what I wanted. It's *exactly* why I said what I did.

Yet somehow I'm not relieved.

I end up dreading math class, because the more I think about it, the worse I feel about sitting right next to him for that whole hour after what I said. Which is ridiculous, because I haven't done anything wrong.

Still, today I try to think of a way out of it, a reason for me to skip class and go home.

Am I sick? I could go to the nurse's office.

Maybe my parents need me at home.

Could I write a note to excuse myself?

Or maybe I could just not show up at all.

But of course I go.

I hardly ever miss class, no matter how I feel. And besides, to miss class because of *this*, because of Teddy Taualai and his blushing cheeks and strange expression . . . it would defeat my goal of focusing on school.

So I go, and Teddy walks in just after I do and flops down at the desk right beside me. He doesn't say anything, doesn't ignore me either, but he definitely doesn't talk to me, and I am a bit confused because I never noticed before how close our desks are. So close that when he bends down to pull his books from his bag, his messy hair almost brushes my arm.

Almost.

I spend the lesson staring straight ahead at the board, aware of May turning around in her seat to frown at me, and more aware of Teddy sitting beside me, his body lounging across his desk like everything is totally fine. He seems bigger now than I remember him being, and when he turns the pages of his textbook I feel like his arm will touch mine, skin on skin.

But of course it never does.

"Bye, Alice."

I look up, startled that class has already finished and Teddy is on his feet, that he's swinging his bag over his shoulder, ready to go. He kind of smiles when he says it, and it seems casual, but really I think it might be strained.

"Bye," I answer, but he's already walking off, the bell ringing loudly as everyone scurries to pick up their things and get out as fast as they can.

"What's going on with you guys?"

It's May. She watches Teddy Taualai as he disappears into the hallway, swallowed by the stream of kids outside.

"Nothing," I say uncertainly. Suddenly I realize that I'm still sitting at my desk, my math stuff lying unorganized and unpacked before me, and quickly I grab my bag and shove it all in.

"It didn't look like nothing," May says. "Did you do something to him?"

I snap my head up, my face flushed.

"Why me?" I retort. "Why do you think it was *me* who did something? Maybe it was him."

May frowns. "Sorry, I was only asking." She takes a step back, as if I'm making her nervous. "It's just, he's been acting weird, so I thought . . . never mind."

"*He's* the one who keeps getting me into trouble," I snap defensively. "*He's* the one who keeps doing stuff to *me*."

"Okay, okay! Sorry."

64

I know I'm being mean; I know it. And even worse, I know she's right.

It *is* my fault.

I *did* do something to Teddy Taualai.

May shifts on her feet in silence, and then finally asks, "Alice, is everything okay?"

I nod, my focus locked onto my bag as I say words meant to convince myself as much as her. "Yeah, everything's fine. Nothing happened."

I stand up, wondering why I'm so good at hurting people.

May has been my best friend since kindergarten. We're really different, but she's always been there for me. She's the only real friend I've ever had.

It's just that things feel as if they're surging forward, out of my control. And I like being in control. I know that May is better at embracing change than I am. Lately I've been watching her, and I think she craves it.

Which is kind of hard for me to understand.

But still, she's my best friend. She always will be.

A surge of emotion rises in my chest, and I lean in and hug her.

"I'm really sorry," I whisper. "You didn't say anything wrong. I think I'm just tired, that's all."

I try to smile when I pull away, and though she's still clearly curious, she doesn't ask me anything else.

I'm glad. I don't know what I would say. The whole thing makes me sick.

We walk to our lockers, and as I open mine to stack my books in, May asks, "You're not gonna go on the excursion anymore? You were so excited about it in class."

I frown over at her. "What do you mean? Of course I'm going."

"Well, it's now, isn't it? Everybody probably left already." She glances at her watch.

"They've gone?"

"Yeah, like fifteen minutes ago."

I slam my locker shut, pulling my backpack on as I stumble down the hall. I yell over my shoulder, "I can still make the train if I run!"

Then I stop dead in the hall and turn back around to face her.

"I'm sorry, May," I call, and am relieved when she smiles.

"Go on," she orders. "You'll miss your train!"

I nod, and then I'm tearing through the school toward the front gate, bursting onto the quiet street outside, my feet slapping loudly against the cracked pavement all the way to the station.

By the time I get there, it is a race between me and the train. I win, just managing to slide through the doors of the end car before the automated voice tells us all to stand clear. I collapse onto an empty seat as the train pulls out, my chest heaving as I try to remember how to breathe. Pushing my bag away from me, I wipe the sweat from my forehead and sit there recovering for a few moments, resting and filling my lungs slowly.

By the time the train stops at the next station, I can move again, and I take the opportunity to slip through the door into the next car, searching for Mrs. Kang and my classmates.

The car is packed with people, mostly kids from my art class, but also a lot of randos heading into the city. As the train begins moving again, I shuffle up the aisle, running my fingers over the tops of the seats to keep my balance.

"Alice!"

It's Mrs. Kang, waving at me from the front of the car. "Good, you made it. Take a seat and I'll add you to the list." She smiles at me and then begins writing in her notebook as I glance around for a spare seat.

There are two of them.

One is in a six-seater booth already occupied by sweet-looking, curly-haired Julie and some of her friends, and the other is near the door next to Teddy Taualai.

Of course he is alone. He glances at me and then quickly turns back to the window.

I stand uncertainly for a moment, and then I take a deep breath, May's words still ringing in my ears. *Did you do something to him?*

Yes. I did.

I said something awful to him. Just like gossipy Emily Cooper did out on the oval, nearly three months ago.

I take a deep breath and walk across the heaving floor to his side, hovering awkwardly, trying to get up the guts to speak.

"Can I sit here?" I ask eventually, fidgeting with my back-pack straps, waiting for him to say no.

He immediately jumps to his feet, moving out of my way so I can sit at the window seat. I am taken aback, because I thought he might want to yell at me, or at least talk about it.

But he doesn't.

He just stays silent, sitting down after I've settled in next to him. After a while he pulls his bag closer and leans down to muck around with it for ages, the silence growing thick between us. I don't think he's even doing anything, just pretending to be busy. Finally he stops and then we just sit quietly, listening to everyone else as they shout and laugh, their noise washing through the train like a wave.

I don't know what to say, so I stare out the window, watching as the suburbs flash by. We pass flat dusty lots with towering silos and empty warehouses, and then the cement factory looms up beside the Port River, dominating the sky-line. The sheer walls of it whizz by. I can't help but think how odd it is that a factory this size is nestled right here in the middle of all these tiny little houses and tiny little streets.

We pass the river, and though they're not visible from the train, I know immense ships float like iron giants in the water, ships that have traveled from faraway places I can only dream of. Faraway places I'm always dreaming of.

Time crawls by, and I still don't know what to say to Teddy Taualai.

I can feel him beside me, watching the window, too, now,

and I don't want to turn toward him in case I meet his eye. It's strange because I've never once felt awkward around him before, back when we were friends and he was driving me crazy. Back then talking to him had been easy. I never had to try to think of things to say.

It makes me wonder if maybe being friends with Teddy Taualai hadn't been that hard after all.

"Here," he says suddenly, startling me.

He's holding out one side of his earbuds to me. They're not the big red headphones he usually wears, just normal iPhone ones. He fidgets as he pushes it toward me, as if he's nervous. Slowly I reach out and take it, placing it carefully in my ear. When I do, his mouth curls into a small crooked smile and he puts the other one in his own ear. He fiddles with his phone for a moment before music begins to play.

I readjust the earbud and turn back to the window, letting the music wash over me, instrumental and electronic. I watch the tops of houses grow smaller as the train climbs over the highway, revealing messy backyards and the asbestos roof of a crumbling warehouse.

We don't talk, and the longer we sit there the more nervous I feel.

I can't stop thinking about what I said.

I can't stop thinking about how Emily Cooper called him a psycho months ago and how what I did was even worse, because I was his friend when I did it.

When we reach the city, the train draws into the central

station, moving alongside a glittering research building, the structure made of glass like a surreal looming beehive. We pass under the road into the darkness of the tunnels, and the inside of the train slowly fills with shadows as our eyes adjust after the brightness from outside.

As the train begins to slow, rolling almost to a stop, everything bubbles up inside me, swelling and growing. If I don't say something now, I'll never do it. I'll just feel guilty forever.

"I'm really sorry about what I said," I blurt into the darkness. "I do want to be your friend."

He can't see my face, and everyone else is being so loud, so I don't even know if he's heard me. But then he reaches out and takes the earbud back, pushing my hair from my ear carefully, his hand lingering against my skin.

My body tenses at his touch. Except then I see that he's grinning, obviously aware of how uncomfortable he makes me. And at first that annoys the hell out of me, but then I think it must mean he's forgiven me, and I'm amazed at how easily we've returned to being friends.

Though somehow it's different this time. Maybe because it wasn't an accident that I said it. This time I chose it for myself.

I chose to be Teddy Taualai's friend.

chapter 8

TWO THINGS

The gallery is an old building. Enormous pillars rise up at the front as if it's some old Roman temple, completely at odds with the eucalyptus trees lining the street outside.

The whole length of the street is a bit like that, though, lined with all the city's oldest buildings, the kind that look like they should be in London, not here surrounded by gum trees and fig trees whose roots crack through the pavement from beneath.

But I think they are beautiful all the same.

Inside the gallery it is cool and cavernous, the roof high and curved, with walls covered in a mix of old oil portraits and colorful modern paintings. I've never been here before and immediately I love it. I'm in awe of the artwork, which looks to me like it should sit in some faraway gallery in Europe, not here in our small city by the sea.

I walk through the galleries slowly, soaking everything in, completely forgetting to fill in the questionnaire Mrs. Kang gave us. It stays forgotten in my backpack as I wander through the vast rooms, pausing to stare at all the precious things on display.

There are two particular things I like.

I mean, I like it all, but two things give me a gut reaction, which is what I like so much about art. It makes you feel things.

The first one is a sculpture of a couple embracing, his hands reaching around to grasp at her head and hers draped across his back. Of course Ali and Jacob, who are next to me, both think it's totally hilarious because the couple also happen to be naked, but I try my best to ignore their dumb comments. Unfortunately Mrs. Kang is too far away to tell them they're stupid. I don't bother to do it for her, and instead just wait for them to get bored and go somewhere else. Which they do.

Then I slowly walk around the figures, staring at their bodies and the way they revolve around each other, like gravity is somehow pulling each in toward the other. It makes me wonder what that might feel like.

I think of May and Harry, and wonder if that's what May was hoping to feel with him.

She didn't, obviously, and I think her indifference toward him was pretty clear, even to Harry, which is why they didn't last long. I drink in the figures and then walk away.

I think it would feel terrifying.

Or at least that's my guess.

It doesn't take me long to lose the group, but I don't mind. Mrs. Kang told us where to meet, and besides, I don't mind being by myself.

Hardly anyone is here on a weekday, and the empty space is quiet as I slowly make my way through a small basement room of East Asian art, stopping to pore over a tiny Japanese painting of a woman who sits in a riverboat in the night, gazing at the sky. Next to it is a portrait of a Korean scholar who lived hundreds of years ago, and I am stunned that I can peer at the features of a man who lived in such a different world, so long ago, his face frozen forever by ink.

Afterward I climb back up the stairs to the main hall, and I find Teddy Taualai standing alone in front of an enormous painting I already passed with barely a glance. I move to stand beside him and he grins at me.

"I saw you before, at the sculpture over there." He points at the embracing figures at the end of the vast room. "Is that your favorite?"

I purse my lips, refusing to be embarrassed by what I like. "Yeah."

I pause and then ask, "Have you been here before?"

He nods. "Yeah, I came here with my mum once. A long time ago."

He is silent for a long time but then he glances at me out of the corner of his eye and casually leans over and drapes his arm across my shoulders. It's a simple gesture but somehow it fills me with relief, because he wouldn't do it if he was angry with me.

But still, I make a face and quickly shove him away, because after all, I only said I wanted to be his friend.

Teddy doesn't even notice and just says, "I like this one."

I turn to examine it: an enormous dark painting of a forest, trees rising like pillars with sunlight filtering through a dense canopy of leaves toward the dark damp floor. And lost in the middle of it are three people, dwarfed by the ancient trees, sitting almost hidden around a tiny campfire. I think it's beautiful.

Teddy glances across at me. "Alice," he says.

"Mmmh?"

"You know what everyone says, about why I transferred?"

I blink, not sure how to reply. In the end I just nod.

"What have you heard about it?" His voice is so quiet it almost disappears in the vast empty gallery room.

I shift from foot to foot uncomfortably and shrug. "I don't know. Not much."

"Alice." He raises his eyebrows to show he knows I'm lying. Which I am.

I clear my throat awkwardly. "I don't know. Why are you asking me this? I thought you didn't care what other people think."

"I care what you think."

He looks straight at me, not turning away, his eyes as dark as the painting in front of us. A buzzing rings in my ears, like everything is getting way too serious for me to deal with.

I shuffle a bit more, feeling my cheeks grow hot, and then I quickly step back. "I gotta go find Mrs. Kang. I forgot to fill out her questionnaire and I need to—"

74

He grabs my arm, holding me still. His voice is quiet and low. "Alice."

After the longest pause I whisper, "I heard you beat up a teacher from your old school. So bad he had to go to the hospital. I heard you broke his nose and his ribs."

This time he does turn away, focused on his sneakers.

"It wasn't a teacher, but yeah, that's true. I did."

My eyes widen. "Why?"

"Why is it true?"

I'm in no mood for jokes. "Why did you do it?"

He bites his lips, hesitating. "It wasn't at school. It was this kid at a party. We were drinking, and he kept saying things about . . . it was totally stupid."

He doesn't finish, breaking off and glancing away from me back toward the big dark painting. Finally he says, "I got angry. It all came pouring out and there was nothing I could do. I just lost control."

"And the thing that happened with your teacher?"

He takes a deep breath. "That's not even true. I didn't touch him. I just . . . well, it's true I walked out of class. But I wasn't ever expelled. I just left."

Silence settles over us for the longest time and then finally he asks in a small voice, "Are you afraid of me now?"

I bite my lip and think about it. Am I?

Everyone says Teddy Taualai is violent, that it was an unprovoked attack, that he's a freak and a loser and he's dangerous.

"No," I say eventually. "I'm not scared of you." And it's the truth.

Teddy smiles, a shy crooked smile, and then as he glances down at his sneakers, his face turns serious. "I'll never do anything like that again. Ever. It was a mistake."

I nod slowly, a strange intensity coming over me, startled that it's me he's chosen to tell all this to.

"Okay," I say and I focus on my feet, too.

Suddenly I'm thinking about how no one has let any of it go, even though it happened three years ago. I think about my few short days in the limelight at school, how it felt to be pointed at and whispered about.

"It must be hard at school sometimes," I say to him eventually. "With everyone always talking about it."

He blinks. "Oh. I mean, I guess so. But it's not as bad as other things."

"What other things?" I'm curious now, curious about everything. But he just shrugs, turning his back to me.

"Come on, we better go. It's nearly time to meet Mrs. Kang."

He walks away and I stand for a moment watching him go, and then I glance back at the painting of the forest. At first there doesn't seem to be much besides the shadowy gum trees. But if you peer a little closer, it's dark and deep like a well with no bottom. Anything could be hidden there, if you bothered to look hard enough.

It's the second thing at the gallery that I really like, the second thing that moves me.

chapter 9

REFLECTION

On the weekend I work.

May continues to complain about how I'm young and a teenager and so should act like it. She says we should be going to the movies with a bunch of other people instead of me working at the cinema and leaving her bored and alone.

But I haven't told her yet about my plans for when school finishes.

I haven't told anyone yet.

Mainly because my parents will tell me no, but also because if I talk about it, it might seem less real somehow, like I'd be jinxing it.

So I keep it to myself and I go to work. And every week my savings get better and better.

"Alice! Can you grab some of these chocolate bars from the storeroom? We're running out."

I nod at Adalina, an older girl with bright red hair who

goes to university in the city. I head off, and by the time I return, she's restocking the water bottles in the mini-fridge, taking them from the cartons I left on the floor.

"Thank you," I say as I add the chocolate bars to the shelf and then bend down to help her. "How's university?"

Adalina groans. "There's so much work to do, you know? I kind of thought after high school I'd be able to take a break or something."

I scrunch up my face. "That's silly. University is always going to be way harder than high school. Everyone knows that."

She laughs, but it sounds a little bitter.

"Not for someone like you. I see you, reading your textbooks behind the candy counter when it's not busy." She sighs and adds, "I wish I was that dedicated."

I shrug. "I'm not really dedicated."

I just say it to make her feel better, though, which only makes her smirk. She sees right through me.

Adalina went to my school last year, but we never spoke then. She hung out with a different crowd, and until she started working at the cinema, neither of us even knew the other existed.

"So how's school, then?" she asks me.

"It's okay."

"That boy still following you around?" She grins at me. "Still driving you crazy?"

I turn to her sharply. "Did May tell you that?"

She just smirks. Again.

I get the feeling she enjoys teasing me, maybe because I'm not great at knowing how to react.

I shrug. "Yeah, I guess so." I lean down to pack away more water bottles. "But it's okay now. I don't mind it so much anymore."

This just makes her laugh, and I'm glad when people arrive, needing to be served.

But it's true that Teddy Taualai is following me around at school again. Things just returned to normal after the gallery excursion. It's almost as if the week we avoided each other never happened. The only real difference between then and now is that for some reason, it doesn't annoy me like it used to.

May keeps trying to ask me what happened, why Teddy stopped talking to me and then why he started again. She's desperately curious.

But somehow I never get around to telling her.

I mean to, I want to, but somehow I just never do.

Not that it's a secret, but what happened in the art gallery scared me a little. Not what Teddy told me, more like it scared me that he told *me*, that it was *me* he wanted to talk to about it.

It's almost private, not something I should talk about with anybody else, even though I've never kept things from May before.

But luckily, with things back to normal, May is happy enough to let it go, and as time goes by, she asks about it less and less. I guess she's happy because our fragile little friend group is still functioning like she wants it to. Even Harry still hangs around with us, having slipped back into his sad role of pining over May as she laughs and flirts with other people. May is oblivious to him, though, or at least she seems to be. She's just happy she's never alone, happy that Stacey Green sometimes sits with us at lunch, too, happy our little group is expanding.

I'm standing behind the popcorn counter serving a bunch of girls from my school. It's my least favorite part of working here. I hate seeing people from school.

"Hi, Sophia," I say nervously, wondering if she still hates me.

She does.

She glares as she orders, like I'm a stupid bug she wants to squash. We haven't spoken once since Teddy Taualai stuck the note on her back, but apparently she still very clearly remembers everything about it. And more to the point, her boyfriend Finn clearly doesn't, because he's nice to me and smiles as he buys his Coke, and this is obviously killing her a little inside.

I honestly don't know why she cares. She is pretty, undeniably pretty, much prettier than I am, and she's popular and has heaps of friends. Maybe she's just annoyed that I might dare to make fun of her at all. Because really, if anyone embodies the opposite of popular, it would be me. And May.

Not that May would ever admit it.

May actually turns up right after, like she heard me thinking about her. I notice the way she longingly watches Sophia and Finn as they walk up the stairs with their friends and disappear into the theater.

"Did they talk to you?" she asks me.

"Hello to you, too," I reply, reminding her I'm the reason she's visiting. "But no. Unless you consider asking for popcorn to be talking."

I wipe down the counter because the last movie is about to start, and it's time to shut down the concessions.

"Hi, May," calls Adalina from the other side of the foyer. "You waiting until Alice finishes?"

May nods. "Yeah, if that's okay."

Adalina opens the swinging door to the concessions area, pushing past us with some empty cardboard boxes. "I don't care," she says. "Just don't let our manager see you." She smiles and walks out the back, leaving me and May alone in the small foyer. Actually, the cinema is small, run by a local family, so it's pretty lax when it comes to things like friends visiting. As long as I still get my work done, no one really minds.

I pull out some Styrofoam cups and fiddle with the espresso machine, asking, "You want a coffee, right?"

"Yeah." May flops down at one of the tables nearby. "But don't make it as strong as last time." She makes a sour face and I laugh.

"I didn't do it on purpose!"

"I know, I know." She squirms in her seat, not meeting my

eyes as she casually adds, "Hey, I was wondering, what do you think of Finn?"

I raise my eyebrows at the abrupt change. "Finn? What do you mean?"

May gazes at the ceiling as if she's embarrassed. "Well, he's pretty cute, isn't he?"

I gape at her. "Yeah, but you're talking about *Finn*. As in, Sophia's popular, perfect boyfriend." I pause and stare at her. "And you've never even spoken to him before."

She sighs heavily. "I know that. But what can I do? If I like him, I like him. It's not as if I can just change my feelings."

That makes me examine her even harder. I am quiet as I carry the coffee cups over and place one in front of her, unsure how I should be reacting to this weirdness. Lately May has been all over the place. Ten years of crushing on only celebrity boys, and then suddenly Harry and now Finn.

"You like him?" I say it carefully, not wanting to offend her. "Do you think it's real if you've never spoken to him?"

She is offended, I can tell right away. "Alice, you're my best friend. You're supposed to be supportive." She wraps her hands around her coffee cup and glares at me, making me sigh.

I try again.

"I just mean he might not be what you expect. That's all."

I'm thinking about what Finn told me ages ago, about Teddy Taualai. Maybe it's true that Teddy nearly punched him when he first transferred to our school, but now that I know Teddy better, it makes me wonder what Finn said to him. Because surely he said something. It occurs to me that I don't know much about what sort of person Finn is at all.

And I guess that's what May's thinking, too, because she quickly snaps, "What do you know about it, anyway? You've never even liked someone before. Look at you and Teddy. He follows you around, *staring* at you, and you don't even notice!"

My body tenses up. "What's that supposed to mean?"

She pushes her hands into her hair in frustration. "Ugh, nothing. It's not that. It just upsets me sometimes, you know, all these other girls having such a great time at school, and I keep waiting for it to happen to me, but it just never does."

Her mouth curls down at the edges, trembling as if all her dreams are crumbling down around her, and I can't help but reach over to pat her arm. Even if I find it difficult to understand her.

May didn't used to care about these things. But now she does. And I'm trying desperately to keep up with her, to not say the wrong things.

I wonder if maybe it's the impending end of school, our final year before everything changes? We haven't talked much about what will happen afterward. May never brings it up, and I have my own plans, so raw and secret I'm certain they would break if I ever said them aloud.

So I just bite my lip and squeeze her hand.

"It'll be okay," I say quietly. "And you're right, I don't know anything about it. I think it's probably a good thing to like someone. I think it's brave."

She sits up and smiles widely at me, her eyes shining, and I can tell I've said the right thing this time, which fills me with relief.

She's so volatile these days. A stab of worry pierces my chest, yet if May wants to be popular and like Finn, who am I to tell her it's stupid? What would I know about it? I'll always just be Alice the nerd. Even if he *does* have a girlfriend and the whole thing is crazy. She's my best friend, after all, and I'll always want to support her.

No matter what.

Later we walk home along the footpath by the beach. It's dark, and stars stretch across the sky like a blanket of light above the glittering ocean. The air coming in off the sea is cold; the hot nights are finally drawing to a close. Our breath is showing white around our mouths when we laugh.

We walk slowly, and as the salty wind buffets my hair, flinging it across my face, May tells me how she feels about Finn. She tells me about the moments when they've shared eye contact, and she tells me about how he talked to her in the hall about a biology assignment.

And all the while she's speaking, I am thinking about Teddy Taualai standing in front of the forest painting at the art gallery, asking me if I'm afraid of him.

And I can't get the expression on his face out of my head, the expression he had when I told him I wasn't.

chapter 10

YOU'RE NOT ALWAYS RIGHT

On Sunday I spend all morning studying in my room, listening to my parents moving around downstairs, their voices murmuring quietly. I scowl at the problem in front of me, my vision blurring until all the lines and symbols blend together into a big indecipherable jumble.

It's too stuffy and hot, I decide, wiping sweat from my forehead.

I need a break.

Slowly I walk downstairs, pulling my baggy T-shirt away from my chest and fanning it back and forth. This weather is crazy. Just yesterday it was cold and I thought for sure we were done with the heat. But here I am, sweaty and distracted in a stupid heat wave instead of finishing my homework.

Downstairs Mum sits at the kitchen table reading a newspaper. She glances up in surprise. "Have you finished already?"

I shake my head, moving to the fridge to stand at the open door and let the cool air wash over me. "Not yet. It's too hot to concentrate."

"Turn on the air conditioner."

I shake my head. "I don't like it."

Her lips tighten and she returns to her paper.

I sigh. "Where's Dad?"

"He went to get some groceries. Did you want something? I can text him."

Again, I shake my head. "No, I was just wondering."

I slide onto the chair beside her, sipping a big glass of cold juice from the fridge as my mum watches me.

"Everything okay? It's not like you to give up so easily."

I drain my glass and rest my head against my hand, elbow on the table. "I'm fine. What are you and Dad doing later?"

I wonder if maybe we can get takeout, wonder if we could all watch a movie together on our big flat-screen TV, laughing on our big puffy couch.

"We have to go visit Stu today, remember? He's having some work people over for dinner tonight."

I nod. I had forgotten.

Mum turns back to the paper, and I fan myself again.

The kitchen is like a sauna, though Mum seems fine. She doesn't like the air conditioner either, but she's as perfect as ever, as if she's made from marble and nothing could ever touch her.

Not even me.

The doorbell rings and I jump a little. Mum doesn't glance up from her reading, just absently says, "Can you get that? Your father probably has his hands full. Help him bring the groceries in from the car, will you?"

"Okay."

I push my chair back and run to the front door, swinging it open to find not my father, but May and Teddy Taualai standing on the doorstep grinning at me.

I gawk at them, frozen, and then urgently push them both back, away from the house, stepping outside as I pull the door almost closed behind me. "What are you *doing* here?" I hiss, glaring at May.

What is she thinking bringing Teddy here?

May just grins. "It's so hot! I want to go swimming, and Harry said he'd meet us at the beach, and I said I'd see if you wanted to come, and then Teddy wanted to see your house, so here we are."

I blink at him. He wanted to see my house?

I turn back to May.

"So you just *brought* him here? May!"

Is she serious? She knows what my parents are like.

"Alice? Is that your father?" On cue, Mum's voice rings from the house. Startled, I turn wildly back to the half-closed door.

"Um, no. It's just May. But she's leaving now."

I begin herding them down the path when her voice sounds again. "May? She hasn't been over in a long time. Invite her in."

I stop, turning from Teddy Taualai to May and then back again.

May just smiles as she pushes past me into the house, calling loudly before I can stop her, "Hi, Mrs. Dyson. It's been ages, hasn't it?"

Teddy Taualai throws me an evil grin and then moves as if to follow her, but I grab his arm hard, looking from his sloppy scuffed sneakers to his old stretched T-shirt. His dark hair is full-on bedhead, somehow managing to both stick straight toward the sky and also hang into his eyes.

I stare up at him.

My mum hates messy hair. She hates boys who aren't neat.

"Oh no," I say, and then I'm reaching up to try to pat his hair smooth, pushing it roughly away from his face with both hands and shoving it flat at the sides. His eyes widen, but he doesn't stop me, even leaning down a little closer to make it easier for me to reach. He smiles his small crooked smile, but suddenly I think maybe he's a bit nervous, too.

"Your mum is scary, huh?" he breathes.

I freeze with my hands in his hair, and then say through gritted teeth, "No. Of course not."

"Alice?" Her voice makes me jump as it wafts again from the house.

"Coming," I shout over my shoulder.

I pull at Teddy's T-shirt, trying to move it so it sits straight, but it's all stretched out of shape and useless, so in the end I give up. Teddy just stares down at me, motionless as I fuss over him, his face a little pink.

"I didn't know," he says suddenly. "I would have . . . I dunno, worn a better shirt or something."

"Okay, it's okay. This is fine," I mutter, trying to convince myself as much as him.

I'm so oddly nervous and I don't know why. "Come on."

I walk inside and wait for him to follow me, then close the door behind us. I move through our hall toward the kitchen and, after hesitating a moment, Teddy follows me through.

Mum looks at him in the exact way I thought she would. Like he is a mess and she knows everything there is to know about him just from one glance.

I want to hide my face in my hands as she grills him about his grades at school and what he does in his spare time. She even asks what he's planning to do next year when high school is over, and I know what she really wants to know is whether he's smart enough to go to university or not.

Teddy actually does well, I think. He says all the right things, tells her how nice our big modern house is, how I'm a good influence on him and May because of how often I study, says he does plan to study further after high school. Though he says all the right things, I know it's still not enough.

He looks all wrong to my mother.

He's too messy, too dark, too loud and confident.

The atmosphere in the room is thick and heavy. She doesn't like him.

In the end, May opens her mouth and blurts something that implies Teddy is more her friend than mine anyway, but I know already that Mum doesn't believe it. It's in her eyes as they follow Teddy across the room, like she's identifying a possible threat to my perfect future and wondering how she will neutralize it.

By the time we finally escape the kitchen, I'm exhausted, like I've just run a marathon. The three of us shuffle back into the hall in silence and climb the stairs to my room, May walking slowly at the front of our procession, the atmosphere strange.

Halfway up the staircase I stop, suddenly turning around and almost banging into Teddy as he comes up behind me. May doesn't notice and keeps climbing but I stay peering down at him, standing still on the higher stair.

My hand slides down the banister as I bend to his ear and say firmly, like it means something, "It doesn't matter what other people think."

I'm very serious when I say it, like it's important, and he just watches me, eyes wide. I'm sure he thinks it's a stupid thing to say, but somehow I feel like it's my fault he had to deal with this, and I want him to know that what my mum thinks and what I think are two separate things.

But then I'm embarrassed and my cheeks start burning, so I turn around and quickly follow May to my room. After another few seconds his footsteps begin to climb up again, too.

In my room all three of us collapse on the bed, not say-ing anything. I just lie there, watching my white ceiling fan, with my head resting against May's arm and my leg touch-ing Teddy Taualai's. My mind is blank, and it's still just so unbearably hot, which somehow makes the whole thing even worse.

After a while May's fidgeting gets harder to ignore, her leg tapping against the floor over and over again, like she's agitated and can't stay still. I turn until I can see her face. "What's wrong? Are you okay?"

She sighs, still fidgeting, her arm pulled up to cover her expression. Her voice is muffled and thick. "I'm really sorry, Alice. You told me not to bring anyone over, and I didn't listen."

She sits up and focuses on Teddy, who is on his feet again, shifting awkwardly from foot to foot in the middle of my room, probably worried May is about to cry.

"I didn't think it would be like that." She turns to me and says, "Your mum is always so nice to me."

I sigh.

My mum *is* nice to May, it's true. But she also says May's personality is too flighty, that she can't dedicate herself to any one thing and she won't do well enough in school to get a proper job afterward.

But obviously I never tell May any of that.

May's eyes are filling with tears, like everything that

just happened in my kitchen was her fault. Which clearly it wasn't.

Teddy glances at her. "Shit, May, it's fine. Nothing even happened. You don't need to feel bad."

He grins, and I think he really does seem fine. It makes me angry all over again, because my mum doesn't know anything about Teddy Taualai.

"Let's go swimming," I announce so abruptly that May stares at me.

"What?"

"Isn't that why you idiots came here in the first place?" I stand up and move to my dresser, pulling clothes from my bottom drawer as I try to find my suit. "Besides, it's really freaking hot!"

May grins at me. "Really? You'll come with us?"

I nod.

"What about your mum?"

I just shrug, determined. I find my bathing suit beneath a pile of sweaters and pull it out. "I want to go," I say, which makes May squeal and jump immediately to her feet, her unhappiness forgotten.

"It looks so nice down there today! The sun's so hot; I bet I'll get a tan." She jumps toward my bedroom door because obviously I need to change before we can go, but Teddy just stands there, grinning at me.

"Need any help getting changed?"

I scowl at him. "May! Make him leave!"

May pulls him after her into the hall. "Hurry up," she says over her shoulder. "We'll wait out front, okay?"

When they've gone, I take a deep, calming breath.

Is this my first teenage rebellion? Is that what I'm doing right now? Rebelling?

But I am determined.

I'm going to go to the beach with my friends, no matter what my mum says, and I'll finish my homework when I come back.

But still, when I go downstairs to tell her, my knees feel a little weak.

chapter 11

WATER

Down at the ocean, there's no breeze and it isn't any cooler.

Harry's waiting for us, sitting irritated on the hot sand. He stands and almost shouts, "Where have you been? You took forever!"

But then May is running to him, and the sight of her instantly pacifies him, which kind of makes me sad, because he isn't the one making May's heart beat these days.

Teddy and I walk over much slower, and when we do finally reach them, we all decide it's too hot on the sand anyway and that we should leave our stuff under the jetty in the shade.

It's not the most popular beach in the city, so the sand here is covered with piles of dried seaweed. It's spongy beneath my feet, crackling like dried leaves as I walk, and there are shells strewn everywhere. The sun beats on my back, and I wonder when it will cool off for good.

Not a scrap of wind rustles the seaweed, and even in the shade beneath the jetty it's stifling, the air warm and muggy with the scent of ocean. We pile our stuff on the sand, and because May is braver than me, she takes off her dress right there in front of both boys, revealing her suit. She has on a pretty bikini with little bows at her hips, and I think she looks cute. Which I'm pretty sure is what she thinks, too.

I envy her a little bit, envy her confidence, but since everyone else is busy ripping off their clothes, I have no choice but to follow, pulling my T-shirt off to reveal my rather boring one-piece swimsuit. My mum bought it for me ages ago when I had to take swimming safety at school, so it's suitably modest.

I'm still embarrassed, though, even if Teddy clearly isn't. He stands there shirtless and staring at me openly until I turn away, my face flushed. And when I glance back he's still grinning shamelessly at me, which makes my skin prickle all over.

"Come on, Alice," May screams, grabbing my hand and dragging me excitedly toward the water. I let her pull me with her because it's much better than staying near Teddy, and we splash into the shallows, the water clear and so much cooler than the heavy hanging air.

Within moments I'm drenched from her splashing, and then Harry bounds in after us, pushing both of us over into the cool waves as May screams with laughter.

I burst out of the water, clutching my glasses in my hand and sweeping streaming hair away from my eyes and giggling, too. It's a fun thing, to hang out with friends at the beach.

It makes me wonder why I've never tried it before.

The sky is empty and cloudless, stretching out in the distance until it meets the blue ocean on the horizon. It's so bright that it's impossible to tell where the water ends and the sky begins, and I think it's like they just merge together, as if the tiny black cargo ships float on the edge of the sky.

I turn back when May shrieks. Harry has picked her up and throws her into the deep water, and then she is bursting back up laughing, immediately swimming toward him to get her revenge.

I smile at their antics and sink down into the water to float on my back, staring up at the blue empty sky just as two seagulls fly overhead, squawking loudly. I think they're trying to get the attention of a family eating chips out of white butcher's paper on the nearby jetty.

With my ears beneath the water, the sounds of my friends playing nearby are muffled, their happy shouts and splashing muted by the endless wash of waves. I let the water carry my body over the swells, listening to their voices, until a hand touches my back from beneath and I yelp, shooting up to find my feet on the sand below.

May cackles happily, her face dripping water as she emerges from the waves behind me.

"May!"

She giggles. "Look at them."

I put my glasses back on as she lifts her arm from the water and points at the end of the jetty just as Teddy throws himself off the edge and does a crazy flip into the waves below. Harry follows him, dropping like a pin into the deep water, and then they both crash back to the surface in a flurry of white spray and loud laughter.

"I want to do it," says May.

I blink at her, shaking my head. "No way! I can't do that."

We watch silently, bobbing gently in the waves, as the two boys climb the rusty metal ladder onto the pier, crawling over the railing before throwing themselves off all over again.

"No way," I whisper, but May grasps my hand tightly beneath the surface and I know exactly what that means.

Which is how I find myself standing on the jetty next to the family and their chips, peering over the edge of the rotting wooden railing into the waves far below. The family's dog is sniffing at my ankles, its hot nose pressing against my skin.

"No way," I say once more, shaking my head.

"Aww, come on, Alice," May whines. "I want to!"

"Then you do it."

"You know I can't do it without you. We have to do it together."

She pulls my arm and propels me against the railing. "Don't you want to try something daring?"

Her eyes are shining, lashes glistening as she pleads silently. Harry and Teddy climb up the ladder, and then Teddy is beside me, his black hair streaming water over his face. "You gonna jump?"

"Alice is afraid of heights."

He turns to me. "Really? I didn't know that."

I grit my teeth, still focused on the water far below. "That's not true. I'm not. I just don't like jumping from high things. It's totally different."

"Come *on*, Alice!" May drags me to the side, squeezing through the small gap between the railings until we stand on the very edge of the splintery wooden platform, swaying where it drops off into emptiness.

May turns to me with wide, shining eyes, and I know I won't resist her. Maybe it's time I give her what she wants. I am terrified, my hands shaking as I grasp at the rough painted railing behind us, but I nod.

Her face opens up into a brilliant smile. "Yes! We'll hold hands and jump together, okay?"

I can't even answer, my chest growing tight.

"Okay, ready?" May shrieks. "We'll count together. On three!"

My throat turns dry, but I am ready, one hand grasping May's fingers and the other gripping the wooden railing, my knuckles straining.

I've never done anything like this before, and my heart beats hard against my ribs, pounding loudly in my ears. And then Teddy takes my hand, prying my fingers from the railing and engulfing them in his own. He smiles at me, the small crooked smile, and then as May begins to count he yells the numbers even louder. His fingers feel warm against mine, reassuring and strong.

"One!"

"Two!"

"Three—aaaiieeee!"

May screams the whole way down, her hand letting mine go as her arms freewheel through the air.

I don't scream, and Teddy doesn't let go.

We plunge into the water below in a chaotic jumble of arms and legs and kicking feet, and then we burst to the surface, taking huge gulping breaths of salt-tinged air. We all swim back to the ladder, Teddy hoisting himself up first and then May and me following, still laughing, my heart still pounding.

At the top we find Harry leaning against the railing talking to Julie. Her hair is ruffled and salty, a sweet smile curling her lips.

I smile at her and nod, but May goes running over to say hello, and I know she is excited at the prospect of making a new, even more popular friend. I watch her go and wonder how she manages to push me so far out of my comfort zone, and why I always enjoy it in the end, no matter how hard I resist.

"Wanna go again?" asks Teddy, but I shake my head.

"Once is enough for me, at least for today."

But I am smiling, happy, the terrifying jump having washed everything else away, my mum and the suffocating kitchen forgotten.

"Fair enough," Teddy answers, then his face splits into a wide grin. "Hey, you wanna go get an ice cream? I think I bet you for one, right?"

He smiles as I attempt to remember. The dog comes over to my feet again, and I crouch down to sink my fingers into its fur, making a face as it licks sloppily at my skin. I can't help but smile, even though it's kind of gross.

"Are you going to buy it for me, then?" I say eventually.

"Ha! No way! You lost the bet, remember?"

He hovers real close, triumphant as I try to remember what he's talking about, but then I realize he's right.

On that very first day, he bet me everyone at school would forget the dancing video by the next week, and he was right.

But I still push him away, feigning ignorance.

"I did not! I'm pretty sure *you* said you'd buy me one." I laugh and back down the jetty as he steps quickly after me.

"No way. You *owe* me," he shouts.

"Whatever!" I roll my eyes and then launch toward the shore, giggling, the little dog yapping as it runs with me. It gets tangled in my feet, spinning me off balance as I totter across the wooden planks. Teddy catches me straightaway. He laughs as he grabs my arm to stop me, pulling me from the yapping dog until my back hits his chest. He leans close. "A bet's a bet. There's no way I'm gonna give up."

I wriggle out of his grip, sticking my tongue out. "It's not a real bet if I never agreed to it."

I end up buying him an ice cream anyway, and we sit on a bench near the kiosk, trying to lick the liquid sliding down our cones before it drips onto our hands.

"Man, this shit is so messy," Teddy exclaims, licking where

the pink ice cream has made a trail down his forearm. He makes a face. "Salty!"

I giggle, turning to locate the others who are still standing way out on the jetty. May is chatting animatedly with Julie as Harry watches. She looks happy, I think, excited at this rare chance to speak with one of the prettiest and most popular girls at school. After Sophia, that is. I've barely spoken to Julie before, but she seemed okay during the whole video-stalker investigation thing. She wasn't mean like Sophia, and I don't particularly remember her laughing at me or Teddy when the others were making fun of us.

I watch them a while longer and then shrug. I still don't understand May's sudden need for new friends. I glance over at Teddy and think that having a friend like him takes up more than enough space in my life. I can't imagine needing more.

But of course May doesn't think like that. We are different, after all.

I think it was easier when we were younger, before May started watching all those perfect-summer-romance movies, before she got so caught up in the fiction of it that she felt like something between us was lacking.

I used to be enough for May.

Or maybe it was easier back then because I hadn't been so focused on my studies. I wasn't so fixated on working every weekend to save money. We spent a lot more time together.

A hollow feeling slides into my belly when I think of how it used to be. The two of us sharing secrets on May's bed, trying to fend off her annoying brothers. Or walking down to the shore and sharing hot chips together with her parents, oil soaked into butcher's paper and salt on our fingertips.

I remember May wrapping her arms around my shoulders and crying just as hard as I did when my mother grounded me for not acing another test. And I shared her misery and tears when her rabbit died. I remember planting trees in May's backyard with her mum, learning how to fertilize and water and clip branches. It used to be my home away from home. My other family. Sometimes I felt closer to May's mum than my own.

Always, I did.

Yet I hardly ever go over there anymore.

I don't know why.

I sigh and shake it off, wrapping my towel more closely around my shoulders and swinging my feet back and forth, my toes grazing the top of the thick green grass.

Teddy smirks suddenly, and he reaches over to wipe the corner of my mouth, his fingers lingering against my skin. I raise my eyebrows at him.

"Ice cream," he explains with a grin. "You're so freaking messy. It's dripping all over you."

"Messy?" I scoff at him. "I'm not messy. You have no idea. I'm practically a neat freak."

I reach up with a sticky hand to fix my hair. Right now I definitely don't seem like a neat freak, with my salt-encrusted hair and hands covered with ice cream.

"Well, normally," I say by way of explanation, but he just reaches out and pulls my hand away from my head.

"It looks good on you."

I frown at him. "You think mess looks good on me?"

He grins again, wide and slow as he leans closer. "Yeah, it always has."

I lean away, making a face. He has no sense of personal space.

"How would you know?" I say. "We've only been friends for like . . . three months."

"Nah, it's been longer than that. I mean, we weren't friends or anything, but . . . it was longer."

I frown at him again and then shrug. "Whatever," I say.

He doesn't know what he's talking about.

I keep swinging my legs, enjoying the shade and the view over the white sand and blue water. "Hey! A breeze," I exclaim as the wind picks up to blow cool air off the ocean. "Maybe it's going to cool off again."

I turn to him and see that he's watching me. "What? Is it more ice cream?"

He shakes his head. "You don't remember, do you?"

"Remember what?" I frown at him, confused.

"The first time you talked to me."

"In the library? Oh, in the hall when I said it was your fault."

"No."

"No?"

I rack my brain, but honestly I can't remember ever

talking to Teddy before the video thing. "I don't think so," I say slowly. "The hall was the first time we spoke. Unless we talked in class. Did we?"

He shakes his head, and I think he seems suddenly odd. Like he's disappointed or something.

"So when?" I ask. "Aren't you going to tell me?"

"I don't think so. You have to remember for yourself."

I frown. "How am I supposed to do that?"

Teddy just shrugs and stands up abruptly. He announces, "I'm going to go find Harry." And then he's gone, leaving me sitting alone on the bench, wondering what just happened.

When the others finally come back from the jetty, Teddy isn't with them.

At first it doesn't bother me, and I hang out with May and Harry and Julie as they all laugh about school stuff. But later they decide to go to the kiosk for chips, and it gets darker and darker and Teddy still hasn't come back. I begin to worry that something is wrong.

I walk alone down the grassy track toward the beach and eventually find him sitting by the water.

The sun has set and the sky is growing dark, a blue glow falling across the sand. The pine trees behind us hide dark storm clouds, rolling in off the hills, purple and black.

I watch his back for a moment, the way he sits so still, peering out across the ocean. Then I clear my throat and call. "Hey, Teddy."

He turns, the last of the sun reflected in his black eyes,

making them glitter in the near darkness. "Alice," is all he says.

I sit down beside him on the sand, not especially close, watching as the choppy waves lap at our feet. Suddenly I am afraid, like I've done something wrong again, like I've somehow ruined it without knowing how or why.

"What's wrong?" I ask him in a tiny voice. I run the cool sand through my fingers and feel afraid of his answer.

Teddy shakes his head, focusing on the sea. "Nothing."

"Is it . . . is it because of before?" I ask uncertainly. "Is it because I don't remember it, when we first talked?"

"Nah," he says straightaway, shaking his head with a soft laugh.

I should be relieved, but somehow the sound of it is strange. Not like a real laugh. Or at least, not like a happy one.

"It isn't that," he continues like he really means it. "I always knew you didn't remember that anyway."

He smiles at me, but it's obvious something is wrong. Just like the laugh, it doesn't feel quite real. But he says, "You haven't done anything. I'm just feeling tired is all. I think I'm gonna head home in a sec."

I pause.

"Okay," I agree, but neither of us moves. We just stay on the sand, watching as the sun's last light disappears and the shadows grow longer and darker across the dunes.

Eventually I lean back, tired after the long day, yet somehow still not quite ready to go home and face my mother. The sand is cool on my back and I lie with my arms stretched above my head and my knees bent toward the sky, watching as stars pinprick the darkness overhead.

I wonder how long it will last, this beautiful clear sky. The black clouds are slowly moving closer, and it's growing colder and windier, but I don't mind. I like the sound of the wind rushing across the dunes. I like the way the pine trees are pushed back and forth, wavering in the night.

Teddy's face hovers into my line of vision, blocking out the sky.

He leans over me, one hand reaching across to rest in the sand beside my head, his face angled down over mine. He doesn't speak, just stares, his eyes glittering in the darkness and his hair moving with the wind.

"Alice." His voice is quiet and thick and strange. Like something else is moving beneath the surface, something complicated I could never hope to understand.

"Alice," he breathes again, "can I kiss you?"

My breath catches in my throat and I grow utterly still.

I stare up at him, and I don't know how to answer, am completely incapable of moving my mouth to make words, so I just remain silent, staring.

For too long.

For so long it becomes clear I'm not going to answer at all.

And then Harry's voice rings out from behind the dunes, calling for us to come back before it rains. Teddy turns toward the voices and I stare up at his throat, at the lines of it reaching from his jaw down to the little indent of his collarbone, at the shape of his shoulders beneath his crazy stretched T-shirt.

And then I roll out from beneath him and stumble to my feet, staggering quickly across the sand toward the dunes and toward Harry's voice. I almost barrel into him as I come running up the track.

"Whoa, Alice," he grabs me to stop me from falling. "Are you okay? Where's Teddy?"

I don't meet his eyes, just pull away. Heat rises in my face.

"He's coming."

"Cool. I think it's gonna rain any second now. May's just up near the kiosk, but Julie went home already."

"Okay, I'll go on ahead," I tell him quickly, because I think Teddy's heavy footsteps are coming up the sandy track behind us.

Before he gets any closer, I am gone.

chapter 12

THREE YEARS

I spend a lot of time over the holidays thinking about Teddy Taualai. About the beach and his face hovering over mine, the night sky stretching behind him. Mostly about the disappointment in his black eyes when he realized I don't remember the first time we talked.

It makes me want to remember. *Need* to remember. But it's like wisps of smoke, intangible and beyond my grasp.

Until it isn't. Until finally, in the dead of night, I wake with all of it on the tip of my tongue, as clear as it was three years ago . . .

I am waiting in the school office, biting my fingernails and worrying about the English test I have to take later in the afternoon. Of course I have studied for it. I mean, I tried my best to study for it.

But still, you never know.

And I really do have to do well this time.

Yesterday Mum said that I didn't score high enough on my math test last week. She didn't even tell Dad what I got because she said it wasn't good enough to bother him with. Like her, he's busy, too busy to deal with a bad grade like that.

Bad grade. That's what she called it, but I mean, my score was fine.

It was much better than May's, obviously.

But still, I know Evelyn Tait scored even higher. So I guess it wasn't good enough. Not good enough for my mom.

I bite my fingernails harder. The tips have nearly all disappeared.

I jiggle my legs nervously as I sit waiting on the orange plastic chair. Mr. Handley finally comes out of the principal's office and I stand up, hefting the massive stack of photo-copies against my chest. Why didn't he ask someone else to deliver the stupid assignments? Someone bigger. Someone with nothing better to do than sit in the office for twenty minutes while the receptionist feeds all the sheets into the photocopier that keeps jamming, over and over again.

I don't have time for this. I could be doing a million better things right now.

"Oh, Alice," Mr. Handley says when he sees me, as if he is surprised that I've been waiting here the whole time. Like he didn't ask me to do it. "I have to go meet my wife in the parking lot for a moment. Would you mind waiting here for the rest of the printouts? Then if you can just take them with you to class, that would be great. Thank you."

I nod, because he's a teacher and that's what you do if a teacher asks you to help. You don't scream at them about how they're wasting your time and then start tearing your hair out because maybe, just maybe, you haven't prepared for your English test in the way that your mother told you to. In fact, you don't manage to do anything quite the way your mother wants you to. Mr. Handley breezes past me, the door swinging shut behind him.

I flop back down on the stupid orange chair. A crack in the plastic keeps catching my skirt, the material pulling every time I move, little bits of thread breaking and twisting.

I shouldn't have gone to May's house yesterday. That's the real problem.

I shouldn't have spent the whole day playing video games with her brothers and jumping on her trampoline. I shouldn't have let her mom talk me into staying for dinner.

I should have stayed home and practiced how I would write the assignment. Or I should have memorized the layout of the sample article. That's what I should have done.

My mind is whirring, tearing through all the *should haves* and *could haves*. But we're already halfway through second quarter, and there's no time for that. I need to get better. I need to *do* better. Otherwise, Mum was talking about that other school in the city.

The idea of transferring to a brand-new school halfway through the year when everyone else already has friends makes my chest hurt. I would have to sit by myself at lunch instead of with May.

And I can't leave May.

We've been together since kindergarten. It just wouldn't work without her. Besides, how would she survive without me? She's so boisterous and always acts without thinking, saying whatever comes into her head. I know the other kids whisper about it, act like she's weird.

She's not. But without me here, who would she hang around with? She'd be left all alone. There's no way I'd do that to her.

My throat turns dry as dust, but I tell myself it'll be fine. I just have to do better.

I just have to change. I just need to be perfect.

The door to the office slams open and I quickly jump to my feet. It's a teacher whose name I don't know. I think she's a substitute. She walks in and points to the plastic orange chair beside me, currently covered in my pile of test copies.

"Sit," she says to the boy who trails in after her, and I scramble to pick up my printouts as the teacher disappears into the principal's office.

The room is silent after she's gone, and I glance over at the boy.

He's short. Shorter than me, with dark skin and dark eyes and dark hair.

His hands are shoved deep into his pockets and he

slouches in the chair beside me with his head bent low. He doesn't say anything, just leans forward until his elbows rest on his knees, his hands pushing through his hair and his face turned toward the floor. He kicks at his schoolbag, and it rolls over on its side against the chair leg.

He's angry, I think, eyebrows pulled together in a dark straight line, his mouth a grimace. I don't know who he is, but I remember Mr. Handley talking about a transfer kid.

Is this him?

I think about the new school in the city. I think about having to start again, to be alone. To be as upset as this kid. For May to be alone, too, left behind.

I open my mouth and ask, "What school did you come from?"

The boy glares at me from beneath his hair and I notice a faded bruise stretching out across his cheek. He doesn't say anything, just scowls fiercely at me like I've done something wrong.

This is why I don't bother with other people. This is why I should just be concentrating on my schoolwork so I can stay here until the end of high school. I don't want to transfer. I don't want to end up like this stupid, angry boy.

"Don't you already know?"

I turn in surprise at the sound of his voice. He's still glaring at me.

"What?"

"Don't you already know which school I came from? I

already heard people talking about me in class this morning. Everyone knows already. And it's only my first day."

I stare at him, because when he said the last part his voice got all quiet and strange, like he was trying very hard not to cry.

I am slightly fascinated. "Talking about what?"

He glares at me. "You *know* what. Everyone already knows. I'm not *stupid*!"

A surge of anger curls in my chest. I don't have time for this. I need to study, not be here talking to this idiot.

I scowl right back at him. "I never said you're stupid. You're the one getting all defensive. And I don't know what you're talking about."

The boy has his hands over his mouth, elbows still on his knees. His eyes are sharp and dark as he watches me, assessing. "You really don't know?"

I roll my eyes at him. "Why would I? You said it's only your first day."

His hands still cover half his face. "I dunno. Everyone at this school keeps talking about it. They're whispering behind my back."

I frown at him, curious. "About what?"

He looks at me sharply. "I'm not gonna tell you. Just ask one of your idiot friends."

That annoys me. "Not that it's any of your business, but those people being mean to you aren't my friends. And I'm pretty sure *my* friend isn't the kind of person who would be cruel like that, just so you know."

He is silent, and I sit huffing for a while, slamming the big pile of papers onto the floor at my feet. Where the hell is the receptionist? There are only fifteen minutes until class starts. I won't get any time to go over my notes.

"You said *friend*. You only have one?"

I blink in confusion. "What?"

"That's what you said," he continues. "Your *friend*. Not *friends*."

"Yeah, so?"

He is so irritating.

"You're not very popular then, are you?" he says.

I turn to him sharply, except he's grinning now. Teasing me.

"I'm more popular than you are!" I snap. "At least I *have* a friend. That's more than you!"

Silence blooms after I say it, and sickness immediately swells in my belly. I'm not like this. Not normally. It's just today, because of the test, because of what my mother said about transferring. I'm all twisted inside.

"Sorry. I didn't mean . . ." I stumble over my words, my face burning red. "That was really mean. It was a horrible thing to say. Sorry."

The boy shrugs like he doesn't care.

"I'm used to it. It doesn't matter."

"It *does* matter." I am slightly horrified. "Of course it matters. And if people here are mean to you like that, you shouldn't listen to them. Everyone here is an idiot. It doesn't matter what they think. Just do your best."

He stares at me, his black eyes wide. "O-okay."

I huff, completely embarrassed about my outburst. I don't know what's wrong with me lately. I'm all over the place. Hot and cold. I tap my fingers as I watch the second hand on the clock creep along excruciatingly slowly. At one point I'm sure it even moves backward.

"Hey," the boy says, still watching me. His voice is softer now, like he's not trying quite so hard to be tough. "Why are you here anyway?"

I turn to him and make a face like he's stupid. "This is my school. Of course I'm here."

"No, I mean, why are you in the office?" He rolls his eyes at me like it was obvious.

"Oh," I answer, because I suppose it *was* obvious, then I point at the printouts on the floor. "I'm helping Mr. Handley. We have an English test."

"Oh," he says. "I thought maybe you were in trouble."

I blink at him. "I never get in trouble." It's true. I might not do completely great at school, but I am quiet and good. I never cause trouble. That would just be stupid.

We are silent for a while longer, but then something about his question makes me turn back to him, curious now. "Well, why are you here, then?"

He peers at his hands, starts fidgeting. "Oh, nothing. I just gotta see the principal. Some jerk here, he just . . . he said some stuff."

I cock my head to the side. "What stuff?"

He shrugs. "I dunno, just . . . mean stuff."

"If he was the one who said mean stuff, then how come you're the one in trouble?"

He fidgets again, growing awkward. "'Cause I kinda got angry and shoved him a bit."

"That's stupid," I say. "The teachers will never like you if you do dumb stuff like that. Especially on your first day."

I frown at him because obviously it's important the teachers like you, and I'm surprised he doesn't know this. My mother told me *everyone* knows this. Well, everyone who wants good grades, anyway. She says studying isn't everything; you have to make sure the teachers like you as well. She says it's an important part of doing well.

I glance at the transfer boy because he's gone all quiet now. "Don't shove people," I tell him and he glares at me but then nods slowly.

I think maybe he wants to say something, but then he must change his mind. The silence draws out between us, and I figure he doesn't want to tell me what the other boy said, so I just shrug, taking a deep breath as I jiggle my legs. I squeeze my eyes shut and clench my fists.

I have to do well on this test. Please let me do well on the test. Please don't make me transfer. I don't want to leave May behind. Please let me get a high score.

Please.

And then, if I get a good score, I will study harder. I will.

I promise.

I repeat it over and over again, like a prayer. And my hands clench harder with every word, my breath growing shorter and shallower.

And then this thought pops into my head, this one horrible, terrifying, awful thought that makes me freeze still.

What if this is all there ever is?

What if after high school, I start at university and it's just the same?

I snap my eyes open.

My chest grows tight, like my rib cage is closing in on my lungs, squeezing them smaller and smaller until it becomes hard to breathe. Is this what it'll be like when I'm at university? And afterward, when I get a job? Will it be the same? Will I always feel like this?

I shake my head. No. Absolutely not. I can't do it.

Finish school, yes.

Work hard to stay here with May until my final year, yes.

But I won't do it again afterward, not after high school.

Which means I need a plan.

"Alice?"

The receptionist sticks her head out of the copy room, and I jump to my feet.

"The photocopier keeps getting stuck," she says. "I don't think I can finish them. Do you just want to bring the ones I already printed with you to class? Tell Mr. Handley I'm sorry, but otherwise you'll be late."

I nod eagerly. Yes! I will get out of this office. And in three years, I'll get out of this school, too.

And after that?

Well, I'll think of something. And I'll commit to it, and I won't ever look back.

I reach down to the floor and heave up my stack of paper.

"You forgot one," says the transfer kid. He picks it up and places it carefully on top of the pile in my arms. "Alice."

He says my name funny, like he's suddenly shy after all that glaring and scowling he was doing earlier. I huff at him, but still say thanks. And the boy again opens his mouth as if he wants to say something else, but my mind is already moving so far ahead of him and this test and this school. My thoughts have run all the way through high school to what lies afterward.

The future.

I walk carefully to the door with my massive pile of papers, turning to use my shoulder to push it open.

As I leave, the transfer kid stares after me with deep, dark eyes, sitting alone on the plastic chair. And then the teacher is calling out for him to come into the principal's office and fear flashes across his face. But then I'm walking down the hallway.

Dreaming of my future.

Lost in the possibilities.

chapter 13

ABSENCE

After the holiday break, I'm still feeling strange about what happened on the beach.

I haven't told May about it, even though I know she would want me to. Even though I know if it were reversed she would have told me straightaway. A few years ago I would have told her.

But now I don't.

Actually, even if I had wanted to tell her, I'm not sure I would have gotten a chance to. I did see May a couple times over the holidays, but she didn't stick around long when she came over. She was like a mini cyclone, arriving in a flurry of excitement and then leaving again almost immediately.

It kind of reminds me of how she used to be. About the time we turned fifteen, it was like May suddenly became aware of other people. Of boys. Of all the little groups at our school. She didn't become shy exactly, but it was like she realized for the first time that people noticed her, were judging her. That sometimes maybe they found her a little weird, because she was always speaking up in class, always being loud and excited.

She started holding herself back. Fading into the background at school.

At first I missed the old May, but I guess that's around the time I changed, too. I got serious about my future. So I got used to it. And I didn't have much time to ponder it because I was busy.

These days May seems more like that old self. Like she's stopped holding back. I know this because when she visits, she tells me that she finds me boring. She says it straight to my face. I suppose it must be true. Since the day when May brought Teddy to the house, I've been staying home and studying every day, trying to atone to my parents for that one small act of defiance.

Mum didn't ever speak to me about Teddy Taualai, not about him being a bad influence or a distraction from my studies. I kept waiting for her to bring it up, but she never did. And I guess it doesn't matter now anyway, after what happened at the beach.

I ran away, and now it's been two weeks. Two weeks away from school on holiday, two weeks of studying and working and staying home. And two weeks of thinking he would turn up at my house or at the cinema, just turn up out of nowhere and demand an explanation about why I ran away and didn't answer him. Just thinking about it stresses me out.

But of course he never did.

And now I've run over what I might say in my mind a million times, but the truth is I still have absolutely no idea what I will do when I see him.

School starts again, and I'm dreading seeing him in class. So I end up just avoiding him.

Stupid, I know. But I'm so nervous I don't know what else to do. The whole thing is just so embarrassing, and I don't know what he meant when he said that to me on the beach, except surely he couldn't have been serious. There's no *way* he was serious.

Boys like Teddy Taualai are never serious.

And if he was . . . I don't even think about that option, because clearly he wasn't.

So in the morning I purposely arrive right when the bell rings for the start of class, so there's no chance of accidentally running into him in the hallways. And then afterward I take the long way to English just to avoid his locker, because I know he always goes there to pick up his books.

At lunch I avoid the library, where he knows I usually am, and also the oval, where he goes to play soccer, and instead I huddle in an empty classroom, eating the sandwich I brought, just so I don't have to go to the cafeteria and face him.

But of course it can't last.

In the afternoon I have math, and in math I sit right beside him.

Outside the classroom I take a deep calming breath. I'll

just act normal, like nothing happened. I will smile and wave and bicker with him, just like I always do.

When I walk in, his desk is still empty, and I sigh in relief. If he's late, there won't be a chance to talk until after class anyway, so that's another hour I don't have to think about any of this.

Obviously I am pleased, at least until Ms. Breannie tells us to open our textbooks to start the lesson. Because by then I've realized that Teddy Taualai isn't coming at all.

And I should be relieved.

Yet somehow I'm not.

First I worry that maybe he's upset with me; maybe that's why he isn't here. If I didn't want to kiss him I could have just said so. I didn't have to run away like an idiot. I bet he wouldn't even understand why I did that, why I felt so nervous. To him, kissing girls on the beach probably isn't a big deal. He wouldn't understand that it was a big deal to me.

He wouldn't get it at all.

And that thing I didn't remember, about the first time we spoke? He was upset about that, too. Or at least, *something* was upsetting him. I could tell *something* was going on.

My fingers keep tugging on the hem of my skirt as Ms. Breannie reads from the book. And even though I like math, and even though it's my last year of high school, my most *important* year of high school, I'm not listening to a single word she says.

When class finishes I just drift through the rest of the day.

Everywhere I go, I'm waiting to see Teddy Taualai, except he isn't there, and by the time the final bell has rung, I finally accept that he isn't coming in today.

Which somehow makes everything worse. All I want is for things to go back to normal. But if he doesn't come back, then they can't. And it's driving me crazy.

"Hey, Alice!"

I turn around at the front gate, my backpack sliding off one of my shoulders. I heave it back up as I watch May run down the path toward me, her shoes slapping against the concrete.

"Hey," I say, sounding gloomy even to my own ears. I just want to go home.

"What's wrong?"

May watches me curiously, moving all around in a circle as she inspects me.

"Hey! Stop that. Nothing's wrong."

"Are you sure? You seemed kind of distracted today."

"No, I didn't," I protest loudly.

I walk quickly out the gate toward the train station, May scurrying after me, trying to keep up.

"Well, I thought you did. Anyway, you know how I was hanging out with Julie a bit over the holidays?"

"No," I say, because I didn't know that.

"Well, I was. Anyway, today she invited me to sit with her group on the oval, and Finn was totally talking to me during lunch! And he was so sweet, asking me how my holidays were! Did you see?"

"No."

"Well, he did! I didn't see Harry, though. I thought he was skipping school like Teddy, but then he was in biology."

I stop walking.

"Teddy skipped school today?"

May stumbles against my backpack. "Huh? Yeah, I guess so. He wasn't here, so that's what I figured. Didn't he tell you anything?"

"No, of course not."

May just shrugs. "He'll be back tomorrow probably. Did you hear Julie is planning a party at her house for her birthday?"

I don't answer, and May just prattles on about the party without ever stopping to take a breath.

Teddy Taualai will be in school again tomorrow; that's what May said. So I tell myself I'll just talk to him then. I can do it. I can be normal, and then everything will be fine. I'm sure of it.

Except on Tuesday he doesn't come to school either.

I notice straightaway this time because I'm waiting beside his locker, right up until the first bell rings. I think about texting him but then feel weird about it. First, I don't have his number and would have to ask Harry for it, and second, I didn't contact him over the holidays at all, so it seems strange to do it now.

Besides, he might be busy. Or he might think I'm stupid. So I tell myself to leave it alone. He'll come back when he's ready. I just need to leave it alone.

I only last until lunchtime.

As soon as we're let out of class, I head to the oval to find Harry. He's playing soccer like Teddy usually does, and when I wave he comes jogging over to me. The weather has gotten cold quickly, and he shivers as we stand in the shade of a pine tree, rubbing his arms to keep warm.

"What's up, Alice?"

"Yeah, hi." Everything is so awkward. I bite my lip. "Um, Harry, I was wondering, have you heard from Teddy lately? Like why he isn't in school?"

Harry just shrugs like it's not at all weird that I'm asking. "Nah, I haven't talked to him. I figured he must be sick."

"Sick?"

"Yeah. He seemed a bit off over the holidays. I saw him a couple times, like, down at the beach and stuff, but . . . I dunno. He was distracted."

"Was he not . . . okay?"

Harry shakes his head. "He was kind of weird, I guess." He scowls for a moment and then blurts, "Is May into that Finn guy now?"

"Huh?" I blink, startled by the abrupt change in topic. "Um, I don't know."

Harry snorts. "Sure you don't."

He runs his hand over his face, annoyed. "He's got a girl-friend, you know? Does she know that?"

"Um . . ."

"Of course she knows that. Everyone does!"

I scuff my shoe against the dry grass in silence, unsure what I should or shouldn't say.

It seems everyone has their own concerns, their own thoughts filling up their heads to the brim, leaving no room for anyone else. Definitely not for Teddy Taualai.

I shuffle from foot to foot. "Um . . . listen, Harry. Do you maybe have Teddy's number? Or his address?"

He's still annoyed, distracted, glancing across the oval to where Sophia and her friends are sitting. May is there, too, sitting beside Julie with a huge smile plastered on her face, soaking up the feeling of sitting with the cool kids.

"Harry?" I say, reminding him that I'm still standing here. "Do you have Teddy's address?"

He runs his hand through his hair, still peering across the oval.

"Nah, I've never been to his house. I already tried texting him and he won't reply anyway. I wouldn't bother, Alice. He'll be back tomorrow. Probably."

With a final scowl in May's direction, Harry runs off to rejoin his friends on the oval, and I slowly walk back toward the school buildings.

I wonder if Teddy Taualai really is sick. If he is, it must be pretty serious if he was feeling bad all break, and now he's still missing two days of school. Or maybe he just doesn't want to see me. That's the thought that keeps running through my head, even though I know it's stupid. It's a self-centered thought, as if there aren't a million different reasons why Teddy Taualai wouldn't come to school.

But then I think that maybe something else happened. And if that was true, none of us would even know.

When the final bell rings, I make my decision.

I find her in the art room, packing the materials from class back into the supply cupboard. I walk up behind her. "Mrs. Kang?"

She glances around, looking surprised.

"Alice! What brings you here?"

She smiles, mostly because she likes me, but also because she likes the idea that I'm seeking her out after school.

I guess it's mean to use her trust so blatantly, but really I am sincere. Mostly.

But I also know she's the only teacher who might actually give me what I want. Because there's no way I could ask Mr. Jenner for Teddy Taualai's address. He'd just call my parents instead, tell them I was getting involved with a bad crowd.

But Mrs. Kang is different. I tell her I need his address to give him notes from math class. I tell her he's sick and I don't want him to fall behind.

And Mrs. Kang likes me. She trusts me.

And she gives me what I want.

chapter 14

HOME

When I get home from school to my empty house beside the sea, I search for the keys to the shed and go out into the backyard to unlock the doors. Inside it is dusty and filled with cobwebs, and it occurs to me that it must be years since any of us came out here. I search the dark shadows and move some old musty boxes until I find it: my bicycle.

I almost laugh when I see it, remembering how badly I wanted it. How I'd been dreaming of it all summer. And then all those months later I got home from school to find it sitting in the middle of the living room. A present. A prize for getting a good grade on my English test.

And I had been so happy, so elated.

I'd been so nervous I wouldn't do well on that test, but I did. And my parents were so proud of me they bought me the bike I'd been longing for. Except by then it was nearly winter.

And I no longer needed my parents to tell me to work hard. I did it all on my own.

So in the end, I only used my precious bike a few times. Just once or twice before it was stored neatly away in the shed. To be forgotten. To gather dust.

I pull it out now with some difficulty, and then I spend the next twenty minutes searching for the bike pump because both tires have gone completely flat. After that I spend another eternity trying to figure out how to actually use the pump, which is when I notice the black widows crawling out from underneath the seat. Shrieking, I run inside to find the bug spray, and then I'm jumping around the backyard, emptying the whole can over every inch of my bike, trying not to get too close.

When I'm absolutely sure they're all dead, I pick up the hose and wash away all the cobwebs, finally deeming the whole thing safe enough to ride.

It's been a long time since I was on a bike. Such a long time. And it's cold and the wind coming in off the sea is strong, and I'm so distracted by the thought of spiders possibly still being inside my helmet that I can't think straight.

But somehow I still manage to make it to the train station, hauling the too-small bike in before the doors swing shut. I travel in silence for five stops, watching as the houses outside the window grow smaller and closer together, their front yards tiny square patches of brown dirt beside the road.

I've never been here before. It's the opposite direction

from school, a different route from where May's house is. It's strange because it's not all that far away from home, but it somehow seems different. Everything around here is just a tiny bit less shiny, just a little bit smaller and more closed in.

When the train stops at the station, I climb out, pulling my bike across the gap between the train car and the concrete platform. Two other boys are getting off here, too, both of them older than me with hoods pulled over their heads to hide their faces. They are laughing loudly and swearing, making me nervous, but when my wheel gets stuck in the gap near the train they both run over to help me. And then guilt surges in my chest for being scared of them at all.

Once the boys are gone I wheel my bike down onto the road, peering around.

Everything is dry. The grass is brown and dead, the dirt by the pathways turning into clouds of dust, blown about by the rushing wind. All the trees are twisted eucalyptuses or scrubby bush-type things I don't even recognize. And behind the houses a factory rises, two spires looming up against the blue sky like sentinels, spewing cloudy smoke across the horizon.

I consult my phone for directions and then climb onto my bike and pedal down the street, following the winding roads toward the river. The top of the factory is the only thing breaking the wide sky overhead, its chimneys and walkways sending long-reaching shadows across the houses as they burn with the orange afternoon sun.

It takes a while to find it, and even when I do I'm still

unsure. An old woman kneels in the yard, a plastic bucket sitting on the brown grass beside her as she pulls spindly weeds from the driveway.

I stop across the street, pushing my helmet back over my head and adjusting my glasses. I think it's the right house. One of the smaller cottages, built right against its neighbor, with a wire fence surrounding the small front yard. I peer at the older woman, wondering who she could be. Her skin is darker than Teddy's, but she could be related to him, I think.

I roll my bike across the road to stand awkwardly just outside the fence, staring at her.

"Um . . . hi," I say, thinking this might not even be Teddy's house. I'm such an idiot. I don't know what I'm doing here, or what I'm supposed to say to this woman. I feel like an intruder.

She peers at me. "Hello. Are you all right, love?"

"I was trying to find Teddy Taualai's house. Is it this one? I might have it wrong."

She lets go of the plastic bucket and stands up, examining me more closely now. Her expression isn't unkind, though, more just interested. "No, you're right. I'm his nana."

"Oh," I say stupidly, half glad I have the right house and half horrified because now I'll have to see him.

A nana is a grandmother, right? Teddy's family lives with his grandmother.

I didn't know that.

"Did you come to visit him?" She is smiling at me now,

as if she's trying to reassure me. It makes me think my awkwardness must be completely obvious, which just embarrasses me even more.

I nod. "He didn't come to school," I answer by way of explanation.

Her wrinkled mouth turns down at the corners. "It's always a bit hard on him this time of year, so I don't make him go to school. This is the first time someone came to check on him, though."

She smiles at me, and I think maybe she's grateful, which is odd.

"This time of year?" I ask, and after I repeat her words, I wonder when exactly it was that Teddy Taualai transferred to my school. Was it around now, three years ago? Is that what his grandmother means? Maybe he still gets upset when he thinks about that fight. Maybe he feels guilty.

"What's your name, love?" Teddy's nana startles me, her question snapping me back to the present.

"It's Alice Dyson."

She smiles. "I'm Violet. It's nice to finally meet you. Teddy's been talking about you for such a long time."

I stare at her, letting those words sink in. They sit there in my chest, leaving me unsettled.

She opens the gate to let me in, pointing to the front wall of the house. "Just leave your bike over there. Teddy is inside. You can just go straight in if you want. I think he'll be happy to see you."

I am not so sure.

I think again of his face when he almost kissed me. He was so strange, and now I'm beginning to wonder what's really going on. If he isn't upset at me or sick, then it must be something else.

I turn back to his grandmother, suddenly nervous. "Are you sure I can just go in?"

"Yes, yes. I still have a bit left to do out here. You go on ahead."

She actually sort of pushes me toward the door, which freaks me out. She doesn't even let me knock, just opens the screen and hustles me inside, saying, "Tell Teddy to give you a drink, okay?"

"Uh-huh," I agree, though I'm pretty sure I won't. It'll be hard enough for me to speak to him at all.

Teddy's grandma goes back outside and I'm left standing alone in a tiny entrance hall, a compact kitchen clearly visible at the back of the house. Everything inside is dark, like the curtains have all been pulled down, and I definitely don't see Teddy anywhere.

The whole thing makes me uncomfortable because obviously I did want to visit him, but still, this isn't exactly what I was imagining. I try my best to push down the panic, forcing myself to shuffle forward.

"Hi? Teddy?" There's no answer.

I walk down the hall, the open door to my left revealing a living room that opens onto the tiny kitchen. A TV sits in front of a big window, the curtains are drawn, and a small worn couch sits in the middle of the room.

And Teddy Taualai is on the couch. Lying on his back, sleeping.

I stare at him from the doorway.

He's wearing sweatpants and one of his stupid stretched T-shirts, the bottom of it folded up to show the curve of his hip and side, bare skin right to his ribs. His chest rises in time with his heavy breathing, and he's all tangled up in a white comforter that's twisted around his legs. I stare, keep staring, and then suddenly realize I'm staring, so quickly look away and back down the hallway, the image of him seared into my mind.

"He's asleep," I say when I get back outside.

The sunshine is bright and blinding after the darkness of the house. Also, I'm pretty sure my face is burning to match the sun, and I hope Teddy's grandma doesn't notice.

Violet glances over her shoulder, blinking, like she doesn't understand what I mean. "You can wake him up. He won't mind."

"Oh, I think maybe I'll just go. If he's asleep and all, I don't want to disturb—"

"Nonsense! Don't be silly. *Teddy!*"

She screams out the last bit, making me jump.

And then an answering shout comes from inside the house. "What?"

He sounds half-asleep and pissed off.

She peers at me with Teddy's black eyes and says, "There, you see. He'll be awake now."

I nod miserably, wondering why I even came here. But I slowly drag my feet back into the house.

"Hey," I say unhappily when I arrive back at the living room door.

Teddy jumps up so fast he kind of half falls onto the floor, his legs still tangled in his blanket.

"Alice? Wha . . . what are you doing here?"

He blinks at me, dark eyes heavy with sleep and his hair sticking up like he just got out of bed.

Which, I remind myself, he just did.

I keep focusing on my feet. My face is burning and I know I have to say something, but I still have no idea what it is, so I open my mouth and babble, "You didn't come to school and Harry said you were sick maybe. And I got your address and came here and your grandma let me in, but you were sleeping. And I didn't want to wake you but she wouldn't let me leave so . . . so I . . ."

I trail off as Teddy slowly sinks back down onto the couch.

He doesn't look annoyed. He doesn't seem to think I'm stupid for having come here. He doesn't tell me I should leave.

Which makes me feel a little bit better.

Except maybe he is unwell, dark circles blooming underneath his eyes. When I'm looking right at his face, I think he looks . . .

Like he's been crying.

I stare at him until he turns away.

And then I realize I was staring and that reminds me of when I saw him sleeping, which makes me blush. Quickly I turn away, too, glancing across the small living room, taking in the shelf covered with books and the dresser in the corner with clothes hanging out of it. A little table is nestled beside the couch, a coffee table like the kind my mum would have covered in special books, the books meant for visitors to flick through, art books, even though my mother doesn't even like art. This table is empty except for a photograph, the frame sitting facedown on the wooden surface. My eyes keep moving everywhere and anywhere that Teddy Taualai isn't.

My heart thumps against my chest because if he was crying then clearly I've intruded on something that has nothing to do with me, and I bite my lip, completely mortified, wishing I hadn't come.

"I'm sorry," I say slowly. "I didn't mean . . . I shouldn't have come. I just got worried when you didn't come to school."

I steal a glance at him. He's staring at me, startled, like my words are unexpected. "Thank you." His voice is low and strange.

"Um . . . you're welcome."

I don't know what he's thankful for. Everything is just awkward and awful.

"You can come in," he adds after a while because I'm still hovering in the doorway. "It's okay." He sounds more normal suddenly, but still tired.

But his words break the aching awkwardness, and I step farther into the room. Teddy yawns and settles back onto the couch, folding up his long legs as he rubs at his eyes.

"Did Nana say anything to you?"

I frown at him. "No. What do you mean?"

He shakes his head. "Nah, nothing. Do you want a drink or something?"

"I'm fine, thank you."

"How was school? Anything happen?"

I shrug. "Not really. When you're not there, it's kind of boring."

I can't believe I said it. But I did.

When I glance at him he's grinning. "That's good," he says slowly. "I'll be back tomorrow."

My face is burning. "Will you?"

He nods, and then the stupid silence stretches out between us again. I keep waiting for him to fill it, but he says nothing, just sits there quietly peering at his hands. It's like something is wrong with him, I'm sure of it, something he's not telling me. But I don't know how to ask because he's almost brittle. Which is such a strange thing for me to think, especially when I imagine him jumping off the jetty into the ocean. Back then he was unbreakable, so much stronger than I was.

But now . . .

I want to ask him what's going on, but I don't even know where to begin.

So instead I wander around the room, examining the books on the shelves, just to keep moving, to avoid the awkwardness of the silence.

"Are these books all yours?" I ask, for the sake of asking something.

He just nods, though, the strange heaviness still filling the air. I run my fingers over the spines. It takes me a moment to figure out they're mostly all schoolbooks. Textbooks from last year and this year. A similar collection sits in my own room at home.

I take in the dresser in the corner of the room. They're *his* clothes hanging out of the drawers, his school uniform and his gym clothes. His sneakers rest in the corner next to the TV, and a skateboard leans against the tiny kitchen bench. I think of the house, of the few open doorways that I saw in the hall.

I look at him sharply. "Is this your *bedroom*?"

I glance around the room. The house is so tiny. And Teddy Taualai sleeps here in the living room, right next to the kitchen. In front of the TV. And there isn't even a door.

"So?"

He says it in a low voice and doesn't meet my eyes, and heat flares across my cheeks because I wish I could take it back. I didn't mean to blurt it out like that. I didn't mean to make it sound like it would matter if it were.

I wonder how I've managed to make this all go so horribly wrong so quickly, and to hide my embarrassment I step closer to the couch. I reach out for the photograph sitting beside him, the one lying face down on the coffee table, and I pick it up. As soon as my fingers close on the frame he has jumped to his feet, his hand trying to grab it back again.

But it's too late.

I freeze, holding tightly onto the frame with his hand wrapped around mine, his body rigid and so close. My face is right near his neck, my shoulder brushing against his chest. And when I see the picture, it all just falls into place. Like the pieces of a puzzle.

He lives here in this tiny one-bedroom house with his grandmother.

Only his grandmother.

The photograph is of a woman. She is maybe in her mid-forties and her hair falls in a dark wave around her face. And her eyes are just like Teddy Taualai's.

As I peer at the photo, Teddy slowly sinks back down onto the couch, his hand still clenched tightly around mine, around the photograph.

I stand frozen, words on the tip of my tongue, but not one of them good enough to say. My breathing is shallow, my gaze locked on him.

Still gripping my fingers with one hand, Teddy uses his free hand to cover his eyes, his head sinking down until his hair hides his face. My chest is thumping as I say, "Is it your mum?"

He nods, just the slightest of movements.

"She's not here anymore?"

He nods again, and I know she is dead.

For such a long time we just stay like that, frozen—him sitting, me standing over him—but then gradually, little by little, he has slumped forward until his forehead is resting against my body, his head heavy against my side, resting just above my hip. My body is stiff, tense. I'm so out of my depth, with no idea how to handle what is happening right now. I don't know if he's crying; I can't see his face. I think maybe he is.

I focus on the top of his head. His dark hair is sticking up, his fingers gone white from holding my hand so hard. Slowly I reach out, my free hand hovering just above his head. I hesitate, then softly touch his hair, sinking my fingers into it, brushing the mess of it back gently. We stay like that for the longest time, just us in the quiet darkness.

When Teddy finally lets go of my hand he does it really quickly, pulling away in one big jerky movement that has him on his feet and striding across the room away from me. He turns so I can't see his face. "Give me a sec." His voice is strange, and then he disappears through the kitchen into some other part of the house.

When he's gone I sit down heavily on the couch, my breath escaping all at once.

I can hear the sound of Teddy's nana outside, still scratching away at the driveway. I sit with my hands folded between my knees and stare at the photograph of Teddy's mum on the coffee table. She smiles back at me. And then after the longest time Teddy comes back and his face and hair is dripping wet like he dunked it in the sink.

"Wanna go for a walk?" he asks, still not meeting my eyes, and I nod.

Outside is a good idea. I want to get out of this heavy room.

I watch as he moves around, grabbing a baseball cap and then collapsing beside me on the couch as he shoves his feet into his sneakers. I don't move, and the space between us is thick and charged like it's a solid thing. I'm so aware of every movement he makes, every moment in which his body almost touches mine but then doesn't, of how the couch sinks under his weight, drawing me toward him. I hold my breath until he stands up again, pulls on a jacket, and picks up his skateboard, and then I follow him out the front door.

"Hey, Nana. Me and Alice are gonna go down to the river for a bit, okay?"

Teddy's grandmother stands up. "It's cold down there, Alice. Are you sure you'll be warm enough?"

I nod, pulling my sweater more closely around me.

She frowns. "Teddy, why don't you go find her something to wear from inside?"

"She said she's fine, Nana," Teddy complains, and his voice sounds so normal I dare to look over at his face now.

"Oh, all right, Mr. Know-It-All," his grandmother answers. "But you should be taking care of her. She was nice enough to come all this way to visit you, after all. Come here." She pulls her towering grandson down and wraps her arms around his neck, and he glances at me, his cheeks pink. He's embarrassed, like he wants to be somewhere else. But then his grandmother says in a worried voice, "Are you sure you're all right?"

And after she says it, Teddy reaches down and hugs her back, mumbling quietly, "Yeah, I'm fine. Promise."

She sighs and lets him go. "Well, off you go, then. Don't be too late. It'll get dark soon."

Teddy grins and grabs my arm, propelling me down the path and outside the gate. "You're such a worrywart," he shouts with a laugh. And then he slams his skateboard onto the road and is speeding away across the street, leaving me scurrying to catch up.

chapter 15

GHOSTS

It's cold and windy on the way to the river. We don't talk much. Teddy just rolls off ahead on his skateboard, flying back every now and then to make sure I'm still following. It's like he doesn't want to stay still. Or like he can't.

But I don't mind.

The road is wide, and I like walking by myself. I like the way he appears again for a moment and then zips off, smiling at me like he's glad I'm here, like it makes a difference even though we aren't talking or even walking together.

My flip-flops scuff at the pavement as we enter a new neighborhood, an array of tiny modern houses all lined up on one side of the street and a scrub-covered shoulder on the other. Beyond that is a field of silos, towering along the riverbank like white giants, and then the next field is filled with huge shipping containers, stacked together like colored Lego blocks.

It takes a long time to reach the river.

The road grows wider and emptier, until it's just us two on it, Teddy way up ahead doing tricks on his skateboard, falling over and then getting back on again, and me following along behind. And as we go deeper into the industrial area, the tops of cargo ships rise above the warehouses, the massive cranes on their decks reaching into the sky. Clouds roll in, gray and dark.

It's strange how empty it is here, this place so close to my house where I have never been.

Seagulls cry overhead in swarms, and in the distance cars hum along the highway. And through the noise is the constant scrape of Teddy's skateboard against the asphalt, over and over again.

He turns and speeds back toward me now, messing up his stop so he has to jump and run on the road to keep from falling, his skateboard skidding away to hit the curb. One of his elbows is bloody from an earlier fall. After he's picked his skateboard up again he comes over to me. "You all right?"

"Yeah. Are you?"

He falls into step beside me and grins. "Yup. Have you been to the river before?"

I shake my head. The wind picks up as we near the water, blowing strands of loose hair across my face. "No, never."

"It's nice. I used to come here with my mum when I was little. We'd go fishing whenever we visited Nana."

"How come you never told me about her?"

He shrugs. "It happened ages ago, just before I transferred into school here. And besides, it's a weird thing to just bring up, isn't it? If no one asks."

I bite my lip. "I should have asked."

I'm thinking of his confession at the art gallery.

I glance over at him. "When you told me about the party, I should have asked what that boy said that made you want to hit him." I pause and then add, "It was something to do with your mum, right?"

Teddy just shrugs again, is silent for a while, and then admits, "Yeah."

"Why did you go?"

He raises his eyebrows at me. "You mean, why did I go to a party if my mum had just died?"

I blush, but still nod as we keep walking down the middle of the wide, empty street.

"I dunno," Teddy finally answers. "No one's ever asked me that before."

He hesitates, thinking. "I was really angry. And this guy from my school was having this big party." He looks at me and adds, "You know, those big, once-a-year kind of parties? The ones you don't want to miss because everyone will be talking about it for weeks afterward and you'll feel left out?"

I don't really know what he means. I've never been to a party before, but I think May must feel like that every time she hears about a party she isn't invited to. So I think I can understand.

I nod.

"Well, it was six weeks after she died." He scuffs his sneakers on the road as we walk, dragging his feet and kicking at loose gravel. "And I just wanted to feel normal again, you know? But I was so angry. I shouldn't have been drinking anyway. But I guess I thought it was helping me forget. I was an idiot."

"You were sad."

He glances at me. "Yeah. It was dumb, though. I should've just stayed home."

"What happened?"

He sighs, and I wonder if I shouldn't be asking. But he keeps telling me anyway, so maybe it's okay.

"At the party everyone was acting really strange around me, 'cause I hadn't been to school in a while and they'd all heard what happened. And no one was talking about it, like they were all just pretending it didn't happen, or not talking to me at all. I dunno, I started feeling like a buzzkill, like they wished I wasn't there. And then this arsehole kid said something about my dad probably not showing up to the funeral and I just . . . I went crazy."

"What an arsehole!" I repeat.

Teddy laughs. "It sounds weird when you say it." He chuckles a bit, and I don't mind him teasing me because it's nice to hear him laugh.

But then he startles me by suddenly yelling out at the sky, a loud wordless shout, the sound of his voice echoing down the empty street. I look across at him as he stretches his arms into the air, face turned upward. It's cloudy now, getting darker, and he shouts again before folding his arms down over his head.

He glances over at me, pushing his skateboard along with his foot so it moves in time with our steps. "You know, I haven't really had to talk about it in forever. No one at school even knows."

"Harry doesn't?"

Teddy shakes his head. "Nah, he hasn't come over to the house, and it never came up before, so I never told him. We started hanging out about two years ago, and by then the rumors had died down at school. He never even asked about them. I kinda liked that he didn't, so I never brought it up."

"You don't have to talk about it. Unless you want to . . ." My voice trails off. I am so bad at this stuff. I peer at my feet like a little inexperienced kid.

No one I know has ever died. Even my grandparents are all still alive, though they live far away and I hardly know them. Whatever I say to him surely couldn't ever be enough.

But when I look at him he's smiling, shrugging. "Nah, this time of year it's all there anyway, you know? It doesn't go away, so I reckon maybe it's a good thing I get to talk about it. Besides, it's just my nana and me usually, and she knows it all already."

I steal a glance at him and wait, because I think that means he does want to talk about it with me.

"It was last Friday, actually," he says, voice too casual, too easy. "Three years ago last Friday. A car accident." He keeps his attention on the approaching river, on the huge looming cargo ship that rises into the gray sky before us. "I was with her in the car."

My stomach lurches but I stay silent.

"She was driving me home from soccer practice after school. She came straight from work to pick me up, and I hadn't seen her all day but I was wearing my headphones in the car and listening to music. I didn't even talk to her." He shrugs, like it's no big deal, but I remember how he was in the house before, so I know how much it must hurt, how guilty he must feel.

"I think that part's the worst, you know? Just that I didn't even bother to talk to her. I could have asked her something, like what she'd been doing at work. Or I could have talked to her about school. Or, I dunno, just talked about something."

He shrugs again. "There were no last words. No last conversation. It was fast." He moves his hands so his palms collide loudly, like a demonstration of how it was, and the gesture kind of shocks me.

I don't know what to say.

Teddy Taualai isn't like everyone thinks he is.

He's nothing like what everyone says.

A heaviness settles in my chest as I try to untangle my thoughts. All of it turns me cold, like I'm being sucked down into a deep hole, and I don't know what to do or say. And I hate how unequipped I am to offer any help. Except then Teddy reaches over and wraps his arm around my shoulders, pulling me closer so I stumble against him.

I hesitate. Normally I would just push him away, but right now everything is awful. And I can't get the image of him crying out of my head. And isn't this when people offer hugs and kind words? That's what people do in the movies.

But I have nothing to say. I don't even know what to do to comfort him.

So I waver halfway between pushing his arm away and letting him stay. Except then I see that he's grinning.

"If I'd known all I had to do was tell you a sad story, Alice, I would've done it months ago." He laughs, and it sounds a bit evil, like he's enjoying himself. He bats his eyelashes at me. "Are you going to date me now?"

He reaches out with his other arm as if to pull me in for a hug but I duck away out of his grasp, my face burning red.

"Stop it," I snap, embarrassment flaring. I power walk ahead to get away from him.

Teddy is still chuckling, and though I'm mostly glad he's okay, I'm also annoyed that his recovery came at my expense.

He's always doing that, always saying things to tease me. I can never tell what's serious and what's just messing around.

Like what happened on the beach.

I sigh. "Yeah, yeah, so funny." Then I call out over my shoulder, "Hurry up, we're almost there."

And we are.

The warehouses open onto the river, a wide space with huge docking stations lining the distant bank. Teddy throws his skateboard onto the gravel in the empty parking lot and then runs ahead across the scrubby grass down onto the shore, leaving deep footprints on the sand.

He runs straight for a group of gulls, scattering them as they take to the skies squawking and screaming, floating above the lapping waves before the wind catches their wings and they are borne away across the water.

When I finally catch up to him, he's out of breath, hands on his knees as he grins at me. He says, "Did you know you can call dolphins here?"

"What do you mean?"

I crouch beside him at the water's edge. It's cold and the wind cuts into me, blowing my hair across my face.

"Mum told me," he says. "She had a friend who used to kayak out here every day, and she'd just click her fingers under the water and the river dolphins would come straight to the sound. They'd swim all around the kayak."

I watch him, not sure if he's teasing again. "No way. Why would they do that?"

He just shrugs, "I dunno. That's just what Mum said. She told me when I was a kid. But she said it never worked for anyone else, just her friend, because the dolphins got so used to her visiting. Maybe they knew she wasn't going to harm them."

Teddy sits down on the damp sand to pull off his shoes and roll up the bottom of his sweatpants. He sticks his foot into the water and makes a face at me.

"What are you doing?" I laugh. "It's freezing!"

But he just splashes into the water anyway, gasping at the temperature, before plunging his hands deep underwater. I can't hear anything but can only presume he's trying to call the dolphins, and that just makes me giggle all over again.

He's so serious and silly, crouched in the icy water with sand all over the bum of his pants and the wind whipping his hair into a frenzy, trying to signal dolphins.

"You're ridiculous," I call from the shore. "Your feet are going to get frostbite."

"Shh, Alice. I'm whispering to the dolphins. You're going to ruin it." He frowns with such disapproval I can't help but laugh again.

And just when I open my mouth to shout back, a fin crests a wave out on the choppy water. I scream and Teddy jumps, following my pointed finger to the other side of the river, where a dolphin slides easily between the waves near the bow of a docked cargo ship, tiny against the colossal red metal hull.

"Did you see it? Did you see?" I'm so excited I am squealing, and then Teddy is splashing up out of the water, running toward me and shouting something dumb about being the king of dolphins. And when I realize what he's planning to do, I am screaming and running away fast across the sand, my chest heaving as I gulp in the salty air, the wind whipping my protests away across the river.

"No! No, don't!" I'm giggling too hard to run properly. When he catches up to me, his wet hands grab at my sweater and he heaves me up, my feet leaving the ground as he turns back toward the river. I scream at the thought of being dunked into the freezing water.

"The dolphins told me to do it," he is yelling. And I am struggling against his arms, unable to control my laughter even as real panic runs through me, too. His hands are freezing against my skin where my sweater rides up, and I struggle like crazy until he can't hold me anymore, and we both collapse into a heap on the cold, damp sand, a pile of limbs and tangled arms.

I roll over, trying to pull myself away, but Teddy grabs my arm and I end up collapsing back down onto the sand beside him, my chest heaving, exhausted.

He props himself up onto an elbow. "You've got sand all over your face."

I snort. "Whose fault is that?"

He smiles at me, small and crooked. "Mine," he answers. He reaches over and carefully pulls my glasses off.

The world's details turn blurry, but it's obvious he's wiping them clean on his shirt, getting the sand off the lenses.

I turn to the sky.

It's so cold, but I don't even care. I like how the wind rushes over my body, how the wet sand soaks into my clothes. I try to remember the last time I had this much fun, the last time

I felt so calm on the inside, like I didn't have to worry about school and home and May.

But then I remember.

It was weeks ago, the day I went to the beach with my friends.

With Teddy Taualai.

I glance over at him just as he finishes with my glasses, and I lie still as he places them carefully back onto my face. I wonder what it means that he can make me feel this way.

A tingle spreads in my chest and in my toes, like somehow things are changing.

A loud booming startles both of us, a horn blaring from a ship. Teddy rolls over, oblivious to the amount of sand he is smearing himself with, seemingly not bothered by the cold. "Hey, look."

I sit up.

An enormous ship floats slowly past our little beach. Tiny people scurry around the top and two tugboats bob in the water beside its hull, guiding the massive ship in to berth next to the factory upriver. We watch it in silence for a long time, and then Teddy clears his throat. "Where do you think it's from?"

I point at the hull immediately. "Spain. Or South America, more likely. Look, the name's in Spanish."

He squints. "How do you know that?" He leans closer as if he'll take my glasses for a better look, but I push him away.

"I'm learning it. I can speak a little, actually."

I'm proud as I say it. It's not something I've done for my parents, but something I do only for myself.

"I learn it online," I explain. "At home."

Teddy looks surprised. "Why? Don't you already do Indonesian in school? Isn't it confusing?"

I just shrug, thinking about the future. "It's not too bad. I can do it."

Teddy grins. "Of course you can do it. You're like a super-woman at school. You do better than anyone."

I am surprised and I don't know why. It's what everyone always says, yet when Teddy says it, it sounds like a real compliment, like he means it. Not tinged with jealousy, not like he's actually making fun of me for being a nerd. It sounds nice. I find myself smiling shyly.

"You said you're coming back to school tomorrow?" I ask.

He nods. "Yeah. I will." He makes a face and flops back down onto the sand. "Can't wait."

I just shrug. "School's not so bad."

He peers up at me. "Well, it got a lot better this year, that's for sure." He grins, eyes locked on mine, as if daring me to not grasp the meaning of his words. My skin flushes hot and quickly I turn away.

More teasing.

Changing the subject, I babble, "Well, lots is going to be better this year. It's the last one, after all. After this, we'll all have to try to be adults."

Teddy scoffs.

"Adults? Can you really imagine some of the people at our school as adults?"

I giggle and shake my head, thinking of May blindly chasing after Finn.

But it's also mean. Who am I to judge how she wants to spend her final year? Just because I don't want the same things she does doesn't mean what she wants is less important. I sigh and Teddy sits up.

"What?"

I shiver. "Nothing. Just May. She's changing a lot this year, I think."

Teddy says nothing, just waits.

"I just mean . . . lately, I think she wants a lot more than I can give her. That's why she's trying to make friends with Julie, right? I think she's trying to get in with that crowd at school. Because I'm not enough for her anymore."

"Does it upset you? If she wants to be friends with them?"

I blink at him.

I have to think about it for a long time before I answer. "I don't think so. It shouldn't matter if she wants to make more friends than just me. No, it doesn't upset me."

Teddy leans over and nudges me, a grin breaking out across his face.

"It doesn't upset you because you've got me now, right?"

I frown at him, but he just looks pleased with himself. "Don't worry, Alice, you're definitely enough for me. I don't need anything else. Just you."

I stare at him. Is he teasing again? I can't tell. He peers at the river as the gulls circle overhead and land one by one back on our little beach. He doesn't even glance my way, just sits all calm and relaxed like it was a completely normal thing to say. I peer down at my hands and don't reply.

I don't think people should be allowed to say stuff like that if they don't mean it. I shiver, wrapping my arms around my body to combat the cold, a strange uncertainty shifting inside my chest, as if the world has slid off-kilter.

"Come on," Teddy says, climbing to his feet before offering me his hand. "We better go. Nana will get worried if we aren't back by dark."

I peer up at him and then slowly take his hand.

On the way back to Teddy Taualai's house he teaches me how to ride his skateboard. He holds my arms and slowly pulls me along the empty roads, the skateboard rolling and skidding loudly over loose gravel. It's scary, and no matter how hard I try, I can never balance right, and Teddy almost falls twice because he's trying to hold me upright.

But it's fun, too, something simple and normal, like how it is at school. Easy.

And clasped around mine, Teddy's hands are warm and strong.

chapter 16

AGES AFTER

"I guess he's cute. A little young if you ask me."

"Adalina!" May's irritation is written all over her face. "He's only one year younger than you. We're *all* only one year younger! You always act like we're kids or something."

Adalina just shrugs as I watch silently, my fingers curled around my coffee cup.

We're all sitting in the empty foyer of the cinema, waiting for the last show to finish. The place is deserted.

Usually I love May's visits to my work; usually I love sitting and drinking coffee with her. But tonight all she wants to talk about is Finn, and I think Adalina is getting frustrated.

"Look, it's not my fault if listening to your high school crap gets boring," she snaps. "Sometimes you all sound like kids. Once you start uni, you'll know what real problems are."

May's eyes turn hard. "I don't know what *your* problem is, but you don't know anything about me." She's getting angry now, and I reach out a hand to try to calm her down.

I glance at Adalina as she rubs at her forehead, and I think again how tired she is tonight, how stressed she said she was about her exams. She's already told me she thinks she might have failed at least two of her subjects, and she doesn't even know if she wants to study pharmacy anymore.

But, of course, May doesn't know about any of that. As far as she's concerned, Adalina is just being difficult.

"You're jealous," May snaps at her. "Just because you weren't popular in high school doesn't mean you have to take it out on me."

I open my mouth to say something to stop them, but Adalina interrupts me. "No, Alice. It's fine."

She turns back to May like I'm not even here.

"I know enough about you, May. I see you staring at that guy every time he comes in here. He has a *girlfriend*. Or is that not a problem for you?"

May gasps dramatically, and I quickly say, "I think everyone should just calm down."

But no one is listening to me.

"Yeah, he does," May says, and now her lips tremble as if she's about to cry, "but that doesn't mean anything. Sophia's not even nice. He should be with someone better, someone kinder."

Adalina scoffs. "What? Someone like you?" She rolls her eyes. "Anyway, you think this guy is so nice he deserves someone better? If that's true, why is he with his bitchy girlfriend, then? How come this nice boy of yours is so happy spending all his time with a girl who's horrible?" She smiles and adds, "I bet she's hot, right?"

My heart sinks, but Adalina doesn't stop.

She scoffs. "Yep, he sounds like a total catch!"

"You don't know anything," says May. She's really upset now, fighting tears.

"Whatever," Adalina answers with a shrug. She slides up from the table and turns to me. "I'm going outside. I'll come back before the show finishes."

"Okay," I agree. I think that's a really good idea.

When she's gone I reach out and touch May's hand. She smiles weakly at me and sniffles.

Over the last few weeks May's been hanging out with the popular kids more and more. I don't really mind it because I want to study anyway, but still, things have been different. I tell myself it doesn't matter; things were always bound to change. And even though she doesn't talk about anything except Finn every single time we hang out, I tell myself that's fine, too.

I take a deep breath and shrug off my thoughts, squeezing her hand. "Are you okay?"

She sighs, wiping at her cheeks. "Yeah, I guess so. How come she's so mean? What a bitch, right?"

I make a noncommittal grunt, though I definitely agree Adalina was out of line. "She told me she's real stressed about university," I try to explain. "I think she's having a bit of a crisis actually, like she isn't sure she wants to do what she's doing anymore."

"Yeah, well, she didn't have to take her problems out on me."

"No," I agree.

May's face clouds over. "I know he has a girlfriend, Alice. But it doesn't change the way I feel. And what Adalina said about him being with Sophia because she's hot . . . well, he isn't like that. I *know* he isn't."

I nod. "Okay."

I watch her and bite my lip. It's funny that we've been so close all our lives, since we were kids, and yet now that we're older sometimes I can't understand her at all. This need she has for other people, to be popular, to have a boyfriend like Finn—I don't get it.

"Alice?"

"Yeah?"

May's big watery eyes plead. "Julie invited me to go to the markets at the Port next week. Everyone's going. But I'm scared. It'll be my first time hanging out with them all out-side school and I was wondering . . ." She pauses and sniffs sadly again. "I was hoping you might come with me. I can't go alone." She bites her lip.

I am caught off guard. And maybe it's the puppy-dog eyes, or perhaps I'm still feeling guilty over Adalina's outburst, but I end up doing something I never ever do.

I agree.

The second I do, I know I've been had.

May bounds off her chair, all her sadness forgotten, her tears washed away like they were never there. "Thank you!"

she squeals happily as I wonder what I've just done. "I'm so glad you said yes!"

She sits back down and leans close to my ear, whispering, "Finn is going to be there, and Alice, I need to tell you something: I think I might love him."

I jerk back to stare at her, slack-jawed. "What?"

But May isn't even embarrassed, a dreamy smile curling her lips.

"How—how can you know that?" I stammer the words out, a disoriented feeling washing over me, like my best friend has just leaped light-years ahead of me into a world I have absolutely no knowledge of.

May just shrugs. "I dunno. I just do. I can feel it."

"Feel it?"

"Yeah, like I can always tell if he's in the same room as me, even if I'm not near him. Or, like, it makes me feel happy to be talking with him, and upset if I don't get the chance some days. And I think about him all the time."

I can't turn away, fascinated by her confession, so utterly lost in her explanation of being in love. I keep thinking of the sculpture from the art gallery, the one of the couple embracing. Is that what May is feeling? I wonder how you can tell you're in love if you have nothing to compare the feeling to.

When I say as much to May, she just laughs. "I told you. You just know."

"You just know?" I echo. "But what if you can't tell?"

May leans forward, like she's going to impart a secret. "I think you can tell if you're in love when you think someone is different from everyone else you know."

"What do you mean, different?"

"Like they're more interesting, and you want to get to know them better. And obviously you also think they're cute, of course!"

She giggles again, and I wrinkle my nose.

But then she suddenly gets all serious, frowning at me. "Look, Alice," she says. "It's obvious what you're thinking about, and I'm going to tell you straight out: it's not love."

"What are you talking about?" I frown at her.

"Well, you keep asking about how you can tell, so obviously you're thinking about Teddy. You're wondering if you're in love with him."

I blink, my skin turning hot. I had not been thinking about that at all. I really hadn't.

"I know Teddy follows you around at school, and I know he's nice to you, but there are so many cool guys at our school, and if you put in a little effort you could do so much better than Teddy Taualai."

Her words shock me and I sit silent for a moment, trying to formulate a response.

I don't even know what to say.

Half of me wants to deny I feel anything like that about Teddy Taualai, and the other half wants to berate May for talking about him in such a callous way in the first place.

Saying I could do better than Teddy implies there's something wrong with him.

And there really isn't.

Despite all my efforts to say something, I just end up tongue-tied and silent. But May isn't either of those things.

"What about Lucas? He isn't totally popular, but he's not a complete loser either. And he hangs out with Finn sometimes, too."

An image of Lucas with his floppy blond hair and goofy grin appears in my mind. Along with the unpleasant memory of him teasing me in the hallway about the viral video.

I lift my hands to protest, except May still isn't done. "Everyone likes Lucas. Plus he's pretty cute. Cuter than Teddy Taualai, anyway. Teddy always has such a scary expression on his face, like he's going to hit someone. That's what Jenny says."

I stare at her. "Who the hell is Jenny?"

May recoils because I sound angrier than I mean to. But her words are strange, like they're not her own, like they belong to a different May, someone I hardly know. It's freaking me out.

"You know, Jenny Pakulski? She's friends with Julie and Sophia. How can you not know her? She's super popular."

I don't know what to say as she adds, "Just think about it, okay? Lucas is a nice guy, and if you put a little more effort into making yourself pretty and tried to get to know him, I reckon you'd really suit each other."

I gawp at her.

"May," I eventually manage to choke out. "I'm not interested in trying to find a boyfriend. And I don't even know Lucas."

I've never even spoken to him properly. I think again about how he teased me about the dancing video.

My voice is shaking as I add, "Saying stuff like that about Teddy—it doesn't sound like you. I thought you liked him. I thought he was your friend."

She waves her hands, oblivious to my discomfort. "Yeah, I mean, he's fine and all, but if you go out with him, it won't help you in school. People are already gossiping about how much time you spend with him, and it would be better for you to choose someone like Lucas who everyone likes. You'll see I'm right. Lucas is a nice guy. I'm sure you'll like him."

She smiles as if satisfied with herself and our talk, like it's gone well. And I just sit there silently, horrified. It's almost as if the May I used to know, the girl who would stand up for someone like Teddy Taualai in front of gossipy Emily Cooper, is disappearing into this new person before me.

This new girl I don't even know.

She stands, saying, "I gotta run! Oh, and next week we can go to my house straight after school. I want to get changed before we go to the markets. I know Sophia is stopping by her house to get changed, too, and I don't want her to look better than me. Then we can catch the train together, okay?"

She grins at me, all shining happiness, focused only on her chance to hang out with Finn. And I just nod dumbly, wishing I had said I wouldn't go.

chapter 17

A FIRE

When the alarm rings I am sitting in the library, studying by myself. I sit up and rub my face, annoyed.

A fire drill. And it's freaking freezing outside.

I glance out the window at the gray sky that stretches over the oval right toward the sea. The alarm keeps clanging, and eventually I close my books and join the stream of students in the hall outside.

I'm thinking about May as we all shuffle along, shoulder to shoulder, down the staircase toward the main entrance. Everyone is excited, like a fire drill is a truly fun experience and no one can think of a better way to spend their afternoon. As I walk I am enveloped by the giggling, squealing masses, swept outside toward the emergency meeting point. May's short hair is visible ahead, bobbing up and down beside Julie in the crowd.

She's changing so quickly I can barely keep up. Every day

that passes brings something new. Maybe a word I've never heard her use before, words like *slag* or *slut*, words that make me flinch when she says them. Or a nasty comment about a girl at school I thought she liked, like Stacey Green. Or she'll repeat something one of them said to her, something Finn or Jenny said that I think is mean and doesn't sound right coming from her mouth.

But lately something even worse has happened.

A thought has occurred to me, a really bad thought, and now a part of me has begun to wonder if maybe it could be my fault. My fault that she's changing. Because if I had given her more of what she wanted, agreed to go with her to parties, been more open to hanging out with other kids at school, made more friends with her, then maybe she wouldn't be trying to change herself so much just to fit in. Maybe if I had helped her, we could have done it more naturally. Maybe she could've become popular without losing herself.

And even though it was nearly a week ago now, the stuff she said about Teddy is what worries me the most.

When he first started hanging out with us, back when he was squeezing himself into my life and making things difficult, she loved it. She thought of him like some kind of savior who was opening her path to a real high school experience. And she liked him, too, and stood up for him when people whispered behind his back.

But now she says I could do better than him.

As I shuffle outside into the winter sun, I think about Teddy at the art gallery, and in the darkness of his house when he was crying. I picture how he looked when he jumped off the jetty at the beach and how he held my hand and didn't let go. And I think about how I felt with him down beside the river three weeks ago, and how his hands felt on mine when he was teaching me how to ride his skateboard.

And it occurs to me that I couldn't.

I really couldn't do better.

"Whatcha thinking about?"

I jump in surprise, my face immediately growing hot as Teddy Taualai appears at my shoulder.

"N-nothing," I stammer. He raises his eyebrows and I add, because I feel like I have to add something, "Just homework stuff."

I glance away because that sounded lame and I'm sure he'll see right through me, but he just grins and shrugs. As much as things with May have been changing at an alarming rate, things with Teddy Taualai in the last three weeks have been exactly the same.

He follows me around at school, always turning up wherever I am. And I'm used to it. It's normal. It's normal to have him sitting beside me while I study. It's normal for me to share my lunch with him every day, and it's normal for me to shove him away every time he tries to touch me or hug me or pinch my cheek. All of it is routine.

And yet, for the last three weeks, it's been different, too.

Because of me. Because I feel like it's different somehow.

But I don't know what has changed.

"Look, there she is," Teddy is saying. "And Harry, too."

He points to where May is standing in the crowd on the oval, then grabs my hand to pull me through the press toward her. And I focus on his fingers wrapped tightly around mine and feel strange, like my world is slowly becoming askew. May is becoming weirder and Teddy is becoming . . . he's becoming . . .

"Alice!"

May is excited to see me, like we weren't just sitting together an hour ago in class. I smile because I like it, her reaction. I'm glad I still mean something to her, even though she's made all these other new friends. I'm glad she doesn't want to leave me behind.

"Alice," she exclaims, her face shining. "I was just telling Harry about Julie's birthday party. She's having it at her house this weekend." She lowers her voice. "And her parents are away!"

Harry rolls his eyes. "Yeah, but that's only because her older brother is going to still be there. Otherwise they never would've said it was okay." He shakes his head at Teddy, like he thinks May is being silly, and I wonder from his reaction if he still likes her. He's more exasperated now, like she's being overly dramatic and ridiculous. It makes me think how quickly people can change. One day he's mooning over her in class, upset that she isn't interested, and a few weeks later he doesn't seem to care at all.

I wonder if that's all love is, fleeting and shallow and quick.

I glance across at Teddy, and once again I'm trying to work out what it meant to him when he asked if he could kiss me on the beach that night.

I wonder if it meant more to him than it meant to May or Harry.

"I live across the street from Julie," Harry is explaining to me, and I drag my attention to his face, trying to concentrate. "We went to the same primary school so I've known her forever. And her brother, too. He's pretty cool, actually."

I nod absently, realizing this is how May made friends with Julie in the first place—through Harry.

May is smiling excitedly. "Alice, you can come over to my house to get ready, and I can help you with clothes and makeup and stuff."

She winks at me, and I know she's thinking about stupid floppy blond Lucas, but at least no one else notices the hints beneath her words. "My house is closer," she adds. "We can just walk from there, and then you can stay the night with me."

She grins at me, her eyes shining, her body practically shaking with excitement.

Feeling overwhelmed, I lift my hands to protest, to tell her I'm not the slightest bit interested in going to Julie's party.

But I don't.

Instead I think about how things might have been different if I'd supported May more, if I had met her halfway and gone with her to parties instead of always insisting she live her life the way I wanted to, without other people.

I didn't need anyone else. But May did. She always did, and I just ignored it.

Slowly I nod. "Okay. I'll go with you."

Silence blooms as the others all turn to me in surprise, Teddy and Harry both staring. Even May, who asked me like she had no doubt I would agree, is still shocked not to have to fight me on the subject.

But the next moment she has thrown her arms around my neck, chattering on and on about how she's going to do my hair and makeup, and do I have any contact lenses because my glasses are ugly, and can we go shopping on Saturday to buy me new clothes.

And her excitement makes me feel guilty again, for ignoring what she wanted all these years, for forcing her to be like me when really she wasn't.

I smile and agree to it all while Teddy stares at me, and Harry rambles on about Teddy staying the night at his house if he wants to go, too. I see Teddy nod out of the corner of my eye, and I'm so glad he will be there, too, because truthfully I am terrified.

I've never been to a party before. I have no idea what I'm meant to do or say, or how I'm meant to act. At school the other kids don't scare me because I know my place. I am Alice the nerd. I spend my time studying in the library, and no one expects anything different from me.

But going to Julie's party is different. It's like I'm trying to engage in their world, a place where they all belong and I do not. I am completely out of my depth, and it is horrifying.

But still I smile at May and try to share in her excitement, try my best to feel even the tiniest little bit of what I know she is feeling right now.

But it's hard, because mainly I just feel sick.

chapter 18

THE OTHER ONE

The next day after school is the trip to the market. May changes her clothes, she changes her hair and changes her face, and then finally she is ready to catch the train to the Port to meet the others. I didn't bring any different clothes, and she tells me I'll be the only one there in our school uniform but I don't care. I tell her I'm not trying to impress anyone.

But it turns out that is exactly what May was hoping I would do, because when we arrive at the huge covered market, Lucas is there, too, watching me, a wide grin plastered across his face. He stands behind Finn and Sophia near some other people from school I recognize but whose names I don't know.

I glare at May, finally understanding why she was trying so hard to make me wear her clothes, telling me to at least do something to make an effort. Seeing Lucas standing there, I am doubly glad I didn't listen to a word she said.

"Hi, everyone!" May calls happily when we meet up with the group. I stand beside her silently. I'm nervous. Really nervous. My hands are sweaty, and I wipe them on my school skirt, praying I will get through this evening without sounding stupid or loitering around awkwardly on the corner of this very big group of people I barely know.

May and Julie begin to chat eagerly about the birthday party, and I notice Sophia narrowing her eyes at May. Finn stands near some other guys, talking and laughing, but I see him catch May's eye and smile.

Sophia's expression worries me, because it makes me think that maybe May's crush isn't as delusional as I've been thinking. Maybe there really is something on Finn's side, something Sophia knows all about. And Sophia is a frightening girl. I wouldn't want to be on her bad side. I've heard about what happens to anyone who is. Like when Finn danced with Stacey Green last year at some house party I didn't go to. Apparently the next day at school was the first time people started using the words *slut* and *Stacey Green* in the same sentence. And that rippled so out of control that Stacey stopped going to class, and her parents had to be called in.

At least that's what May told me. I was too busy studying and didn't notice. Sophia rules the school, and no girl will reach out to someone Sophia doesn't like, not if they don't want to be targeted by her and her friends. Sophia can make a girl's life living hell if she wants to.

She frightens me so much that as we walk around the

market I steer clear of her, immediately finding myself on the outskirts of the group, wondering exactly how I ended up here. It makes me dread the stupid party even more.

"Hey," says Lucas. He walks over and smiles at me nervously. "Alice, right?"

I nod, knowing full well he knows who I am, remembering him laughing at me about the dancing video. He obviously remembers, too, because the next thing he does is apologize for it, calling himself an idiot. And that surprises me enough to make me examine him properly. His light hair hangs in his eyes and his goofy grin isn't actually all that goofy today. In fact, it looks kind of shy. He's still wearing his school uniform, too, making us the only ones.

He leans over and whispers secretively, "Actually, I don't even know what I'm doing here. My mate Jamie, you know Jamie Gorecki? Well, he hangs out with Finn sometimes, and he's part of that whole crowd, so I got roped into tagging along." He shrugs and glances at the others who stand nearby, loudly joking together. "Pretty much the only person I actually know here is Jamie. You?"

I glance at him in surprise.

"The same," I answer after a moment. "I came with my friend May."

He grins. "Should be a fun evening then, right?"

I can't decide if he's being sarcastic or not so I just nod, noncommittal.

We stand for a moment in silence watching May and the

others, and just when the awkwardness is rising to unbearable levels, Lucas grabs my arm and drags me over to a candy stall.

"You want one?" His enthusiasm is obvious, his gaze sweeping across the multicolored lollipops. "Oh man, so many flavors! Look at that one. It's cherry cola!"

He's a little too excited, I think, but still I stand next to him while he muses over his options, babbling away about the merits of fruit-flavored licorice.

I have nothing better to do, and besides, May is lost in the middle of the group, standing close between Sophia and Finn, and I don't want to be involved in any of that.

And I decide Lucas isn't so bad after all.

He's even kind of funny.

So the next hour we spend trailing after the others and examining all the random stalls isn't as excruciating as I'd expected.

Except when May glances at us over her shoulder all pleased with herself, like I'm exactly where she wants me.

Later she peels herself away from Finn long enough to join Lucas and me outside, and the three of us sit on the wharf beside the river, our feet dangling over the edge of the jetty above the cold green water. Lucas buys us both hot chocolates, which is nice, and we sit huddled in our jackets, shivering against the wind as we sip them.

Lucas asks if I'm going to Julie's party, and May jumps in, enthusiastically answering for me, "Yeah, she said she'd go with me."

She sounds so pleased that I feel guilty all over again for being a bad friend. I reach out and rest my arm across her shoulders, and when she looks at me I just shrug and say, "I'm cold."

"Yeah, I'm gonna go, too," Lucas is saying. "I think everyone in our whole year will be there. It's gonna be pretty mental."

May nods in agreement. "I know. I'm so excited. It's gonna be awesome."

I sit and listen as the two of them go on and on about how totally completely amazingly fantastic the party will be, their adjectives getting more and more creative with each exchange. Soon I can't possibly imagine any party living up to their high expectations, and I wonder if half the excitement of parties is just the lead-up, when everyone is dreaming about it and wondering what wonderful things will happen to them. I don't know if any night could really measure up to such excitement. For May's sake, I find myself hoping it will.

"Alice is going to come shopping with me tomorrow," May is telling Lucas, like it's something he would be interested to know. "And she said she'll let me choose her clothes and makeup and stuff."

I roll my eyes at Lucas over her head, because I'm pretty sure he doesn't care about my makeup plans. He grins back at me, a teasing glint in his eyes as he jokes, "Yeah, I think Jamie is planning on picking my outfit, too. He said he wants us to match."

May pouts at him. "What do you know, Lucas? You have no idea how nice she's going to look tomorrow night because of me." She smiles knowingly at him, an expression I don't enjoy because I know what she's thinking. "I'll bet you'll be thanking me then."

Lucas just shrugs and smiles.

I'm glad, and I lean over and nudge May in the ribs to glare at her.

"Stop doing that," I whisper.

"Doing what?" She smiles innocently at me and I sigh.

We spend another hour at the riverside markets, strolling around the different stalls and peering at the animals in the tiny pet store in the corner. The whole thing isn't nearly as bad as I thought it would be, mainly because hanging out with Lucas turns out to be okay. Okay as in a normal okay, and definitely not a romantic kind of okay. Lucas is nice, and I'm glad he was there, but I'm not interested.

But the main reason my evening wasn't as bad as I'd expected was that no matter how many times May flitted off to talk to her other friends, or to stand silently next to Finn for a while, she always came back over to me. She never left me alone for too long.

And I liked that.

I liked how she never forgot I was there with her.

chapter 19

BAD VIBES

I spend Saturday with May at the mall, and she drags me
absolutely everywhere until my feet hurt and my back aches
and I truly don't want to ever try on more clothes again in my
entire life. And then we start on the makeup.

When we finally go back to May's house, I collapse on her
bed, exhausted and glad to get a rest in so I can recover before
the party starts. I lie still as May buzzes around me, all energy
and excitement. She doesn't shut up about the party, saying
we have to wait until at least ten before we can walk over to
Julie's house. She tells me that's how it's done at real parties;
you don't go too early or you end up looking desperate.

Or something.

Of course I tell her that's stupid, and if she's supposed to
be Julie's friend she should go early and help Julie get the
house ready. I tell her that's what I would do if the party was
at May's house.

And of course after I say that, we have to get ready much more quickly and I regret it, because now I have way less time to rest and way more time hanging around awkwardly at Julie's party before Teddy and Harry come.

By the time we're ready to leave, May is all dressed up in a very short flowy dress, her hair pinned back, and her feet strapped into tottering heels.

She looks good, grown-up and different. I imagine it's exactly how she wants to look.

And me, I'm wearing contacts and way-too-short jean shorts and a tight white tank top May chose for me. It was the most casual outfit I could talk her into, and even that was hard work. But she wanted me to be different, she said, and if I wouldn't agree to flowery prints or sparkles or a dress, then shorter and tighter was apparently the only possible alternative.

And in the end I agreed with her, because really that's what all of this is about, giving May what she needs.

And apparently what she needs is for me to be wearing very tiny shorts.

I am standing in the hallway of May's house, fidgeting next to her as she poses excitedly for her mother's camera while her two younger brothers watch and make smart-aleck comments about my clothes and my hair.

"Muuum," May whines, and her mother finally orders both boys back upstairs, smiling at May with such pride that something twists in my stomach. I catch myself wondering if my own mother would ever look at me that same way for something as simple as dressing up or being pretty.

I think May's mum must read something in my face because she quickly says, "You look lovely, Alice. And your hair is so nice when it's loose like that. I never knew it was so long."

May makes a face. "I always tell her but she never listens. Look how pretty she is when she bothers to make an effort." She giggles. "Wait, I meant when *I* make an effort for her."

"Well, I think you *both* look very pretty. Though it's different seeing you without glasses, Alice. I've gotten so used to them now."

I nod because it's weird to be without them, and I feel strange with my contacts and makeup and my new clothes and artfully messy hair. I catch a glimpse of myself in the hallway mirror and admit that I don't hate it. It's an interesting thought, that people might find me pretty.

It makes me wonder what Teddy Taualai will think.

And then I feel stupid for wondering.

"Are you sure you don't want me to drive you?" May's mum is asking her again. "At least call me to get you when you're done."

"I already told you, we'll just walk home. It's not far."

May's mum holds her hands up in surrender. "Okay, okay, just promise me you won't get in a car if the driver has been drinking, okay? Just call me. It doesn't matter how late."

"Mum! It's not like there's going to be much drinking there anyway."

Her mother scoffs.

"I was young once, too. I know the kind of things you kids get up to. I did it all myself."

"Muuum!"

May rolls her eyes at me, like the thought of her mum being young and rebellious is gross, but I think her mother's honesty is nice. And her worry for her daughter's first party is nice, too.

I didn't even tell my parents about the party, only that I would be staying the night at May's house because we had a group project. I don't think they would have stopped me from going, but Mum wouldn't have approved. She would have thought it was a complete waste of my time. And Dad would have been disappointed. It just seemed easier not to mention it in the end. And I know that's a bad thing, but a part of me is reckless, because at the end of the year, when I tell them my plans for the future, it'll be even worse, so it's not such a big difference to start now.

May drags me toward the front door before her mother can offer any more advice. "Bye, Mum! We'll definitely call you if we need a lift. But we won't need one!"

She pulls me down the path toward the gate, but then just before we leave she turns back around and relents, "We'll be safe, I promise. Love you."

And I smile as we walk down the dark street outside, because I don't think May could ever stop being decent. Not fundamentally, not truly. And that thought fills me with utter relief.

After May knocks on Julie's front door, we both stand shivering and waiting.

May glances at me and smiles, her excitement written on her face. But she's in for disappointment, because when Julie opens the door we're literally the first ones to arrive and her house is empty and quiet.

May throws her arms around Julie. "We came to help," she exclaims, and Julie stares at me over May's shoulder, pushing curly hair from her eyes.

"Wow, you look different, Alice. You look nice."

I nod, wondering if it's weird that I'm here, considering I don't know Julie all that well. "Thank you," I answer stiffly.

"Wait until she takes the hoodie off," says May. "I had this nice tailored jacket—it was so much nicer—but she totally refused to wear it." She sighs and pouts, and once we're inside the house she literally paws at me to get my hoodie off, like I'm a doll that she's proud to show off.

After Julie's finished admiring May's handiwork, we give her our warm stuff and she motions us to follow her, saying, "You can leave these in my room. Come on."

The house is warm, which is nice because I'm not wearing a lot. Neither are May and Julie, though, so maybe that's the point. We follow Julie to her room, which is big and spacious, her bed covered by a bedspread with horses printed all over it. She grins sheepishly. "I went through a horse phase." She shrugs and then adds in a loud stage whisper,

"Actually, I still like them, but these days I keep it on the down low."

I smile back, because I like that such a beautiful, popular girl would admit to what Sophia would think of as a totally dorky obsession. I feel a bit braver after her admission and say, "What's not to like? Horses are pretty cool, right?"

I giggle and Julie does, too, which is encouraging because I didn't expect us to get along.

"What about you, Alice?" she asks, sinking down on her bed beside May, who is examining her friend's makeup bag. "What are you into?"

I sit back on the couch in her room. Because she actually has a couch in her room.

I shrug, awkward again. "I dunno. Nothing really. I just study."

I bet she thinks that's stupid. Girls my age should be into more than just studying, and I wonder if I've killed our conversation before it even started. This would be why I'm a nerd and Julie is super popular.

Except Julie doesn't seem to notice, which only makes me like her more.

"No way. That can't be true," she protests. "Everyone's into something, right? What's your thing?"

She smiles at me so easily that I'm compelled to answer, suddenly at ease as if I'm just chatting with May and no one else.

"I guess . . . the world?" I say after a moment. "I'd like

to see something different from here. Go visit somewhere incredible."

I smile just thinking about it before noticing May watching me.

"What about you, May? What are you interested in?" Julie asks, distracting her. May just shrugs, but then suddenly grins mischievously.

"Finn."

She and Julie both explode with laughter as I watch quietly. I hadn't known Julie was aware of May's crush. Or May's love. Whatever it is.

Julie holds up her hand, telling us to wait, and then she disappears away down the hall. When she returns she's struggling with three glasses of orange juice. She hands around the drinks and then holds hers up into the air like she's proposing a toast.

"Well, May, with a little luck, and a little help"—she pauses and glances pointedly at the orange liquid, which turns out to be something entirely different from orange juice—"I think tonight could be your night! Go for it!"

They both grin manically at each other and then down their glasses, leaving me lagging behind. I lift my cup to my lips and take a sip of the bitter drink.

And then another, making a sour face at the taste.

"Is this Alice's first time drinking?" Julie says as if she finds me cute, like I'm a little kid, and some of my warm feelings for her fade away.

May nods. "Yeah, it's totally her first time. She's so innocent."

And now May is sitting there with that same expression plastered over her face, too, like she needs to guide me through life.

I frown and down the rest of the bitter liquid, warmth tingling in my toes. I wonder if Julie knows that it's May's first time drinking, too.

I doubt it.

Except then it occurs to me that maybe it *isn't* her first time. May and I haven't been spending as much time together lately as we used to. I glance between her and Julie. Maybe it's something they do together. Would I even know?

"Alice hasn't even kissed anyone yet," May is saying now. Julie gasps and I bury my face in my cup again before remembering I've already finished it.

"What? Oh my god! I thought you and that Teddy guy were—"

"No way!"

May interrupts before Julie can finish whatever embarrassing thing she was going to say.

"She and Teddy aren't like that at all. He just follows her around. Seriously, he's totally in love with her. It's so annoying."

I blink at May and then notice that Julie is refilling my drink, and once she's finished I drink more. The alcohol sends a strange warmth spreading through my body, and a slight softness invades my mind as I try really hard not to think about what May just said. Because obviously I should be getting angry with her for being so rude about Teddy, but a tiny part of me can't get past the part about love. My chest keeps thumping jaggedly, and my face flares hot.

In love, she said. Like it's obvious.

In love with me.

I drink more, hiding my face in my cup again.

"Seriously?" Julie fills my glass again, and then fills May's cup, too. She says thoughtfully, "Yeah, I heard a lot of rumors about him. I've never talked to him, but Harry always does so I thought he must be okay, but I know Finn really doesn't like him. And neither does Jenny, actually."

"Heaps of people don't," agrees May.

"I got told he bashed some teacher up at his old school," continues Julie. "And I heard that he even hit a girl at some party and that's why he transferred. Emily Cooper says her cousin used to go to that school and told her that Teddy was totally violent."

"He *is not*," I interject, scowling at May, daring her to say anything different.

Julie glances at me, surprised by my outburst. Finally she says, "He isn't like that?"

"No, he's not," I answer more quietly. "And he didn't do any of that stuff people say. Not like that, anyway. It was completely different."

Julie leans in, and I can feel how interested she is. "Really? Harry never talks about it. What *did* happen?"

May is watching me with a strange expression on her face, and suddenly I feel guilty that I never told her Teddy shared that stuff with me. As best friends I know she thinks we should tell each other everything. Or at least, she used to think that. I don't know what she thinks anymore.

I hesitate and then finally say, "Nothing. I mean, none of that, anyway. He isn't violent. It's all just dumb rumors."

Julie is clearly a bit let down, but nods after thinking about it for a moment. "Yeah, well, you'd know. And it's not like I've ever really talked to him anyway." She turns and grins at May. "Besides, Harry isn't the type to hang out with a psycho."

I wonder how Julie knows so much about Harry though they never talk at school. It makes me wonder if she hangs out with him at home but not school because people can see her there.

I wrinkle my nose, and more of the warmth she created from our horse talk disappears. It's so fake that I have to cover my expression with another gulp of the orange drink.

Then May says, "I think Lucas is so much better for Alice, though, don't you think? He's cute and funny, and totally gets along with everyone."

"Oh my god, do you like Lucas, Alice?" Julie squeals in excitement. "I did notice you two seemed to get along well at the markets yesterday. That's so cute! You should totally hook up with him tonight. And you look so good, too. I reckon he'd be totally into it if you made a move." She pauses and then gasps. "And it would be your first kiss, too! Oh my god!"

I blink. My head is light, a buzzing inside my skull making it impossible to focus properly. I lift my hands to try to stem her torrent of terrible words, trying to make sure she doesn't get the wrong idea about Lucas, but she's grinning like everything is already settled, and then the doorbell is ringing and Julie and May both squeal, falling over each other to go answer it.

I am left alone in Julie's room, looking at her horse bedspread and wondering why everyone I know is so complicated.

I lift my cup to my lips and drink again, waiting for May to come back.

chapter 20

HOW YOU FEEL, AFTERTHOUGHT

Everything is loud. So loud.

The sounds of it all twist deep inside my skull, filling every part of me until my entire body is throbbing with the steady beat of the thumping music. It's dark inside the house, with only a few lamps left glowing through the shadows. And people are everywhere. Standing in the kitchen pouring drinks, draped over the stairs and across the couch, filling the living room until it's impossible to move.

And none of it is as bad as I thought it would be.

It isn't scary at all, maybe because my head is buzzing and my body has turned soft and relaxed. I suppose I must be drunk, but if I am I don't mind it, because now May and I are good again, laughing and giggling at everything. Back to how it was before. At least until Sophia shows up and drapes her body over Finn's. Then I think May's about to cry.

I wonder if all parties are like this one.

Nearly everyone from our school year has turned up, and I think that's unusual. But maybe Julie is just special and everyone likes her and wants to celebrate her birthday. I don't know.

Or maybe no one wanted to be that one kid who didn't show up, that one kid with nothing to talk about on Monday morning at school.

Lucas tells me this party is even huger and more awesome than Sophia's was, way back at the beginning of the year. He reckons Sophia must be pissed, but I can't tell. She is as beautiful as ever, swaying prettily in Finn's arms to the music, surrounded by people.

I am surprised by how much I like it, the darkness and the lights, the reverberating music that makes the floor bounce beneath my feet and makes talking impossible unless you draw together until you touch. May is standing by my side, and she is watching Finn and Sophia dance together, and her face swings from determination to fighting back tears. I can't tell if she was always this emotional or if it's just the alcohol. Either way it's clear her night is dissolving into a tangled web of missed moments with Finn that she will regret forever. Or at least that's what she tells me, her hands clasped around my shoulders and her breath hot against my ear.

It's hard to concentrate on what she says. My body is warm, and I like how everyone is moving slower than normal. The darkness brings a sense of anonymity, tearing down the barriers between us, with kids making out in the corner or talking with people way beyond their normal groups. Or perhaps that's just the alcohol, too.

May grabs my hand and drags me away from Finn and Sophia into the front hall. It is crammed with people. I am unsteady on my feet and rest my back against the wall as she presses against me and hisses hot into my ear, "I thought tonight would be different. I want to dance with Finn. And I can't believe you're so drunk!"

I push the hair off her face and giggle. "I know. Imagine if my parents knew."

She sniggers, her pain over Finn abruptly forgotten.

"Such a rebel," she laughs. "My best friend, Alice!"

"Who's such a rebel?"

It's Lucas speaking, appearing at our side again with Julie, his smile small and shy. The two of them are like ghosts, following my every move.

"Alice is a rebel," repeats May, making Lucas come close to hear her over the throbbing music. "She told her parents she was studying tonight."

His eyes flick to me as I giggle again, touching my hot face with my hands and sweeping my hair back, still unfamiliar with wearing it down. It keeps getting in my way, getting stuck on things. Like on my fingertips right now.

"Alice? Did you hear what I said?"

I glance up at Lucas. He's looking at me. May and Julie are

whispering next to us with arms around each other's necks, no doubt talking about Finn again.

He leans down against my cheek and shouts, "You're totally sick of all the Finn stuff, right?"

I stand back, unsteady, and try to smile, shaking my head. "No, it's fine. I don't mind." I'm curious though, and ask, "You know about that, too?"

"Yeah, of course I do. Everyone knows. Finn knows. Even Sophia knows! May tells everyone. Come on, don't lie. It's totally driving you crazy, isn't it?"

I shake my head again but somehow can't stop myself from giggling, ruining my protests. I lift my fingers to indicate it may be just a tiny little bit frustrating, and Lucas nods in satisfaction, pleased with himself.

He draws close. "I knew it," he says into my ear. His breath is filled with sweet alcohol smell.

"I feel bad to admit it," I shout with another laugh. "It makes me feel guilty!" I sway a bit, unsteady on my feet.

"Don't feel guilty."

He looks at me differently now than he did yesterday, and I think it must be because of my hair and my clothes. He leans down again, breathing, "Alice, I'm glad you snuck out and came here. I never would have picked you for that type of girl." He stands closer, and the way he stares makes me nervous.

I move along the wall, sliding out from under him and stepping back against somebody else who is hovering right next to us. An arm slips around my shoulders from behind, and I don't even need to look to know that it's Teddy Taualai, finally turning up just when I was beginning to wonder if he wasn't.

I smile, the stuffiness inside my head suddenly becoming clearer.

When I glance back at Teddy, he's staring hard at Lucas, but then he pulls me closer against his chest, wrapping both arms around me. And instead of pushing him away I just let him do it, leaning back against him. Maybe because I'm a little drunk. Maybe because tonight nothing feels normal anyway.

Or maybe because it isn't all that bad, pressing close against Teddy Taualai.

"Hey, everyone. Happy birthday, Julie!" Harry is there, too, and he is shouting above the music. He pulls his jacket off as he squeezes through the crowd of people. "Sorry we came so late!"

He leans across to hug Julie and then he gives her a card, which I think is nice. No one else gave her anything, even though it's her birthday.

Julie smiles at him warmly. They keep talking, leaning into each other, but the music is too loud for me to hear them. I wave at Harry as he looks my way, his eyes widening when he notices how May has dressed me.

"Are you drunk?" Teddy's voice draws my attention and I twist my head back to see his face. He grins, his arm still slung around me and his eyes moving back and forth across my face. And my body. "And what are you wearing? Did May do this?"

I nod. "Yeah, I let her."

193

"You look pretty," he says, like it is a simple fact and not a compliment at all. "You always do, though. I think I miss your glasses."

It makes me smile, and I glance over at May, who worked so hard to make me look nice, to make me look different. I wonder what she would think of that.

Actually, she is watching us with a weird expression on her face, but I just smile at her and wave. My head is buzzing too hard, thick and slow. It's impossible to guess what she's thinking. I turn back to Teddy because he is saying something against my ear, his breath warm against my skin. Distracting.

"I was worried you would push me away." His voice is filled with teasing.

I just smile, and then I look him directly in the eye. "I don't mind it."

His eyes widen and he grows still, frozen surprise flickering across his face. It wasn't the answer he expected. Now that I'm letting him touch me, he has no idea how to act.

I burst out laughing when he drops his arms. It was fun to shock him, to actually say something to surprise Teddy Taualai, but then I wonder if I'm flirting with him, and that makes my face burn hot, so I turn away.

May is glaring at me.

"Hey, Alice." Harry turns to the others. "Hey, is she drunk?"

May nods and Julie is giggling. Harry shouts, "How long have you guys been here, then?"

"Alice and May got here first," interjects Lucas, talking

straight at Teddy. "Just before me. We've been drinking together for ages before you got here."

"Yeah, it's been awesome," adds May loudly. "You guys should've gotten here earlier. You totally missed out!"

She is glaring over at us again but Teddy doesn't notice, instead asking me quietly, "Is that true? Have you guys been having that much fun?"

I giggle and lean real close against him, whispering into his ear. "No. Mainly me and May were just watching Finn dancing with Sophia. I don't think May's even having a good time."

"Uh-huh." Teddy is staring at me in a strange way, clearing his throat. His face is close to mine, cheeks flushed.

"Actually, I think she's pretty upset," I tell Teddy, leaning in close again. "Stuff lately with May has been kind of—"

Suddenly May is right in front of me, pulling at my arm and cutting me off. "Come to the kitchen with me?" She pleads with wide eyes. "I want another drink, and I can't go by myself."

She tugs on my arm and shoves Teddy back, literally pulling me along with her and jostling against Lucas, who is apparently coming with us.

I glance back at Teddy, catching his eye. When I smile at him a grin spreads across his face, wide and slow, and then May has dragged me through the crowded hallway into the living room.

This room is much louder, dark and filled with swaying

bodies all moving sort of in time with the thrumming music. The darkness is so deep that for a moment I can't make out the faces in front of me, but May just pushes past everyone until we reach the kitchen.

She leans against the island in the middle of the room, pulling me in close to her. "Lucas, can you get me a drink? And Alice, too?" She droops against the counter, touching his arm.

He nods, grinning. "Sure. What do you girls want?"

"Anything," May answers. "I don't care."

The second he's gone, she wraps both her arms around my neck, pulling me toward her to hiss, "What was that back there? I thought you liked Lucas now. You could've totally ruined it all by acting like that."

I frown at her. "I never said that. I never said I liked Lucas."

May's looking at me like she's really pissed off, but I'm totally out of it, finding it hard to concentrate. She glares at me.

"What? Lucas is totally into you! I heard him tell Julie you looked hot. And he's *popular*, Alice. So many girls are into him. Of course you like him!"

My attention travels to where Lucas stands pouring drinks with some other guys bunched around him. His eyes are glazed and his cheeks are red from the alcohol. May glares at me. "All you have to do is kiss him. That's *all*."

I burst out laughing. I can't help myself, giggling uncontrollably as her face turns bright red. Obviously somewhere inside me I know it's the wrong thing to do—she's clearly getting furious—but I have no control over my body. None. So I laugh and laugh, unable to comprehend how she could possibly be getting so angry over something so utterly stupid.

Really, the whole situation is hilarious.

Except May isn't smiling, and my giggles stop abruptly, like a tap has been turned off. I stare at her and then the words just come pouring out. "May, why does this even matter to you? Why does *any* of this stuff matter to you? Being popular? I don't get it."

I take a step toward her, and suddenly I'm extraordinarily upset, my emotions swinging from one extreme to the other. "You've changed so much this year. Do you even know that?"

Her mouth twists. "What?"

"You have," I say, reaching out to press my hand against her arm. She flinches at my touch. "I've been trying hard to understand it. Really I have. But it's confusing. I don't get why you care so much about what they think of you. Why does it matter?"

She glares at me, leaning back on the counter, staggering slightly.

"What's wrong with it? What's wrong with wanting people to like me? I like how things are now."

"But next year it'll all be over anyway. Everyone will be somewhere else. School's nearly finished!"

"You didn't answer my question, Alice. What's wrong with wanting to be popular?"

Her lips are trembling now, like I've said something cruel

and uncalled for, and a tidal wave of hurt rises inside my chest. I wonder if I'm about to cry.

"There's nothing wrong with it," I say, taking a deep, shaking breath. "But it's not you. The stuff you were saying about Teddy? That's not you. He's your friend, and you've been really mean."

She jerks away like I've slapped her.

"Mean? You think I've been mean?" She exhales sharply, the sound bitter and hollow. "You have no freaking idea! Just because you're happy being a nerd that no one even likes! But it's different for me. I have to listen to what everyone says about you! Do you know how that makes me feel? I was just trying to protect you. Don't you get it?"

She's breathing heavily now, tears filling her eyes as she shouts, "Being with someone like Lucas would change everything for you. It would make people like you! You're such an *idiot*—you don't even know."

Everyone in the kitchen is so loud. Someone jostles against me, the two guys next to us are shouting at each other and pushing, but I try to ignore them, focusing only on May. Through the haze in my mind it suddenly strikes me how defensive she got when I talked about next year. The thick sludge of alcohol parts for a moment, and I wonder if May is afraid of the future.

And I blurt it out.

"What are you planning to do next year?"

She flinches. Turns away. "That's got nothing to do with this."

I grab her arm, hold on to her with wide eyes. Waiting. We never talk about it.

"Seriously," she yells, "it's got *nothing* to do with any of this! Who cares about next year? Not everyone has their future paved out for them like you, Alice. With your good grades and your good parents and good university."

I freeze, hurt blooming inside my stomach. That isn't even true. Yet I never told her the truth. My own secret plans for next year remain unsaid between us, like a wall that pushes us farther apart.

But May isn't finished yet.

"*This* year is what matters. And you're so stupid you don't even get that!"

She pulls away from me and smacks right into Lucas, who has come back carrying drinks.

"Whoa, shit! May, watch it!" Liquid splashes everywhere, and May squeals.

She whips around to Lucas and shouts, "Get out of my way!" Pushing him in the chest, she shoves past, making the drinks in his hands slop around all over again.

Lucas turns and watches her go with his mouth open. May shoves her way through the crowd. He turns back to me, his eyebrows raised. "Everything all right with you girls?"

No. Everything is terrible.

I take deep, heaving breaths. I don't know how to explain it, but the fact that he saw us fighting makes me even more worried. Making an effort to be heard over the pulsing music,

I say, "May's just going through some stuff. Lucas . . ."

I gesture for him to lean down so he can hear me better. My mind is thick and slow, and it's hard to find the right words. "Please don't tell anyone what you heard, okay? I don't think rumors and everyone gossiping is going to fix it. It'll just make everything worse."

He nods slowly. "Yeah, okay. Don't even worry about it."

He leans against the kitchen island beside me and takes a swig of his drink. "You must be a good friend. Heaps of the girls at our school would totally take this opportunity to spread bitchy rumors about her."

I frown at him, wondering what kind of girls he's been hanging out with, as he adds, "I think it's really cool of you."

I turn away. Everything around me is blurry and warped. Lucas is leaning close to say something else and I bury my face in my cup to avoid him, drinking deeply. And the alcohol helps because now I'm not that upset at all, the weirdness of it already fading away. I do wonder where May has gone and if she's okay. But I don't really feel like chasing after her. I just finish my cup and sway back against the counter, losing my balance. And I wonder where Teddy is.

"I'm going to go into the living room for a bit," I tell Lucas. "See if I can find Teddy."

I don't wait for an answer and begin pushing away through the crowd.

Lucas says in a strained voice, "Oh, I'll come with you."

Which is just great.

chapter 21

NIGHT, JUST BREATHE

The darkness of the living room is thick, nothing but bodies, all moving with the music and twisting together. Little by little, I register faces.

Julie and Harry dance together right in front of the deejay. They're doing stupid dance moves, which makes me smile without thinking, because I like the way they're ignoring everyone else around them, just having fun. I start to like Julie again. She obviously doesn't care right now whether her friends think Harry's cool enough or not.

Of course May is there, too, swaying within a group of her friends, positioned right next to Finn, not dancing with him exactly, but her side brushes against his every now and then. She seems better now, as if our conversation is forgotten in the aura that is Finn.

"I was looking for you."

The voice comes from behind me, and I turn to find Teddy

arriving from the kitchen, too, following us through. "Hey Lucas," he adds, scowling.

Lucas glares back at him, "What's up, man?"

Teddy shakes his head, as if to say nothing is up, and then turns to me, crooked smile back in place. "You wanna go see May?"

Lucas quickly interjects. "I dunno if she wants to see May right now, man. Some stuff happened before when you weren't here. You should just go by yourself."

I frown over at him, because I *literally* just told him not to spread rumors about May.

Teddy is scowling back at him, hackles raised. "Uh, okay, *no*, I don't think so." He shakes his head and turns back to me. "You coming, Alice?"

I nod and Teddy reaches for my hand, pulling me into the other people and away from Lucas, moving through the crowd toward May. He leans back toward me as we push through and shouts, "What was he talking about?"

I'm pushed into him from behind, some kid trying to squeeze past us, and I answer, "May and I, we . . . I think we kind of had a fight."

I'm unsteady on my feet, upset all over again. I glance away, trying to hide my expression because hearing myself say it aloud has kind of shocked me. May and I have never had a real fight before.

Teddy stops and I smack into him again. He reaches down and places his arms across my shoulders, and this time his fingers touch the bare skin near my collarbone. He leans down close so I can hear him. "Don't worry too much. It's just because she's drunk and emotional. May will sort herself out, and you guys'll be fine later. Parties are just weird."

A twinge of sickness swells in my gut because here he is defending May when she wants me to go hook up with Lucas and pretend Teddy doesn't exist. I sway a little on my feet, leaning in close to him, taking a long, deep breath. I feel strange. I do. I close my eyes, trying my hardest to forget about May. Everything with her is all wrong, and my brain is so strange and fuzzy. I sigh and then open my eyes. We're standing close now.

"Teddy," I say. "You know, you're just really nice. You are."

Obviously it's an odd thing to say, but I mean it. I lean in closer, reaching up on my toes so our faces are closer, too. "And you smell good."

He jumps a little, but then after a moment it's like he changes his mind. He grins at me, wide and slow. Leaning his face down close, he breathes, "I don't think you should be saying stuff like that to me."

I watch him real close, and it's weird, because he's the same as he always is, but I feel bold and strange, my mind not bothered by all the little things it normally would be. I reach out and touch his hair. I do it because it's messy and hanging down in front of his eyes. I do it because I want to.

"Why not?" I say. I touch his neck, too, at the back beneath his hair, running my fingers down to the top of his T-shirt.

He's grinning at me, his black eyes locked on mine, his face close and his breath warm against my skin.

"Alice, you should stop . . ."

Suddenly Teddy jerks forward as a figure launches onto his back. It's Harry. His grinning face appears over Teddy's shoulder, shouting something above the music. I don't know what he's trying to say. Teddy is bending low beneath the weight of his friend, and Harry just keeps laughing maniacally, like squashing Teddy Taualai is the funniest thing that he's ever done. I notice his face is flushed and his eyes are shiny and bright. I wonder if he and Teddy were drinking before the party. I peer around at May, swaying close against Finn, and at Julie, who is trying to cling onto Harry's arm, her curly head bouncing in time with the music. Everyone is lost in the haze of it, going crazy.

May turns her back to me when Harry and Julie drag us into their dancing group. Her attention stays locked on Finn, smiling at him prettily, a little unfocused and definitely ignoring me. I sigh because the whole reason I came to this party was for May, and now we aren't even talking.

"Come on," Harry is shouting. "Dance! Dance!" He makes goofy dancing motions, like he's trying to explain what to do by demonstrating. Teddy laughs, and the music's deep bass shakes the floor, traveling up my legs into my chest. It sounds good, deep and slow and strange, like I'm listening to it underwater. Everyone around us is moving to it, crushed together in the small dark space of the living room, the air warm and heavy despite the icy weather outside.

I catch a glimpse of Sophia and that girl Jenny out of the corner of my eye, both of them staring daggers at May, who is really dancing with Finn now, arms tight around his neck. I don't say anything, don't think of warning her because I am swaying on my feet, partly in time with the music, partly because standing still is much too hard when the whole room is spinning like it is. I think about that last drink I had in the kitchen with Lucas. Why did I accept that? I didn't need it. Everything around me is dark and blurry and heavy, and then I open my eyes and May and Finn are gone and Teddy is pressed against me, his body warm and his hand curled around mine. I suppose we are dancing—that's what everyone else around us is doing—but really we're just swaying back and forth in the darkness, hardly moving. Teddy's head drops down against my shoulder, and I lift my free arm to stroke his hair. He shifts slightly and his lips brush my neck. The feeling of it turns my throat to fire, makes me think of that night on the beach, of what it would've felt like to kiss Teddy Taualai in the darkness on the sand.

I turn and suddenly Lucas has pushed through the crowd toward us, strange and slow, and then May is there, too, shoving at Teddy, her face furious and her eyes unfocused. I think she's been crying. Because of me? Because of what happened between us? Or because of Finn, because her night hasn't been magical like she wanted it?

I don't get the chance to ask her because she pushes Teddy back hard, peeling him off me until she's managed to shove her body between us by force. She turns to him and jabs her finger at his face. "What the hell do you think you're doing?"

Teddy raises both his hands as if in surrender, stunned. "Nothing! I'm not doing anything."

May is furious. "You were! I saw you. You were kissing her!"

I turn from Teddy back to May again. "I don't think he kissed me, May. I think I would have noticed." I giggle, like I've made a joke, and Teddy grins at me slow, his eyes sparking like I've just given him an invitation.

"Don't you even start, Alice." May has venom in her voice. "He was taking advantage of you. You're so freaking drunk you wouldn't even notice."

I sway and nod. "I am a bit . . . drunk, but so are you. We all are."

"*He's* not!" May shoves Teddy back again. "He's not even drinking. He's just taking advantage of you being stupid. And you're letting him do it."

I glance at Teddy and he just shrugs, and I realize May is right about him being sober at least. And I think maybe I should mind that, maybe it should upset me that he was dancing with me and pressing his mouth against my neck when he was sober, but somehow it doesn't upset me at all. Instead it makes me stare at him, thinking about what May said to Julie at the beginning of the night.

She said that he's in love with me. She said it like it's obvious.

May is ignoring me, turning to Lucas, who is hovering awkwardly behind her. "Help Alice to the kitchen," she orders him. "I want to talk to Teddy for a bit."

Lucas moves forward to take my hand, and that's when I finally explode.

"I don't *like* him, May! Nothing you do is going to make me *like* him! This is so *stupid*! You tell me Teddy's taking advantage of me, but you want me to go make out with Lucas in the kitchen? Because he's popular? What is *wrong* with you?"

All three of them just stare at me, Teddy opening and closing his mouth in stunned silence and Lucas going red. And of course immediately I feel bad, like really bad, and I turn to Lucas and quickly try to backtrack. "I didn't mean I don't like you, Lucas. Of course I do. You're so nice! And I've had a good time hanging out with you. I just meant, you know. Not in that way."

He nods, still red, already trying to back away. It makes me feel guilty, especially because now Teddy is totally pissed off, scowling at Lucas in a way that is definitely less than friendly. But then May's hand rests on my arm. I turn to her and she looks like hell, tear stains on her cheeks and her nose all red. I wonder what happened to her, my anger suddenly softening. "May, what's wrong?"

She only glares at me. "Nothing's wrong!"

She's lying.

Something has happened.

"Alice," she's saying, and I try to concentrate on her words, try to forget the expression I just saw on her face. She glares at me. "You have no idea what everyone at school says about you and him." She points at Teddy, who is still standing silently, watching us. "There're so many rumors, and I've been protecting you. That's why I said you should go out with someone like Lucas! It would change *everything* for you. You could come hang out with Julie and me and the others at lunch." She frowns like she can't understand me. "Don't you want that?"

I shake my head slowly, sickness swelling in my gut, from her words or the alcohol, I don't even know.

"Forget it," May snaps. "Do what you want, but don't expect me to hang out with you anymore!"

I peer after her as she staggers away, shocked by her words. I turn to Teddy with wide eyes, unsure how to react to hearing my best friend say something like that. But he is staring after her, too, and I think he flinched when she said those words, which makes me remember that May is actually his friend, too, and at least I saw this coming.

"Let's go home," is all he says. I can't read his face, but I nod.

The room is spinning, the faces all blurring together. I feel sick, like my head is going to burst open, like I can't breathe. Suddenly everything is too loud, too close and too hot.

I can't breathe.

chapter 22

US, SINCERELY

"Why are you so heavy?"

Pause.

"Alice? Are you sleeping again? Man, you are *so* heavy!"

I'm nauseated, my mind cloudy and my body cold. I am swaying back and forth, too, as if I'm rolling in a boat across the sea.

It makes my stomach turn.

I try to breathe, but that just makes me realize how very cold I am, and now my body shivers and shakes, my breathing shallow.

"Don't worry." Teddy's voice is softer now. More sympathetic. "We're nearly there. You can have a hot shower and that'll help. Man, I'm starving. Are you hungry? I bet you are." He laughs loudly and I scrunch up my eyes and try to tune him out.

He's too loud. It hurts.

The swaying gets worse.

He's complaining softly now, still going on about me being too heavy, something about standing up and walking. I shift slightly, my fingers gripping my hoodie closer to keep me warm. The material smells nice, but not like my clothes, like it belongs to someone else. I squeeze open one eye, trying to figure out what I'm wearing.

A gray hoodie, too big, loose around my arms with the hood pulled up over my head. I don't remember putting it on.

I open my other eye.

It's like someone poured lemon juice on my brain, as if every bit of moisture was squeezed out, and now I'm all shriveled and sick. Pain pounds against my skull and I close my eyes again because it's just so much better that way.

"Did you hear what that security guard on the train said to me? Alice? Hey, wake up! Did you hear what he said?" Teddy keeps rambling on and I'm trying really hard to ignore him but I'm slumped across his back, my head bobbing on his shoulder like a rag doll, so it's hard. But I can't move. I'm empty and gross.

Then an image of May pops into my head, May saying terrible awful things, her expression tight with anger. That makes me even sicker, so I quickly push it away, try to lose myself again.

We keep moving, and the ground rumbles as a train approaches. We're near the tracks. I open my eyes just the smallest slit, watching as the cars roll by, tiny warm lights seeping from the windows and piercing the darkness. For an instant the inside is visible, all the tiny people. But then they are gone, taking the warm lights with them.

I close my eyes again and shift my body, wrapping my arms tightly around Teddy's neck, resting my cold face against his warm skin and breathing deeply.

"Aaah, don't do that!" He flinches away. "Your nose is cold!"

He grunts and stops suddenly, and then he kind of hikes me up, adjusting to get a better grip so I don't slide off his back.

I guess I should tell him I'm awake, except I'm not sure I am. His voice sounds like it's floating in from somewhere far away, and his skin against my face is so nice and warm. I press closer and decide to stay there forever.

Slowly my body thaws, turns a bit more normal, and I shift again, pressing closer.

"Stop it. Move your face back! Oh man, that is cold. And watch your fingers! Ugh."

He pauses and then adds after a moment, "That guy on the train totally thought I was kidnapping you or something. And you didn't help. You kept falling over. Alice? You awake?"

He sighs, his back swelling beneath my body.

"I can't believe you're sleeping. I dunno how much longer I can carry you. Seriously." But then he is laughing, too, so I just hold on tighter, enjoying his warmth and the way my head has slowly stopped spinning, trying my best to ignore his rambling.

But then Teddy says, "The security dude on the train was gonna call your folks."

That makes me wake up more.

"Yeah but, luckily for you, when you're drunk you get all giggly and cute, so you charmed him out of it."

I frown at that, still squeezing my eyes shut, slightly horrified.

"You were all over me, you know." The grin is clear in his voice, and I imagine it spreading across his face. "You kept saying I'm your best friend and you love me. Do you remember that?"

I snap my eyes open. I said that? No.

"He believed you, too."

Teddy shifts his grip on me, leaning forward to get a better hold.

"You said it a lot though, you know," he adds quietly as he moves. "That you love me. I bet you're not gonna remember that when you wake up, huh?"

His breathing is getting heavier, and I wonder how long he's been carrying me. Because wondering about that is a whole lot better than picturing myself telling a security guard that I love Teddy Taualai.

I squeeze my eyes shut in embarrassment, which is when I realize that Teddy is holding me up with his hands on my bare thighs right beneath my bum. He is giving me a piggyback ride, so I'm not sure how else he could do it, but now that I've noticed his hands pressing into my skin, I can't think of anything else. Stupid May and her stupid tiny shorts.

Teddy's voice brings me back. "It was nice when you said that, you know?"

He laughs again, but there's something in his voice now, something different. The tone of it makes me feel strange all over, his hands near my bum momentarily forgotten.

He is quiet a moment longer and then adds, "I think I've been waiting all year to hear you say something like that. Like you love me." Then he groans. "But in my head you were sober when you said it. Which is definitely the biggest difference, because I'm pretty sure you didn't mean it, right? Hey, Alice? You're still sleeping, right?"

He stops talking and I don't move. Not at all. But my eyes are open and locked on his throat, on his jaw. The curves and the straight lines. His breathing is heavy from carrying me, and though he's only wearing a T-shirt, he is sweating. There's no spinning now, no sickness, no pain in my head. Everything is clear, and I can't think of anything else except him, his voice.

His words.

He sighs softly and everything grows silent, just the sound of cars in the distance. The street is empty and dark, and Teddy walks slowly down the center of it, passing the unlit houses with their tiny shadowy yards. It's like we're the only two people left in the world, walking out here in the night under the black, empty sky.

"You know," he is saying, his voice falling flat in the empty darkness of the night. "You shouldn't tell someone you love them if you don't. Because I do. I mean, I really love you."

He suddenly sighs, shifting his grip on me as he mutters, "And what a brilliant time to tell you, when you're completely fucking unconscious. Way to go."

A heavy silence falls, and I'm not breathing, just clutching at him. And I'm sure he can feel my heart beating like a drum through his back. I'm sure he knows I'm awake. He must have heard my breathing change, my arms growing tighter around his neck. He must know.

But he doesn't, because suddenly he's loudly saying, "Hey, wake up! Time to wake up, Alice!" He jiggles me, trying to jerk me awake, but I lose my balance and nearly fall off his back, which makes him laugh like he didn't just tell me he loves me, like everything's completely normal. He grins. "Oops. Sorry."

I slide down off him, my feet hitting the pavement. And then I rub at my face because I really need to hide my expression. I focus on my feet, pushing my hair over my eyes. Teddy stretches and twists his back, all the time with one hand on my side like he's worried I won't be able to stand by myself. And his fingers burn where they touch me and my hair is kind of wet and everything just feels totally weird.

"She awakens!" Teddy shouts this like I'm Frankenstein's monster. He grins at me. "You are super heavy. I don't think we should do that again. Ever. Seriously, my back hurts." He yawns and absently takes my hand, which burns, too, and leads me farther down the road.

"We're nearly there," he tells me, and I glance around, wondering where exactly "there" is. And even though I thought I would never be able to look him in the eye again, I turn and exclaim, "*Your* house? I can't go back to your house!"

Teddy just shrugs. "You told me you didn't want to stay at May's, though."

I make a face at him. "That doesn't mean I want to come home with *you*!" Blood is pounding in my ears and I am sure he'll notice how red my face is.

"Well, it's not like you can go back to your house," Teddy says easily, like it's obvious. "It's midnight. And you told me your parents didn't even know you were going out."

He's right: my parents will most certainly figure out I'm a big liar if I come home from a "study" night at midnight smelling like alcohol and covered in makeup.

And wearing a boy's hoodie.

I shiver and press my arms around my body; Teddy's house is visible just ahead. "Okay," I mumble. "But won't your grandma be mad?"

"Nana? No way. She likes you."

I follow him to his gate. I'm sure his nana will be mad. How could she not be? If she knew I was drinking at a party and that I told a security guard I loved Teddy Taualai, I wonder if she'd still like me then. I wonder if she'd tell me to leave her grandson alone forever because I'm clearly such a huge confused mess and I got embarrassingly drunk even though he doesn't even drink at all. I groan and press my hand over my face, my clothes beneath Teddy's hoodie pressing wetly against my skin.

Which is clearly not right.

I stop walking and slowly unzip the hoodie, peering down at my chest. The white tank top is completely soaked. I stare up at Teddy in horror. "What's this?"

He turns around and smirks. That's when I realize my wet shirt is completely see-through, my bra on vivid display. Immediately I pull the hoodie closed, my eyes wide.

He laughs. "Relax! Believe me, what happened back there was *not* a sexy situation. Trust me." He grins in a way that makes me nervous, like he's not telling the truth, but then he motions toward his foot.

"Look." He shakes his sneaker at me. One whole leg of his jeans is soaked, his shoe, too. "You threw up everywhere when we got off the train. All over your shirt and my leg."

I gape at him.

"And then I had to find a tap in the park and try to wash you. And wash my foot, too." He grins at my horrified expression. "See, totally not sexy."

But then he ruins it all by smirking at me and adding, "Although now, that's different."

I follow his eyes. I'm not holding the hoodie properly, and it's open again. I grasp at it, panicked by all of it. The look in his eye, the thought of me vomiting all over him, and the words he said in the dark when he thought I was asleep. My head hurts again, and now I'm thirsty. So thirsty I think I'm going to die.

"Teddy, please," I whisper and there must be something in my voice that makes him take pity on me because the next thing I know he has his arm around my shoulders and is guiding me through his gate and up to the front door of his tiny house.

Which reminds me of the last time I was here, when I saw him asleep on the couch with his T-shirt rolled up and his body exposed from hip to ribs.

My face is hot and I feel sick.

chapter 23

SMOKE AND MIRRORS

I wake up tangled in Teddy's sheets, sprawled out across his couch. Or his bed. Whatever.

And I feel like hell, eyes burning from keeping my contacts in all night.

Light is streaming through the open windows, late morning sky visible outside. Wind tickles the curtains, and they gently shift back and forth, over and over again.

Slowly I sit up, peering over the back of the couch at the kitchen. It's empty. No one is here. I sigh in relief and think back to last night, when we got in, how Teddy made me take a hot shower and put on some of his clothes. He gave me an old stretched T-shirt with a Power Rangers logo and some sweatpants, then he fed me and brought me water, and I stayed on the couch while he went in to sleep on the floor of his nana's room. I'm embarrassed just thinking about it.

I flop back down, exhausted, and decide that parties suck.

It was bad in a different way from what I expected. I thought I wouldn't have fun, but I did. At least until that thing happened with May.

I press my hands over my face, not ready to even think about that yet.

And it turns out that's not all that hard, because already, even though I have literally just woken up and have a headache that is trying to pound my head in, already I'm thinking about those words Teddy Taualai said when he was carrying me home. They move beneath my skin like living things, making changes to every part of my body they touch.

And it terrifies me.

"Good morning, Alice."

I poke my head over the couch to find Teddy's grandma in the kitchen, knocking things around as she makes coffee. Loudly. But she smiles at me and doesn't appear angry to find me sleeping on her couch instead of her grandson. I take heart from that, and when she offers coffee, I accept it.

She ushers me outside and we sit in the back garden, just the two of us because she tells me Teddy is still asleep. Apparently they have an air mattress, and he woke her in the night trying to inflate it. I sneak a glance at her but she doesn't seem mad when she says it, so maybe she really does like me.

The back garden is tiny, just like the rest of Teddy's house, but unexpectedly lush, tropical almost, which is strange. Creepers grow twisting along lattices propped against the tin fence, and the grass underfoot is lush and green. Two olive trees loom at the very back with their leaves shining silver and green. They make me think of Mediterranean islands. Beside them is some kind of citrus tree I recognize because we have something similar in our garden at home. Ours is a lemon tree.

Teddy's nana and I sit together and sip our coffees, and I keep thinking how glad I am that Teddy made me shower when we got in, even though at the time I didn't want to. At least now I'm not covered in smudged makeup, and I no longer smell like vomit or alcohol. My cheeks burn just thinking about it.

It's funny, because even though we came back so late, Teddy's grandma doesn't ask me any questions. I expected her to grill me. I expected her to want to know.

But she doesn't.

The silence isn't uncomfortable, but in the end I ask *her* questions. Mostly just to be polite, but her answers are interesting, and then I'm asking because I want to hear more.

She tells me about her family and I find out Teddy has two aunts, both with families of their own, one here in the city and the other in another state. After the accident, she tells me Teddy was in the hospital for nearly two weeks, and when he left he came straight here because his aunt didn't have enough room to keep him.

When she says it, I think maybe she sounds bitter, like perhaps she thinks it was just an excuse. I think of Teddy sleeping here on her couch and think that his nana didn't have much room either, but she didn't mind.

Teddy's grandma tells me she moved here from New Zealand when she was young, but her parents come from an island in the Pacific. She tells me about her husband, passed away so long ago that he never even had the chance to meet Teddy or any of the other grandkids. That makes my insides twist, so I take a deep breath and slowly sip my coffee, listening to her talk.

"I was surprised when Teddy said he wanted to go to a party again," she is saying. "He usually avoids them."

"He didn't drink, though," I say, because I don't want her to be angry with him.

She just smiles absently at me, her face crinkled and worn. "You're the first one of Teddy's friends I've ever met," she says instead. "Since he transferred schools, I mean."

"Really?"

I take another sip of coffee, hiding my burning face in my cup.

She nods, still smiling. "I was glad things went well after he changed schools. I was so worried after what happened to his mum and with that other boy. I thought he'd never get over it." Her hands fidget, long fingers curling and uncurling. "It was quite bad back then, love. He wouldn't talk to me for a long time. It was like he just shut down."

Her mouth pulls into a straight line, like just remembering it physically hurts her.

"But at the new school he got his fresh start, thank goodness. He started making an effort, and he talked to me again. When he told me he'd made friends so quickly I was just so happy. Friends are such important support, you know. I think you need good people around to help you at times like that. Don't you think, Alice?"

An awful sinking feeling stirs in my gut.

"He told you about making friends?" I say slowly. "In his first year at our school?"

"Yes." She smiles, saying, "I think a fresh start is what he needed after what happened with the boy at the party." She looks at me seriously and adds, "What Teddy did was wrong, I'm not denying that, but he deserved a second chance. He deserved a fresh start where none of the other kids knew about it."

I feel like I want to cry. Because everyone did know about what Teddy did. And because of it, no one even talked to him. Not really. Not until he joined the soccer team halfway through his second year, not until he met Harry.

And even now everyone still talks about what he did. They never let it go. Not ever.

I take a deep breath and glance at the garden, drinking in the greenness of it, the calmness. And then slowly I stand up.

"I'll be back in a second," I say, and then walk inside to the living room and collapse back onto the couch, my chest pounding and my headache worse. I press my hands over my face, and then, just because if I don't do something to distract myself I think I might go crazy, I go searching for my phone.

When I find it I'm greeted by eleven missed calls and four text messages.

All from my mother.

In the end I decide to wear Teddy's T-shirt and sweats home. It's either that or tiny shorts and a vomit-stained tank, though neither option is particularly appealing. My real clothes are at May's, and though Teddy offers to take me to pick them up, I decide I can't see her right now. Not with the impending anger of my mother looming in front of me. I need to deal with that first.

I called Mum as soon as I saw the messages. She told me she rang May's mum last night to check how the studying was going, and of course May's mum wasn't going to lie about the party. So she told my mother where I was.

I don't know if Mum still thinks I slept at May's or not. I don't know what to tell her if she knows I didn't. Bringing Teddy Taualai into this can only make it worse. Of that I am absolutely positive.

Teddy's grandma offers to talk to her for me, which I think is so nice. Obviously I say no, though. I tell her the real problem is that I lied to my mother about where I was, and now I'll have to face her and explain why.

I don't tell her that Mum would be just as thoroughly unimpressed by Teddy's grandma as she was with Teddy himself.

But I would never put his nana in that position. I think Teddy knows it, too, because when I decline her offer he seems kind of relieved.

Teddy drives me home in his nana's tiny old car. He's cramped up in the driver's seat like a giant at a child's play table. It would be funny if I wasn't so scared. He drops me down the street from my house, and I don't even know what I say to him when I leave the car, my mind already somewhere else.

Inside the house is cool and dark. Dad is out playing golf with his friends like every Sunday, and Mum tells me she hasn't told him yet. She tells me she wants to hear it from me first, that she'll decide whether he needs to know afterward.

And I surprise myself by telling her the truth. All of it.

I tell her how May has been drifting away from me and I thought going to the party with her might change things, make it how it used to be between us. Through it all it's obvious how unimpressed my mother is. And when she asks me if the messy boy she met at the house before the holidays was there, too, I wonder if she was even listening to anything I said. She doesn't ask me anything about May, only Teddy Taualai, and the way she talks about him tells me this is the heart of the problem.

I think about lying, but in the end I don't. I tell the truth. But I can't help mentioning that he wasn't drinking, like that might somehow make her like him more.

It doesn't work, of course, and I'm sent to my room to

study, reminded that I'm jeopardizing my future. Mum says I should know better now that I'm in my final year. She tells me I'm a disappointment.

I hate that. A disappointment. I wish she would get mad and tell Dad and they could both yell at me instead. But of course that won't happen, and the gap just opens wider between us.

When I leave I glance back at my mother from the hallway, sitting alone in our kitchen calmly sipping her coffee, reading the newspaper like her daughter didn't just lie to her and stay out all night. Like nothing happened at all.

It occurs to me that I barely know anything about her. We don't talk about what she feels and thinks about her work. We don't talk about Dad or what she does with her friends when she leaves the house.

And we don't talk about me, either.

Not really. I mean, we talk about my schoolwork and my exams and my assignments, but not really about *me*.

It makes me wonder if things might be different if we were honest with each other sometimes. But it's hard to know for sure, and in the end I just walk upstairs to my room and study like she told me to. And when Dad comes home from golf, she doesn't tell him what I did.

Like it never happened.

Teddy texts me that night, and I lie in bed, staring at the bright screen, watching his words appear from across the suburbs, talking to me from so far away. He asks me if I'm all right. He asks me if I'll be at school tomorrow. He tells me that he liked having me at his house, that he likes it better when I'm around.

I drink in the words, and it scares me how the warmth of them seeps deep into my insides, untwisting everything that's knotted and wrong, loosening it all. How can such small things make such big changes? How can such simple words unlock anything?

But they do.

chapter 24

YOU

At school on Monday, everyone is buzzing about Julie's party. They talk about how Stacey Green hooked up with Lucas in the kitchen, both so drunk they could barely stand up. Lucas gets high fives and Stacey gets laughed at. They talk about how Sophia and Finn had a big fight over May and almost broke up, but then they didn't. They talk about Harry and Julie dancing together all night. And they talk about a thousand other people and things I don't even remember.

And maybe they talk about me, too, being drunk and at a party for the first time, about me dancing with Teddy Taualai and leaving with him. But if they do, no one mentions it to me.

I decide I don't care. I am too busy trying to decide who I want to avoid more, May or Teddy.

May and I haven't spoken since the party.

I wanted to text her on Sunday, but in the end I was too

scared. At least she was drunk when she said those awful things, when she said she didn't want to hang out with me anymore. I don't think I can bear for her to say it when she's sober. I don't want her looking at me in that same way during the daylight.

Clearly the only solution is to avoid her, not even give her the chance to say it, not give her the chance to end our thirteen-year friendship with cruel words and angry eyes.

And then there's Teddy. He scares me even more.

Everything feels different with him, and I can't stop thinking about his mouth on my throat or the things he said when he didn't know I was listening. It makes my pulse race and my hands tingle, like I have no control over my body. I'm sure the second he's in front of me he'll see everything laid bare on my face, and I'm not ready for that. Everything about it terrifies me. Like it's moving so quickly now and I still haven't decided what I want to do.

So I avoid him, too.

And it all goes pretty well until just before lunch when I run into May near my locker.

She looks at me like she's just seen a ghost and then scurries off down the hall away from me.

That's when it occurs to me that maybe she's been avoiding me, too.

Which makes me want to cry, because I don't understand it, how this could have happened to us. We've been best friends since kindergarten and now we can't even bear to be near each other. And it sucks, because I actually do need to talk to her this time. About Teddy Taualai and what's happening to my insides whenever he's around. I need to explain it to her so she can help me, because I have no idea what I'm doing, but May would. She's always been braver than I am. She's always just thrown herself in, never caring about the consequences, never too afraid to try.

That's why I love her. That's why I will always love her. Why I don't want to lose her.

I go outside at lunch, onto the oval to sit by myself.

I think Teddy will probably try to find me in the library after I've been so careful to avoid him all morning, but he won't think to search for me out here. Julie and Sophia sit over near the fence in the sun. Finn is there and Lucas, too, and all the others in their group.

But no May.

I turn my head, trying to spot her on the oval, maybe making her way over with lunch from the cafeteria, or maybe off talking to Harry somewhere.

But she's not there.

It makes me uneasy, because I know I definitely shouldn't be glad that she isn't sitting over there with her new friends that she's chosen over me. I'm sure that would be petty and nasty and not a good way to be feeling at all.

Glad.

Glad she isn't over there smiling and having fun while I'm sitting here alone feeling terrible like this.

I guess it means I'm angry with her. And I've never really been angry with May before.

I think again of her face at the party, how upset she was. Like something had happened. I wonder if Finn finally made it clear he wasn't into her and that's why May isn't sitting with any of them right now, basking over there on the grass in the sunshine.

I wonder if that will make her regret what she said to me and Teddy Taualai. I wonder if that will make her wish she could take it all back.

I hope so.

"Hey!"

I jump at the sound of his voice. Teddy Taualai bounds toward me and throws himself down onto the grass with a grin. He is sweaty and his uniform is covered in grass stains; he's been playing soccer. Which makes me wonder why I came out here in the first place when I should have known it's exactly where he'd be.

He leans into me, raising his eyebrows. "Are you avoiding me or what?"

I jump, startled, turning away from him toward the school buildings. "What? Why would you say that?"

Shifting so he's sitting closer, he frowns at me. "Why do you look so guilty? What's going on?" I don't answer and suddenly his eyes go wide. "Wait, were you *really* avoiding me?"

I still can't meet his gaze but I say, "No, of course not." It doesn't sound very convincing, though, even to me.

He stares at me. "Alice, I'm sorry I didn't tell you I wasn't drinking at the party. I didn't mean to take advantage or whatever, if that's what you're thinking. I wasn't trying to be an arsehole. Shit, you know I didn't mean to freak you out, I just—"

"It's fine," I say, cutting him off.

Each word is clipped because I'm trying to be firm, trying to shut down any conversation that is going to center around Saturday night. I absolutely cannot talk to him about any of that. I refuse.

I need a safe topic, something simple and normal that won't lead anywhere. Something that won't give me away.

"How did it go with your math homework?" I ask, and Teddy stares at me like I've grown an extra head.

"Don't try to change the subject. If you're upset about Saturday, you should just say it. What's the point of not telling me?" He pauses and I think *he's* the one who looks upset. "If you're mad at me then just say so, okay?" Then he sits there silently, like he's waiting for me to fix this problem.

He has absolutely no idea what he's talking about.

Pretending nothing has changed is way harder than I expected. But I tell myself I face hard things every day. I can do this. I take a deep breath.

"I said it's fine." I turn to face him, plastering a smile onto my lips. "Saturday was great. I'm not upset at all. It was really fun."

I'm proud of the way my voice sounds normal when I say

it, like I'm just chatting about a fun yet totally uneventful weekend where absolutely nothing significant happened.

But then I worry maybe I sound a little *too* enthusiastic, because Teddy is smiling at me slowly, like he knows something I don't, lounging back on the grass all sly.

He grins. "So, what you're saying is you liked everything that happened?"

Whoa. No.

I lift my hands in protest. "That is not what I was trying to say! Don't be an idiot."

I glare at him and he just shrugs, like he's enjoying teasing me.

"That's what it sounded like you were trying to say. Are you sure you didn't like it? Dancing with me? You seemed to like it at the time."

"I didn't."

"Are you sure? What about when I kissed you?"

Panic surges in my chest. "You didn't!" I almost shout. Everything is going wrong.

"I did. On your neck. Remember?"

"No. I don't," I splutter, and then, because he's staring at me in a way I really need to shut down, I add, "And that wasn't even a kiss, anyway."

He grins. "It was. You're saying you liked that, too, right?"

"I didn't like it!" I snap.

I should have known he would do this. Surely the only reason he didn't do it already at his house was because of the emergency with my mum. It distracted him for one day. One day of peace before this hell started. I really want to just run away.

Instead I try to stay calm, repeating firmly, "I never said I liked it."

He sighs and sits up.

Suddenly he's completely different. "Yeah, you didn't," he agrees, which throws me off guard. He pauses for a long moment. "You know that night you said that you loved me."

My eyes widen and a buzzing starts in my ears. "No, I didn't," I answer weakly.

"You did," he fires back, and I wonder what he's trying to do right now. Here at school, in front of everyone.

I want him to let it go.

I want him to stop saying it, and I want to go back to how it was before, when I didn't think about Teddy Taualai in a way that makes my chest go tight.

I need to get out of here. That's what I need to do.

I glance at him.

He's still serious, and I hate how easily he's bringing all this up, trying to embarrass me with those words I still can't believe came out of my mouth. He watches me so calmly, yet my skin is burning red, my heart jabbing painfully into my ribs.

"You said you loved me," he repeats, his eyes still locked on mine, and I can't handle it anymore, can't understand why he's being so pushy. I stumble to my feet and gather my lunch stuff, throwing it all roughly back into my bag.

"I don't have time for this," I tell him. "I don't. Everything is a huge mess right now. All of it, May and Mum. I should be studying. Exams are coming soon."

I struggle to my feet, my face still hot, and I guess Teddy finally realizes I'm trying to run away because he jumps forward and chases after me.

"Seriously?" he says in disbelief. "You're leaving? Because I said that? Because you don't have time to talk to me?"

"You know that's not why," I protest.

"Then tell me."

I shake my head. I don't know what's happening. Suddenly it's like we're talking about something entirely different from just Saturday night. Panic swells beneath my skin. I need to get out of here.

"Admit it, Alice." His voice is low. "You did say it. And I know you feel—"

"*You* said it, too," I interrupt furiously, grasping at the first thing in my head to cut him off. "You said it, too, Teddy Taualai, and don't even pretend you didn't."

That was not what I meant to say.

I watch as my words sink in, as he realizes what I've just admitted. Silence draws out between us, and I'm sure I must have ruined it now because everything will have to change. It has to. Me listening to what he said on Saturday night, those things he said to me, if he knows . . . it can't be like it was before. It can't.

Teddy is staring at me, eyes wide, like I've said something important, *admitted* something important.

Maybe I have. I don't know.

A humming grows thick in my head and Teddy blinks, stunned, like he has no idea what he's supposed to do. I turn and walk toward the school building, slowly at first and then faster and faster until I am running. Until my chest is heaving and I can barely breathe, until I'm running through the hall and taking the stairs two at a time.

I find the art room, always empty during lunchtime, and I open the door and burst inside, dropping my stuff and crouching down to slide against the wall where no one can see me. My hand presses down hard on my chest because I still can't breathe.

What did I just do?

Why did I run?

Running was admitting something.

Is that what I wanted? I wonder if that's what I wanted.

But even if part of me wanted that, the rest is just afraid, afraid of things being different. Because if things change between us and we end up like May and Harry, together for a week and then all the feelings just forgotten and dissipated, if that happens, I don't know what I will do.

But that's what always happens, isn't it?

Not just with May and Harry, with so many people at school. They start something and then it just finishes, just ends like none of it was ever real in the first place.

I'm afraid because I think it must already be too late.

I jump as the door crashes open and then Teddy is standing looking down at me, his face flushed. He takes a step inside the room.

"Alice," he says quietly.

I focus only on my feet as he says my name again, shuts the door behind him. His footsteps approach, sneakers tapping on the floor. And then he crouches down right in front of me, hands on my knees, which are drawn up against my chest.

"Alice."

"What?"

He stares at me, black eyes unreadable, and I am losing my breath even though I'm not running anymore. He leans forward onto his knees, pressing against my legs, and he reaches and holds my face in his hand and kisses me.

And it's not like how it is in the movies. It's messy and strange. His mouth is hot and his hands push into my hair, pulling on the strands as they get caught on his fingers, and he is breathless and not composed or cool at all. Our teeth bump and he presses his open mouth against the corner of mine and I'm sure that's not what he's supposed to be doing.

But when he pulls back and stares at me, his breath ragged, hovering close with one hand propped against the wall beside my head, I decide I like it. I like the way it feels, I like everything about it. Because it's mine, messy and confusing, but all mine.

Teddy's biting his lip and blinking, nervous as though he

might have done something wrong. He's so close that his breath touches my mouth.

I reach out slowly with my hand, brush my fingers against his skin, running them to the corner of his mouth, and his eyes flutter closed. I think it's so strange that after all the teasing, all year long, now it's me who is making *him* burn red, me who can make him close his eyes just because I've touched him.

His reaction makes me brave and I move to press my mouth against his softly, like I'm testing it out. He stays so still. Once. Twice.

And then again.

His chest heaves, like he's having trouble breathing, and he makes a soft noise against my mouth, almost like relief. It makes me wonder how long he's been waiting for this.

And then I sit back against the wall, watching him because I can't think of anything else to do, his legs overlapping mine, his knee pressed against my thigh, warm and close.

He opens his eyes slowly and I wait for him to grin, wait for him to break the tension of it with a knowing smile or an "I told you so."

Except he doesn't.

He just stares at me, and it makes me think that something really has changed now, because what he feels for me is in his eyes, and I don't want to be like everyone else and let him down.

And then the bell clangs so loudly we both jerk back, my

head hitting the wall behind me. The door has opened again, quietly this time, and Mrs. Kang is in the doorway, and when she sees us she says, "Oh." And Teddy and I just stare at her and she stares back and then she asks me if I have art next period.

So I climb to my feet and walk to my desk and sit there like I am calm, like everything is normal and Mrs. Kang didn't just catch me pressed against a wall with Teddy's hands stuck in my hair and his knee pressed into my hip.

Teddy stands up, too, mumbles something about his bag and practically runs out of the room, his face so red it makes Mrs. Kang smirk.

chapter 25

WHATEVER

For the rest of the day, Teddy Taualai doesn't speak to me. He just passes me silently, staring with his face all red. I guess he doesn't know how to be normal, so he just says nothing.

Which is kind of funny, because that's exactly what I was worried *I* would do. I thought if I admitted what was going on inside me, if I acted on it, it would ruin everything, because I would never be able to act like myself around him again.

Except it turns out I'm good at pretending everything is normal. It's Teddy Taualai who's bad at it. It's Teddy who has gone all strange and mumbly, like just the sight of me makes him flustered. In comparison I am the composed one, the one who can still meet his eyes and ask to borrow a ruler during math class, just like I would any other day. Any other day that Teddy hadn't kissed me in the empty art room.

It's Teddy who goes all red when our hands touch, it's Teddy who fumbles with the ruler and drops it, and it's Teddy who spends the rest of class with his head down on his desk and his hands in his hair, refusing to look at me.

When I think about it, though, I don't mind it, his reaction. Because it clearly wasn't nothing to him, what happened between us. And it wasn't nothing to me either.

When school finishes, he is waiting for me by my locker, his hands in his pockets and his skateboard threaded through the straps of his backpack. He smiles but I think he's still nervous. Really nervous. He keeps scuffing the tip of his sneaker against the lockers, kicking it lightly, over and over again.

"Hey," he says, and I nod at him, strangely calm, like he is sucking all the terror out of me so I can remain normal while he fidgets and freaks out enough for both of us. It almost makes me laugh, but then I think that's mean because he clearly is a bit distressed.

I open my locker and pack my bag, and then I say calmly, "Do you want to come over to my house?"

"Oh," he breathes. "But your mum?"

I shoulder my bag, shutting my locker as I turn to face him. "She works late. They both do."

He stares at me and fidgets and then finally nods. "Okay."

But his face is going red, and that makes me all flustered and I quickly add, "Just to hang out, obviously, not to, like . . ."

He coughs. "Yeah, no. Obviously."

He keeps scuffing his feet, and now I'm blushing, too. I actually want to put my face in my hands because it's all just so completely disastrous. So disastrous, in fact, that I wonder why people would ever put themselves in this position voluntarily. Staying just friends is clearly the better option. Obviously.

I'm all regretful and awkward as Teddy and I walk toward the school gates, but then I think about what happened in the empty classroom at lunch, and I know I don't want to only be Teddy Taualai's friend. Which only makes me blush harder.

We reach the train station, and now I'm wondering if him coming over to my house was a totally stupid idea. What are we going to do? Talk about what happened today? Set rules and boundaries for this new . . . whatever it is that's happening between us now? Horrifying.

Does he expect me to say I love him back?

That thought makes me freeze up.

Maybe I can just uninvite him. Or maybe he can still come but we don't need to have a conversation about what happened in the empty classroom. Maybe we can just do something else. Like watch TV.

But then that makes me think about sitting on the couch next to Teddy Taualai.

The train ride is silent and fidgety, and by the time we reach my street, the sun is sinking low between the houses. Toward the beach, the last red rays sear the clouds, reflecting on the windows as we approach my house. Soon it will be night.

I walk slowly to the door and take a deep breath before I open it.

Teddy stands with his hands in his hair, his face still a little flushed, but now he's smiling, lopsided and crooked, like he's glad to be standing on my doorstep. I don't say anything, just step aside so he can come in, and then we are in the kitchen together, him leaning across the counter and picking at a basket of cherry tomatoes as I rummage through the fridge.

"You always alone after school?"

I turn to watch him. He sounds so normal, but he's obviously being very careful about it, trying hard to appear casual. I nod. "Yeah, they're always late on weeknights."

He shoves another tomato in his mouth, looks nervous.

"Listen, Alice, I . . ."

He stops, turns away, and grabs at a piece of his hair that hangs into his eyes, twisting strands between his fingers, letting out his breath. Then he says, "What are you making?"

My heart beats faster because I know it isn't what he meant to say. "Just an omelet. You want one, too?"

He has his hands pressed over his mouth, peering at me over his fingers. "Yeah."

When the rain falls outside I think Teddy should probably go if he wants to make it to the train before the weather gets any worse, if he wants to be home before it gets fully dark.

But I don't say it aloud.

Instead I finish making the omelets, and Teddy eats his standing up in the kitchen, watching me with dark eyes as I wash up. We still don't really talk, but somehow now it's strangely calm.

And as my panic ebbs away and my tangled thoughts begin to unwind, I am noticing how different my large empty house is when Teddy Taualai's inside it. The weeknights are always so long and quiet at home, but tonight feels different.

It feels full.

It's so strange how he does it. Spending time with him, something about it calms my insides and makes things lighter.

I glance at him across the room. I like it. I like him. It bubbles up inside me, and when he finally turns his back on me I'm free to watch him, to feel the change in a way I haven't let myself feel before.

He walks around the kitchen, touching things, examining photos, just quiet and busy as I finish washing up. I keep glancing at him and find I like watching him. Something is building up in all this silence, something between us that we're both too nervous to open.

Eventually I tell him I need to study. It's either that or watching TV, and there's no way I'm going to fall behind because of this, this thing with Teddy Taualai. My parents would just love that. I gather up my bag and walk toward the dark living room, setting my books out on the coffee table in front of the couch.

Normally I would study in my bedroom. But thinking about Teddy Taualai in my room at night, when there's no one here but us . . . I think the living room is better. Only marginally better, but still.

The rain outside gets heavier, and really I should tell him to leave.

But I still don't.

Teddy hesitates in the hallway, but then the soft padding of his feet follows me through to the living room. Light spills in from the kitchen and the streetlights outside, and I reach across to turn on the light switch, but Teddy presses his hand down on mine, stopping me. His fingers are warm, and we stand in the dark, listening to the rain pelt down outside.

I know what he's going to do before he does it, his breath loud and strange in the darkness, his body silhouetted by the light still shining from the kitchen. He does it slowly this time, not fast like he did at school when he kissed me the first time. Back then it was like a rush of pent-up emotion, like a fissure in a gas tank. This time he is slow and deliberate, his mouth moving against mine and his hands reaching up to touch me, my neck, my face. I touch him, too. I like the feel of his skin; I like the shape of his jaw where his mouth is moving; I like the noise he makes when I push my fingers into his hair. I even like the way his uniform smells of grass and school and sweat.

It feels different. Like the beginning of something.

That thought makes me warm and calm, because although I'm still not sure I know exactly what love is, this is the closest I've ever come to it. It fills my body up with warmth, seeping inside my chest. It makes me feel like I'm not alone. It's also like I have no control over anything, yet somehow I don't mind. Which is strange because usually I want to control everything.

Teddy is watching me now with dark eyes. He smiles and I nod, even though I don't know why he's smiling except it must just be this moment, this feeling between us.

It makes me think of the sculpture of the couple I saw at the art gallery. It makes me think I can understand a little more of what they were feeling, or of what the artist was feeling when it was created.

I don't say that to Teddy, of course, mainly because the couple in that sculpture was totally naked, and I don't want to give him the wrong idea. After all, today is only my first kiss, or first bunch of kisses, and I'm nowhere near ready to tear his clothes off and make out with him. But then suddenly the idea that one day I *might* actually be ready for that hits me, and the thought makes me burn red and immediately wish I could unthink it.

I stand back from him quickly, trying hard to hide my flushed face in the darkness, fixing my hair and straightening my clothes.

"My parents will be home soon," I say because it's true, and not because I need to collapse on the couch and think really hard about everything that happened today.

"Oh, right. Yeah, I better go anyway." He grins at me and reaches over to flick on the light, like all his cares are over now and he doesn't need darkness to hide anything. He comes closer, his eyes shining, as he says, "Alice, you wanna go to the beach after school tomorrow?"

I nod. "For a bit. Then I have work, though."

He grins. "That's cool. I can walk you there." He watches me for a long moment and then adds in a serious voice, "See you at school."

"See you at school," I echo, and I think that's it, our good-bye, except suddenly other words are bubbling up inside me. I can't help but blurt, "Teddy, I do remember. I remember the first time I met you." .

He slows and grows still.

"It was at school, on your first day." I stare at him as under-standing slowly lights up his face. "You were being bullied. The other kids were being mean because they'd heard what happened at that stupid party. And I told you . . ."

"You told me they were all idiots. You told me to do my best," he finishes. And then he smiles at me, small and crooked, almost shy, and I'm not sure how to react to a smile like that. It makes my insides tangle and dance.

Suddenly Teddy leans in, kisses me quick on my cheek, his breath warm against my skin. Before I can say anything else he's already backing away, a hand lifted in a wave goodbye and a grin creeping across his face.

I realize we didn't really end up talking about anything at all. We didn't talk about what this is, what it means. What happens next.

We didn't talk about whether I love him.

Even so, it feels like we did, like we've made progress, like we took a huge leap forward. And instead of making me scared, I surprise myself by being glad about it. Really glad. Almost relieved, actually.

I watch him as he leaves the room, and listen for his footsteps walking down the hall and the front door opening and closing as he leaves.

I peek out the window and glimpse him disappearing down the dark, rainy street toward the train station, hands in the pockets of his jacket as he rolls casually on his skateboard. I watch him go and then sink down onto the couch.

I reach for my phone because I need to talk to someone about this; I need to explain how much everything has changed for me in only one day, how Teddy has changed it. I need someone to help me examine what I'm feeling and tell me what I'm meant to do next.

But then I remember May probably won't answer if I call her, and slowly I put my phone back down, trying not to let that bad feeling seep into today.

chapter 26

DRIFT

School doesn't change that much, even after what happened between Teddy and me. In the morning he yells my name across the whole hallway, making everyone turn. At first I'm beyond embarrassed because I think now everyone will know, that they will somehow be able to tell that he kissed me yesterday and that everything has changed. Except when everyone realizes it's only Teddy screaming stuff in the hall, no one even cares.

And that's when I remember that Teddy was always like this. Crazy.

When he reaches me at my locker, he flings his arm around my shoulders, and I totally start to shove him away but then think maybe it's weird to push him away if I already let him kiss me, if I already kissed him back.

But this *is* still school, after all.

Teddy must notice my warring emotions because he

laughs, "You don't even know what to do now, right?" And then he leans in to breathe against my ear. "Just be how you always are."

And his teasing is embarrassing enough that I push him away hard, yelling, "Get off! I'm going to class."

I stalk away down the hall with my face all hot and flustered, his laughter following me.

And then I end up doing what he said.

I just act like I always did. At lunch I sit with Teddy and Harry, and Teddy eats half my sandwich before I can stop him. Harry doesn't blink, and I know we are just the same as we always are.

It makes me wonder if that's all love is, just the same as being friends.

If that's true, I like it. It's easy and simple. The only difference between now and then is that I've kissed him. And I can kiss him again if I want to.

Which is something I think about a lot more than I'm sure I should.

Because I want to. I really want to.

And that makes me awkward all over again, and I'm sure Harry will read it written all over my face so I mumble something about the bathroom and jump to my feet, scurrying away.

I find a bathroom and disappear inside, happy that it's quiet and cold so I can calm down. I peer in the mirror for a few moments and watch as my skin returns to normal, then I smooth my hair and take deep breaths.

Just when I'm finally ready to leave, two girls come in: stupid blabbermouth Emily Cooper and some other girl I don't know by name. Emily smiles at me, her expression cold. They stand next to me at the mirror as they continue their conversation. And with every word that she says, Emily glances at me again and again with widening eyes, like she *wants* me to listen.

"That's why no one's talking to her now," she's saying, pushing her hair from her face.

The other girl gapes. "Really? Sophia must be so mad!"

"Ha! She's more than just mad. She told that slut to disappear."

"Oh my god, that's so harsh," her friend exclaims, but she's smiling, too, like she agrees with it, finds it funny. She adds, "May did deserve it. I can't believe she even did that."

"I know," answers Emily, attention trained directly on me. She looks excited. "She was always so quiet and sweet. I think she was just pretending, though. Really she's got no friends and is just a boyfriend stealer."

I stare at them, sickness spreading into every part of my body. "What are you saying?" I whisper, so quietly at first that I don't know if Emily has heard me.

But she has, because she laughs.

"You don't even know, do you? I'm not surprised. As if any-one would bother talking to you long enough to tell you."

They both giggle like that's hysterical. Then Emily informs me, "May threw herself at Finn on Saturday night. She totally tried to seduce him, right in front of Sophia!" Emily turns back to her friend and makes a face. "She wanted him to go home with her."

"What?" I whisper. "No . . . she . . . Who told you that?"

There's no way May would have tried to take Finn home to her house. Her brothers were there, and her parents. It's obviously a lie.

But I hate to admit it: there is some truth sprinkled in there, too. She did want Finn. She wanted him to like her, even though she knew he had a girlfriend. And Sophia knew it, too.

I can't believe I haven't heard about this yet. I can't believe I didn't know what everyone was saying.

And May.

I haven't seen her. Not properly.

I should have known something was wrong.

"Everyone knows about it," Emily is telling me. "The whole school. Everyone knows she's a bitch and that Finn couldn't get her to leave him alone. He told Jenny Pakulski he thinks May's a total slut."

I stare at the two girls and I don't know what to say, my mind blank as the cruel words keep tumbling from Emily's mouth. About May. About *my* May.

Emily just smirks. "Well. Now you know."

And then, finished with their hair and their giggling, they both saunter out of the bathroom, Emily glancing back at me with one last smile.

After they've gone, I just stand gazing at the empty doorway. And then after the longest time, one of the stall doors
swings open and May is standing there, holding her bag like
she was eating her lunch hidden in the stall.

"May," I breathe.

She freezes with wide, horrified eyes. "Alice. I thought
you'd gone."

She steps out of the stall and pulls the straps of her bag up
over her shoulder, walking toward the exit. Like she's seriously just going to leave.

I lunge forward and grab her arm to stop her. She freezes
when I touch her. "May! Has this been happening all week?
Have they been doing this to you all week?"

I am so shocked that I don't know what to do or say. I just
watch stupidly as she slowly turns around, her face streaked
with tears. Then she spits out, "It doesn't matter. It's got nothing to do with you!"

She pulls my hand off her arm and runs out of the bathroom.

The rest of the day is a complete blur. I don't know what I do
or who I talk to. All I can think about is May. And now that
I know, now that I'm actually listening for it, I start hearing
what everyone is saying about her. And it's so much worse
than I could have imagined.

These people I go to school with, these people I see here
every single day, the cruelty they are capable of shocks me,
and the things they all laugh about, I can't even listen to.

Maybe it was Sophia who started the rumors, or maybe it was Finn, because I hear that he's telling everyone May tried to hit on him at the party and how gross he thinks she is. And I know that's a lie, because I remember the way he was watching May on Saturday night. He didn't think she was gross then.

It makes me sick. It makes me hate Finn and Sophia.

And it also makes me think about May's words, how she said it's got nothing to do with me. Like we aren't even friends anymore. Like it's all over between us and she doesn't want to talk to me anymore.

And that hurts worse than anything else.

After school, Teddy and I go down to the beach even though it's freezing cold. I'm still not feeling great, but the wind is strong and fresh, and maybe it's making me a little better.

Teddy's all bundled up, a scarf wrapped around his neck and covering his chin and mouth. I think he looks nice like that, a beanie on his head pulled low so that mostly all that's visible are his black eyes. But I don't tell him that.

It's too cold to walk down the jetty, so we settle for the kids' playground on the shore, both of us sitting on the swings and twisting back and forth in the wind as we talk. Though mainly it's just me talking. Talking about May.

"She said it's got nothing to do with me. I don't know what to do." I scrunch up my face, thinking again about what May said in the bathroom. "She was crying."

Everything is just so twisted and wrong. Even after all these hours I still feel it, the effect of her words. Because when has anything about May had nothing to do with me?

Never.

Teddy swings next to me, watching. He doesn't say anything, just listens as I begin to slowly unravel.

"We've been friends since we were kids. She tells me everything. And people were saying things like that about her all week and I didn't even know! I didn't know."

"That's not your fault, though," Teddy says quietly. "It's obvious that Sophia and Finn are just talking shit. Everyone at school will figure it out eventually." I bite my lip as he continues. "Besides, May is the one who stopped talking to *you*. So it's obviously not your fault you didn't know. Especially after what she said at the party."

I glance over at him in surprise because he sounds angry. But what May said on Saturday must have hurt him. Because she told him he wasn't good enough.

I sigh and lean back on the swing, wondering how things could have become so twisted. I watch the sky half upside down, my hair almost trailing in the sand beneath the swings.

I guess I was angry at May, too.

Or I was until I saw her face today. Now I'm just worried about her. Listening to the awful things people have been saying has wiped everything else away.

"You okay?"

Teddy is leaning over, watching me, and I force myself to smile.

"It's just weird," I answer. "I'm used to having May around. It feels really wrong that she's going through something bad and I don't know anything about it."

Teddy shrugs. "Text her, then."

I falter. "But she said it's got nothing to do with me."

He just smiles at me and shrugs again, leaving me to decide for myself. I sit thinking about it for a while as Teddy stands up, walking over to stand behind me. He presses his hands against my back and gently pushes me, making the swing move.

"It happens, though," he says after a while. "You have close friends and then stuff goes wrong. Not all friends last forever."

I twist to glance at him over my shoulder, wondering if he's talking about himself right now. I never thought about it, but I guess Teddy doesn't talk to anyone from his old school. He would have had friends there. Once. He probably had lots of friends before he transferred here. And then he had none.

That just makes me feel worse.

"I don't want that to happen to me and May," I answer.

Teddy pushes me again and I soar higher.

"Sometimes you can't help it, though. I mean, are you planning to go to the same uni next year? Sometimes people drift apart if they don't see each other enough."

I'm surprised. "Next year?"

I guess that's true. But I never thought that we could drift apart.

"Alice," Teddy says, "what are you gonna do next year?"

He sounds funny, and I try twisting because I want to see his face, but I can't turn enough.

I pause for a long time before I answer. And when I do, my heart is thudding loudly in my ears. "Actually, I have a secret," I say. "I haven't told anyone before. Not even May."

He pauses, then asks, "What is it?"

His hands push against my back.

"I have this plan for after school. I'm going to apply to uni in the city like my parents want, but if I get in I'm going to defer."

A longer pause. His hands are warm and strong against my back as he pushes me higher. His voice sounds thick when he finally talks. "Why?"

It's my first time speaking about my plans out loud, and suddenly I am extremely nervous. But I push forward anyway. "I want to move overseas. I'm *going* to, I mean. I decided three years ago. I've been working since then to save up money so I can afford it."

The silence stretches for the longest time and then he says, "Oh."

I try to catch a glimpse of his face because he sounds weird, but I am soaring so high. I don't feel his hands on my back anymore, but I know he's still standing there, on the ground just behind me.

"Where are you going?" he finally asks.

"To South America. To Chile," I answer, dragging my feet in the sand to try to stop the swing's motion. Talking to him without being able to see his face is making me nervous. "There's a school I've applied for. You live in a dorm and teach English and learn Spanish. Like a cultural exchange. You know I've already been learning, but it'll be different doing it there."

I manage to stop the swing, a little dizzy and disoriented. I stand and twist to face him, my hands gripping the cold metal of the chains. His face is blank, making me nervous because he's so quiet.

Finally he asks, "How long will you be gone?"

I shift my feet in the sand, watching him, and for the very first time it begins to sink in that maybe he won't like this.

"Two years," I say quietly, and he stares at me.

"And when do you leave?"

I hesitate and then answer, "In four months."

He doesn't say anything else. Just stands there watching me. Then finally he repeats, "Four months. Nice."

I stare at him.

His eyebrows draw together, his eyes flashing black. "Are you fucking serious?"

I gape, unable to fill the silence drawing out between us. It lasts forever. I don't know how to fill it. I don't know anything.

When Teddy does finally speak again his voice is so quiet

I barely hear him. It takes me a moment to notice how it shakes.

"Alice, do you have any idea how long it took to get you to even notice I exist?" His voice is suddenly much louder. "Two and a half *years*." He runs his hand over his face. "Four *months*?"

He stops abruptly, breathing hard, his chest heaving and his hands balled into fists. His voice is low, shaking. "I'm such an idiot. I was thinking about—" He stops speaking abruptly and then starts again. "And you were only thinking about four fucking months."

He takes a step back from me, and I open my mouth and then close it again. I don't know what to say. Because he must be right. I must have screwed this up. Because if I loved him, wouldn't I have thought about this? Wouldn't I have understood that being with Teddy and leaving the country are two separate things that don't add up?

"Teddy," I say slowly. He stops moving away, waits to hear what I have to say, and my hands grip the cold chain so hard my fingers are turning white. "I'm sorry . . . I didn't . . ."

"No," he says finally. "You really didn't."

And then he just turns his back on me and walks away.

It isn't until later when I'm at work, much later at night when I'm alone in the foyer sitting with a coffee and waiting for the last movie to finish, that it finally sinks in. Because normally May is sitting there, too, drinking coffee beside me. And normally I would be thinking about Teddy as she talked, but I wouldn't ever admit it to her. I wouldn't even admit it to myself, holding the thought of him close like a secret.

I start to cry, and Adalina runs over and turns red and doesn't know what to do with me. She tries to put her arms around me for comfort, but she is awkward and none of it helps. And I just sit with my head in my hands and I cry and cry and cry, wondering why I never told anyone my plans for the future, wondering why I couldn't just be honest with my friends about my feelings, why it never even occurred to me.

And I wonder why I started thinking that I loved Teddy Taualai if I really don't. And I wonder if it's true that I don't, because maybe, deep down, I think that probably I do.

chapter 27

CAVES AND FISSURES

I want to fix everything. I want it so badly that I'm brave enough to stand next to his locker in the morning and wait. I wait even though his expression from yesterday is etched into my mind, and the thought of encountering that side of Teddy Taualai again, the side that is hurt and angry because of me, makes me want to run in the other direction.

But I don't, because the thing I have with Teddy Taualai is worth fixing.

When he arrives I take a deep breath, ready to tell him something, anything, so he knows how sorry I am that I'm going away. How I'm even more sorry that I can't change my mind. Because when I examined everything, that's the one thing I realized last night when I got home after work.

I can't not go.

Except he doesn't even glance at me. He walks right past to his locker like he doesn't know I'm standing there.

I'm so shocked at first I say nothing, because I'm not used to being ignored by Teddy Taualai. He's become the one person in my life who never leaves me alone no matter how much I sometimes wish he would. The one person who barges into everything I do.

To be ignored by him, for him to pretend I'm not standing right there next to him, does something dark to my guts I've never felt before—a twisting, tightening sensation that makes me want to throw up.

And then he just walks away without a word, without even a look. He just calmly takes his books from his locker and then he's gone, leaving me gaping after him.

The whole morning is horrible. Nothing works. I can't concentrate, I don't answer questions right, and all I think about is Teddy Taualai walking away from me in the hall, pretending I don't exist.

As soon as the bell rings for lunch, I try again. He walks down the crowded hallway, and I stop right in front of him. When he tries to sidestep, I grab his arm, holding him back. He looks down at me, eyes cold and hard. He snaps, "What?"

It isn't going like I hoped it would, and my mouth isn't working properly, my words caught on my tongue. "I . . . Teddy . . . about yesterday . . . it, but . . ."

He kind of laughs, and the sound of it is horrible. I stop trying to speak and just watch him, eyes wide.

"Alice, what are you gonna say? You changed your mind, you're not gonna go?"

I don't answer, because I could never say that. I have to go. I'm unable to speak.

"See?" He unlocks my fingers one by one from his arm and pushes me off. "You can't say it."

"But that doesn't mean anything. I had that plan before everything happened. It's got nothing to do with . . . this."

His eyes flash. "You don't even get why I'm angry, do you? It's not that you're going."

I blink at him, confused. "It's not?"

He leans down close so no one else can hear and I think I've never seen him so angry. "I can't believe I have to explain this shit to you, Alice. You didn't even think to *tell* me about it! You didn't think about me at all."

I shake my head. That's not it. I think about him all the time. *All* the time. He seeps into everything, even when I don't want him to.

"Th-that's not true," I stutter, trying to explain it.

"Don't even bother. I get it, okay? I get it. This whole fucking year, I was just doing this all by myself."

And then he shrugs me off, turning his back on me, and I'm left standing alone in the middle of the corridor watching him walk away for the second time today.

The next few days must be the worst of my entire life. Which is ironic because I get exactly what I always wished for. I go to school and I sit by myself, I go to work and save money for my future, and then I go home and I study in my empty house.

And no one bothers me. Or talks to me. Or asks me to do anything I don't want to do, like hang out, or go to the beach, or eat lunch together, or anything at all.

May walks around school like a ghost. She is shrunken, quiet and small. And no one talks to her. Not even Julie, who encouraged her to chase after Finn. Not even me.

I do try, once or twice. But whenever I draw close, I can't stop thinking about her words, that it's got nothing to do with me, and I wonder if she prefers it this way, if she's really still so angry with me.

So I don't end up approaching her. I just watch her move through the halls like she is sleepwalking. And the horrible rumors don't go away. They are everywhere.

I finally get up the guts to take Teddy's advice about texting her. I spend nearly an hour composing it, trying to get the message to sound right, sound normal. And then when I finally press send, it's only two short lines anyway.

Are you okay? I miss you.

She doesn't reply.

I miss Teddy, too.

At school when he passes me in the hallways, he won't even look at me, his face carefully blank like a mask. And it kills me that he won't talk to me, that every day he just pretends I don't exist, because I never thought he could be like that, so cold and distant. At first I try to approach him, try to catch him alone between classes or when he passes me in the hall. But his eyes slide over me, and it scares me to think how badly I must have hurt him for him to treat me this way.

And then, finally—because even if he does listen to me, even if he does give me the time to explain, I still don't know what I will say—little by little I find myself drawing away.

After a week, I stop even trying, though every time I see him I find it hard to breathe, a pressure building in my chest that never seems to go away.

And that's when it happens.

I'm at home in my room studying, because that's all I can do to get my mind off everything else. There's a knock on the door downstairs, and even through my doubt, it occurs to me it can only be one of them, either Teddy or May, because who else would come here? Who else would bother to visit me?

So I fly down the stairs and throw the door open, and May is standing there.

She seems smaller than before, like she's afraid of what I'll do next, and looks at me with wide eyes, like a lost puppy with nowhere else to go.

And then she bursts into tears.

Immediately I pull her indoors by her elbow and wrap my arms around her as she sobs. And in between hiccups, she manages to get out, "Alice, why are *you* crying?"

And I realize she's right. I *am* crying.

I pull her tighter and wipe my face with the heel of my hand. "Because I missed you," I answer. "Because I hate it when we fight. Because you were having a hard time and you were all alone. I'm so sorry, May. I didn't know what to do."

She pushes me back then, untangling herself from my arms.

"No, I'm the one who's sorry." She hesitates as tears well up again. "I really screwed up." She covers her face with shaking hands. "I wanted to come here every day and say that to you. Mum kept saying I should."

I shake my head. "Why didn't you? I thought you didn't want to see me."

She wipes her face, and the silence stretches between us.

Finally she says in a tiny voice, "I was scared. After what I did to you, after what I said. I was too embarrassed. Because you were right, Alice: I didn't know what I was doing. I was so stupid. And I couldn't come here and tell you because I thought you must hate me."

I shake my head. "May, I don't hate you. You're my best friend. Until Teddy, you were my *only* friend. I don't think anyone else would have put in so much effort for me. Without you I never would've had anybody at all."

I hug her again and she breaks down sobbing.

After a moment I pull her up toward my room, closing the door behind us. Even though no one else is home, this conversation feels private, like it shouldn't be happening in the wide-open space of my living room. I need to speak to her in my room, where we can be alone. Where it feels safe.

I settle May on my bed and then run back downstairs for water, and after she's drunk the whole thing, gulping it down like her tears have drained her dry, she calms down enough for me to ask what happened at the party.

Because I know something did.

May nods. "It was Finn," she whispers. "He didn't act like I thought he would." She drops her head into her hands, saying, "I'm such an idiot. I don't know what I expected. I was trying to make him cheat on Sophia. I guess that's what I was meaning to do. I don't know."

I hesitate and then ask, "So did it work?"

Hurt blooms in her eyes. "Yeah, but not how I thought. I expected it to be perfect, you know? We would kiss and it'd be romantic and then he'd choose me over Sophia and we'd start going out instead. But Alice, he just kissed me and then he got really handsy and too . . . full on. And when I didn't want to, he was just angry and drunk. He said . . . mean things. He said I was leading him on. And then he went and told everyone. Except when I started hearing all the rumors, they weren't even what happened. He just . . . made it up."

I am lost for words as May's tears bubble over again. "I tried so freaking hard to get him to like me, and I didn't even know anything about him. And I spent all this time hating Sophia even though it was me trying to do something awful to her. And I was so mean to you, because . . . because . . ."

She stops and stares at me.

"It's okay," I tell her quickly. "You don't have to say it."

"I do."

She takes a deep breath and I wince, because I already know why and I don't particularly want to hear it out loud.

Because it will hurt. But I can see she needs to say it. Maybe owning up to it is part of her self-imposed penance.

May focuses on the bedspread as she whispers, "I didn't think you were cool enough. I didn't think Teddy was cool enough. I thought you'd both drag me down, make me less popular. I wanted to impress him." She peers at her hands and then whispers, "I'm so sorry, Alice. I'm so sorry. I really hate myself right now."

I take a big shaky breath. I was right. It hurts. But I think maybe I can understand her, too. I always knew May was different from me, that she needed different things from her life than I do. And I think it's easy to make bad mistakes and thoughtlessly hurt other people when you're afraid of not getting what you want, especially if you think you can't live without it.

Like what I did to Teddy. I didn't even once think about what it would mean to him if I went away, because it's what I wanted to do. So I never even bothered to tell him.

May is still crying, so I crawl forward onto my knees, rumpling my bedspread as I wrap my arms around her neck. "What will you do now?" I whisper.

She shakes her head. "Nothing. If people want to believe those rumors, let them. I don't want anything to do with any of them. Just as long as you don't hate me, I think I'll be all right."

She pulls away and watches like she's waiting for me to speak. She looks scared.

"I said I don't." And it's true. It's so easy to make mistakes. It's so easy to hurt the people you care about, just by being selfish. I try to smile at her, and then I say, "I missed you, May."

She nods, wiping at her cheeks, smiling with relief through her tears.

And then abruptly she says, "What's going on with you and Teddy?"

I jump. "What?"

"Don't even try to pretend, Alice. You haven't spoken to him in like a week."

I am silent for the longest time and then finally I say, "No, it's him. He doesn't want to talk to *me*."

And then I tell her everything, all of it, what he said after the party, what happened at school, and how he made me feel.

And I tell her how it went wrong, how I hurt him. And as I do I feel like I'm already getting lighter just by talking, like the words leaving my mouth were heavy as lead and now that they're gone, I can finally breathe again. And mostly, it's just good not to be alone anymore.

"You're going to Chile?"

May is stunned, just like Teddy was, and I nod, regretting my silence all over again. "I don't know why I didn't tell you. It was like it wouldn't be real if I spread it around or something. I don't know. It was stupid. I didn't think about anyone else."

May's sobs return, and I'm feeling guilty all over again, but when I try to comfort her she waves me away. "Alice, it's not that! I mean, of course I'm upset that you'll be gone for so long, but I'm impressed, too."

I stare at her. "Why would you be impressed?"

"Because at least you've thought about your future. At least you have a plan." She covers her face with her hands. "Oh god, I'm such a mess. I don't even know what I want to do next year. I don't know if I want to study or work. And I spent nearly this whole year just chasing after a dumb boy instead of even thinking about the future. While you've got everything figured out."

"I don't think I have anything figured out." I bite my lip. "I still haven't told my parents about what I want to do, and they're going to be *so* mad. I don't know if they'll forgive me."

I take a deep breath. "And even though I want to go, I'm scared, too. And then all this stuff with Teddy. I just . . . I never planned for something like that to happen. It doesn't fit into what I imagined at all. And I think that must be why I ignored it, but now whenever I think about it I feel sick."

"At least you're trying." May sniffles. "At least you're *trying* to do something. I've been such an idiot. All year . . ."

Suddenly she lifts her hand, waving it as she says, "I'm sorry. I'm all right. See? I'm doing it again, making every-thing about me." She sniffs and then adds, "What are you going to do about Teddy?"

I hesitate and then shake my head slowly because I'm still so confused by it all.

"You must have hurt him really badly." Suddenly she smiles, quick like a flash of lightning across her face, just like the old May. "I should know, because Finn really hurt me. And I didn't even really know him. Which I think means I didn't really love him, either. And that *still* hurt! For Teddy this must be so much worse."

"You're supposed to be *helping*," I say.

May leans her head to one side, watching me.

"He loves you, Alice. Everyone can see it. This whole year. You're the only one who didn't get it." She sighs. "If I were you I wouldn't want to give that up, even if you do want to go overseas. He looks at you like . . ." She pauses and then smiles sadly, shrugging. "I don't know."

I don't say anything, and finally May asks, "Don't you love him back?"

Her words make me hesitate.

"I don't know."

She raises her eyebrows. "I think you do, but you're not saying it. What are you so afraid of?"

"Nothing," I answer defensively.

She just shrugs. "Then how come you've been dancing around him all year when it's obvious you like him? Why not just admit it and get it over with?"

I bite my lip. "I don't know."

"It's like you're scared of getting hurt, but it's not like you've ever been hurt before. *That* I think I could get. I'm definitely going to be a lot more careful next time, but you've never even liked anyone before. So just admit it already!"

I hesitate and then shrug. I don't even know what to say, except maybe she's a tiny bit right. Maybe I *am* afraid.

May just shakes her head when it becomes obvious I'm not going to say anything. She sighs. "Okay, try this: if you go away for two years, what if you meet someone else, someone you like more than Teddy?"

I make a face. "That won't happen."

"Two years is a long time. Anything could happen."

I shake my head, adamant. "It won't happen."

I don't know why I'm so sure about it, but I am.

May nods. "Okay, well, what about this, then: while you're away, Teddy finds someone he likes better than you."

I stare at her, silent, horrified.

May smiles. "See? *Now* you're thinking about the future. That's what Teddy was so angry about, that you never even thought about this stuff. He's clearly been thinking about it. So now he doesn't believe you like him, because if you did then you would have thought about all this rubbish by yourself, instead of having to wait for me to explain it for you." She makes a face at me. "But Teddy obviously doesn't realize what a clueless idiot you are!"

I bite my lip. Inside I'm freaking out, my heart thudding dully against my ribs. "What am I supposed to do?"

May just slides off my bed and shrugs. "Why would you ask *me* that? I have no idea what you should do."

I blink at her as she yawns and gathers up her bag.

"I made a mess out of my own stupid love life. You must be crazy to ask me for advice." But then she turns serious. "I don't regret it, though. I mean, obviously I regret how I acted and how I treated you and Teddy. But I don't regret liking Finn." She makes a face like she's not explaining it right. "No, obviously I regret liking *him*, because he's an idiot, but I don't regret that I did like someone. I think it's a good thing, to really like someone else. I think it's kind of brave to try, even if it doesn't work out, you know?"

I am impressed by May. To be so optimistic about it all, even after what happened to her, after what Finn did. She is brave. It makes me want to be brave, too, no matter the outcome. To admit what I'm feeling, instead of always trying to push it all away.

She grins at me suddenly and says, "I missed you, Alice Dyson. I'll see you tomorrow at school."

And I grin back, glad to have my old May again.

chapter 28

ORDINARY, ABNORMAL

It happened after school, when I was walking home alone.

That strange moment between Teddy and me, the moment that started everything.

When we danced together on an empty street.

All that time ago.

I'm distracted, glancing at the top of a big ship that rises high above the street ahead, the lights flashing on the cranes that line its deck as the afternoon sun shimmers, reflected in the windows.

I have my earbuds in and I'm not really paying attention to where I'm putting my feet, not watching where I am. I've walked this path a million times before, from the school to the train platform, the train platform to the school. I don't need to pay attention anymore; it's just routine.

But then I fall into step beside someone else, and we are

walking in time together naturally, the beat in my music matching their steps exactly, like some kind of minor miracle.

I glance across. It's Teddy Taualai, tall and scowling like always, except today he keeps looking at me, matching his steps perfectly to mine. Big red headphones are clamped tightly over his ears, and I wonder what he's listening to, how his music could be fitting my movements so exactly, that it could match the beat of my song.

And then, even though I've never talked to him before, even though we have no reason whatsoever to even acknowledge each other's existence, Teddy Taualai suddenly does this weird worm thing with his body, like a dance move, except it's just so ridiculous no one would ever actually copy it. Not if they didn't want to look like a complete idiot.

And when he's finished he just falls back into step beside me, glancing across and away again. I think he's sort of embarrassed.

Which he should be, because his worm dance was stupid.

I don't know Teddy Taualai. It makes no difference to me whether he does embarrassing things while he walks home after school. I don't care.

So I don't know what possesses me to do it, but suddenly I'm twirling around in a clumsy circle before sticking my hand in the air in some kind of stupid answering dance move. Which is ridiculous. I can't explain it.

And then I keep walking like nothing happened.

Teddy Taualai stifles a laugh with his hand and then does

a hopping swimming move, his finger pinching his nose like he's jumping into a pool and his other hand waving in the air.

I snort because it's hilarious, but quickly I follow him by doing scissor legs and robot arms, which has Teddy Taualai laughing so hard he has to wipe away tears.

I'm somehow triumphant about this, like I've won this . . . whatever it is we're doing. So I turn in a circle, bowing low to my adoring fans as Teddy Taualai waves his hands, fanning me like I'm a true athlete and he's my proud coach.

But then my music finishes.

And I'm left standing there in absolute silence, blinking at Teddy Taualai on the street outside my school.

Suddenly the clanging of the roadblock sounds ahead, the barriers lowering over the street to signal the arrival of the train. Teddy Taualai just stands there as I scream at him, "The *train!*"

He jerks back in surprise, but I'm already pelting away down the road, my feet slapping loudly against the asphalt. I hurtle across the street and up the concrete platform, practically throwing myself into the train just as the doors are sliding shut.

And then I'm left, sweating and exhausted, my glasses skewed and my hair a mess, wondering why the hell I was dancing with Teddy Taualai.

chapter 29

DECADES

On Monday morning May meets me at the train station near school. She's clearly been waiting for me, too afraid to arrive by herself, too nervous to face everyone alone.

But the truth is, after two weeks, it's already dying down. Well, a little bit. She has a reputation now, for being easy or something, and that seems to be sticking. But people are staring less, making fun of her less. Which I guess is progress.

May just continues to smile and pretend it doesn't bother her, her face hiding any pain she might still be feeling underneath. That makes me proud of her, because in the end she's stronger than all of them, holding her head high and ignoring their stupid gossip.

But then, things do begin to get better.

A few days after May and I make up, she tells me that Julie is talking to her again, that she came to May's house and apologized for everything, that she felt really bad for still hanging around with Finn and his group after what happened. She felt bad for leaving May on her own.

And then the unexpected happens.

Julie, pretty popular Julie, one of the coolest girls in school, stops hanging out with Finn and Sophia and Jenny, and instead she comes and sits with me and May every lunch break, sits where everyone can see her, right between the nerd and the social climber.

And of course everyone whispers and gossips, and she gets pulled down into the whole stupid rumor mill, too, added into the story of what happened that night at her party in the stupidest of ways, but Julie doesn't seem to care. She continues to sit with us anyway.

And that is when I decide that I really like Julie, because I think she is brave, too. And then Stacey Green begins sitting with us as well, and some of her friends, and little by little, things die down. Harry sits with us sometimes, too, and it's the first time I've ever seen him and Julie speak at school. It makes me like her even more, because she isn't embarrassed by him, either; she just smiles and giggles at everything he says, and all together we have fun. And it's been forever since I had fun.

Teddy never sits with us.

I think about it a lot. Trying to decide how to talk to him, what to say and how to say it, so he knows I mean it. But I get nowhere, because I don't really have an answer.

But I do decide I need to do something. May holds her head

high every day even when she's bullied, and Julie chooses friends with complications over the easier route. I need to be brave, too. Especially when May tells me she's apologized to Teddy for what she said at Julie's party. If she can do it, then I can, too.

But mostly it's the idea of ending the year without speaking to Teddy Taualai, finishing school and graduating, moving on and going overseas, all without ever fixing it with him, that drives me the most. Because I think that might actually kill me.

So I take the train to his house after school on a Thursday, over three weeks since he stopped speaking to me, and though I don't know if it will make any difference, I want to explain everything to him so he can understand. Or at least, I'll try my best to because I still have no idea what I'm going to say. And after that?

Well, that will be up to him.

The weather is slightly warmer as I walk along the road toward his house, a soft breeze floating off the river behind the looming factory. I can't help but remember the last time I walked down here with him. The words he said keep wandering through my mind.

Outside his gate, I stand for a moment and try to calm my nerves, watching a gray-and-white cat across the street as it explores a neighbor's yard.

And then I take a deep breath and march up the garden path and knock loudly on the front door. After a moment,

Teddy opens it, and I take note that he isn't that surprised to see me. I wonder if I should have come sooner, if maybe he's been expecting me to come here and try to fix it, and I feel stupid for staying away so long.

"Hey," he says.

"Hello," I answer, expecting him to move aside to let me in, except he doesn't, he just stands in the doorway watching me. That makes me nervous, and I shuffle my feet, glancing back at the cat across the street. "Whose cat is that?"

He shrugs. "I dunno. What are you doing here, Alice?"

I frown. "You know what I'm doing here," I say. But then I worry I sound annoyed. I'm here to make him less angry, not aggravate him more. "Um . . . can I come in?"

He sighs and moves aside, holding the door open so I have to squeeze past him, making me shiver when our bodies almost touch.

Inside he walks to the kitchen, forcing me to scurry to keep up. He's still angry. I thought by now he'd have cooled down, that he'd let me talk to him about everything properly. But he is silent and indifferent, and I have to work hard for every response.

In the kitchen he bangs the cupboards, putting away dishes that were drying beside the sink. He makes everything way louder than it needs to be, and I just stand there watching him.

"Where's your grandma?" I ask.

He glances at me over the kitchen island, raising his

279

eyebrows like he doesn't know why it matters. "She's playing bridge."

I blink at him. "What? Bridge, really?"

"Why? You think because she's old she doesn't go out? You think she doesn't have friends?" He sounds so irritated.

"You know I don't think that," I protest quickly, disheartened. This isn't going to be easy.

I try again. "Um . . . does she play a lot?" I try to smile, but his face stays stony and cold as he watches me.

I walk around the island to stand beside him, frustrated.

After another long moment of silence I finally ask, "Are you seriously not even going to talk to me?"

He just shrugs and backs away, crouching in front of the open fridge to do something loud and annoying in there, too. He tugs at the bottom shelf, trying to make it sit back down flat where it's slid in all wrong and crooked.

I step closer, my voice shaking. "Do you want me to leave? Is that it?"

He doesn't say anything, just keeps yanking on the stupid tray inside the fridge, and anger twists my stomach. I can't believe this is where we ended up, after everything.

"If that's what you want," I tell him quietly, my voice shaking, "then I'll go."

I make a move to leave but a ridiculously loud cracking sound turns me back. The fridge shelf has snapped, and a whole bunch of vegetables are rolling off onto the floor in a wave.

"Fuck it!" Teddy shoves it again, breaking it even more. An apple rolls across the kitchen floor toward my sneakers. He slams his palm against the broken plastic and then, like all his energy has been sucked away, he slowly sinks onto the floor, sliding until his back is resting against the cupboard behind him.

And I stop then, because it should be funny, him sitting there surrounded by vegetables and a big head of iceberg lettuce, but instead it's just sad.

He doesn't look at me, doesn't make a move to clean up, either, and for a moment I'm still thinking of leaving, but something tells me if I go now, that really will be it, and that makes me more decisive. I sink down onto the floor across from him, shoving a green pepper out of my way as I draw my knees up against my chest.

He's sitting still, watching me. He kicks the iceberg lettuce away with his foot and says, "Okay. Tell me why you want to leave, then."

I am silent. The kitchen is small, and I haven't been this close to him for weeks. And now he's sitting within arm's reach, his gaze locked on mine and his expression blank.

And I pretty much have no idea what to say.

"Um, I . . ." I close my eyes for a second and take a deep breath. "You know my parents are strict, right?"

"Uh-huh."

"So, three years ago, I wasn't doing so well in school. I mean, I was doing okay, but I wasn't at the top of my classes or anything, and they told me I'd have to transfer to a private school in the city if I didn't do better. But I was scared to go because I'm not really good with people, and I thought I wouldn't be able to make any friends. And I didn't want to leave May, and I was just scared, I guess. So I decided to work harder, because my mum said if I got better grades I wouldn't have to change schools. And that was good, but then . . ."

I pause, glancing at Teddy, who is watching me carefully. I hope this is making sense because it's not something I talk about with other people. It's not something I've even put into words before. And I want to get it right.

"So then my parents started being happy with me, for maybe the first time ever. Which was a relief, but it was difficult sometimes, too. But I wanted them to be proud of me and I wanted to stay at school with May, so I decided I could keep doing it, you know? And then, after a while, the idea of doing it forever, to have them *choosing* everything for me forever, it was suffocating."

I almost choke just thinking about it, even now. I used to get that a lot, moments where I couldn't breathe, where it felt like my lungs would collapse. But then I made my plan to run away, and those moments stopped. And everything got a lot easier to handle.

I need Teddy to understand.

"The idea of going to uni right away, of living like that for another three years. Of studying what my mother chose for me and then applying for the jobs she wanted me to, the idea of going into the city every day and working late . . ."

I stare at him, sickness sharp inside my belly just at the thought.

"I can't do it. I won't." I take a deep, shaky breath. "So I decided I had to do something drastic. And I think they'll hate me forever when they find out. But I decided to give myself two years to do what I want, then I'll come back here and live how they want me to, to make it up to them."

I hesitate, willing him to understand. "Teddy," I say breathlessly. "If I stay here, I think I'll go crazy."

And then my words run dry and I just sit there all stiff and tense, waiting for him to say something. And the whole time, he is watching me with his hands across his mouth, his eyes glinting in a way that makes me uncomfortable enough that I almost wish I could leave.

"Okay," he says quietly. "So that's why you want to go. What do you want me to do about it?"

I stare at him, wondering if he can still be angry, if he didn't understand what I just said.

I extend my foot and nudge his. Hard.

And then I take a deep breath because there's something I need to tell him. I falter, end up only saying, "I like you. A lot."

It's not what I really mean.

His eyes flick to mine and I know it's not the thing he wants to hear either. "Then why didn't you tell me about it?" Silence stretches between us until he adds, "You made me feel stupid, Alice. Like I was embarrassing myself this whole year."

"You weren't," I say. But Teddy clearly doesn't believe me, so I continue, "I don't know why I didn't say anything. Except maybe you scare me a little."

He raises his eyebrows. "I scare you?" He looks hurt.

"No, I mean . . . I'm no good at this stuff . . ."

"Clearly."

"It's harder for me to admit if I'm feeling . . ."

"Feeling what?" He watches me closely, eyes dark. Daring me.

"I already said it," I mumble, and he sighs.

"So you want to go out for the next three months because you like me so much, and then you're gonna just leave? Nice."

"No! It's not like that!"

He sits up, moves closer. "And I'm just supposed to be okay with that?"

"Teddy, please don't . . ."

He slides forward, knocking aside the stupid pepper and the green apples, coming closer.

"Okay," he says easily, but he's still pissed off, and the word hangs in the air, at complete odds with the expression on his face. His eyes burn black. "If that's what you want, we'll do that. Let's go out for your last three months." He leans in closer, smiling like he's challenging me, except even the smile is angry. "But I won't make it easy for you."

He leans closer and I don't know what he's doing, because

nothing about what he's saying feels normal or right, and I know we haven't solved anything. I know he's still angry. But it's really hard to think about what that all means when his hands are moving to my hips, and his body is so close to mine. He reaches forward and presses his open mouth down on mine, grabbing my arm and pulling me closer against him, half lifting me up to my feet, pressing me against the kitchen counter with his body.

And because I'm not thinking, because everything else except him is out of focus and not quite as important, I reach up and clutch at his shoulder, my fingers pulling at his stupid stretched T-shirt as I kiss him back. And I think this must be what they're describing when people say they lose control of themselves. I push my hand into his hair, pulling him closer, and Teddy is gasping against my mouth like he can't breathe, like I'm stealing all his air, and the whole thing is half terrifying and half amazing. Like a moment you know is a bad idea, but you just throw yourself into it anyway.

So unlike me, so unlike everything about me. Alice, who is careful and deliberate and slow.

Without stopping, Teddy has lifted me, carrying me toward the couch so he can fall on top of me, his chest hard and solid. His mouth opens against mine, his teeth, his tongue, his hands holding me closer so I can't breathe. I'm yanking at his hair, and then we have somehow fallen off the couch onto the floor, his body breaking my fall.

I almost laugh, but he catches my mouth with his, still

serious, and then he's sitting up, his kisses harder than before, and they're angry kisses, not normal ones. And his hands slide from my hips, fingers bunching up the material of my skirt, raising it higher up my thighs with each tug.

And that scares the hell out of me, because I know what he's doing right now isn't about being romantic, or liking me or even loving me. It's just about proving a point. That it won't be easy for me to be with him and then just leave when I'm done. He wants to burn himself into me so I won't ever be able to forget him.

So I shove him away, dragging myself with effort off his lap, disentangling myself from him until I'm standing near the door, my chest heaving and my legs shaky.

Teddy just sits there.

Finally he lifts himself off the floor back onto the couch, sinking down and leaning his elbows on his knees, half covering his face. He doesn't look at me.

A long silence draws out between us, and I can't drag my eyes away from him, everything inside me moving and crashing like a storm.

"Sorry," he mumbles finally, so quietly I almost don't hear him.

In that moment I know I can finally tell him. I don't know what has changed or why I know it. But I do.

I step forward, until I'm standing right in front of him, towering over his bowed head. I reach out, hesitating with my fingers just above his hair, waiting.

"I love you," I whisper. I think I've never meant anything in my life as much as I mean this.

He stiffens at my words, shifts to look up at me with dark eyes as I slowly and carefully sink my fingers into his hair.

"Really?" he asks.

"Yeah."

I flop down beside him on the couch, tired suddenly, like all my energy has been stripped away, leaving me empty like a rag doll. Leaning my head on his shoulder, I fold my arms across my body, closing my eyes. It's a good feeling to be sitting beside Teddy Taualai again. Like coming back to where I'm meant to be.

"Are you okay?" I whisper when he doesn't move, doesn't speak.

He just nods and then slowly lowers his head to rest against mine, his cheek pressed against my hair. "I missed you, Alice."

I shift to press closer against him, thinking about the future, how everything is blurred now, murky and uncertain in a way it hasn't been for years. I don't know what will happen to us, but for the moment at least, for right now, this will have to be enough.

I curl my fingers around Teddy's hand, and he squeezes back.

chapter 30

THE FINAL VIEW

Things change, little by little, as the year draws to its end.

The weather grows warmer, the air hot and dry until we sweat during our classes and swim at the beach after the day has ended.

I study hard. Probably harder than I ever have before in my life. I barely have time for anything else, but that's fine because no one else does either. It's like a void has pulled us all inside, and we only surface for air after the exams are finally done, when the true end of our high school lives is really here.

The school holds a formal dance at a convention center near the city. It's a big carpeted room with no windows, and we all sit like adults in our assigned seats, eating dinner and talking about how great school was, even the kids who never really liked it.

After we eat, everyone gets up and dances, and when I need to rest, I find Mrs. Kang to say goodbye. She smiles wistfully, asking me what I'll do next, and because I'm trying to be more open now, I tell her. When I say that art was always my favorite subject and she was my favorite teacher, I swear tears glitter in her eyes. We sit together for a long time and she tells me I should follow my own interests, that studying business or law like my mother wants would be good for career opportunities, but that there are always other options, too, options my mother still might approve of. She tells me about this dream she had when she was younger, of working in an art gallery, of organizing exhibitions from all over the world. She changed her mind in the end, decided being a teacher was her true path, but she told me that she still thinks about it sometimes.

And her words sink deep down inside me, like a seed being planted somewhere hidden. Not for now. Not yet. But later, I might examine them again. If I decide I want to.

At the formal, Harry and Julie make out on the dance floor where everyone can see, and Teddy whispers that he always saw it coming. I think May is surprised, but she manages to act normal, to dance and sit with all her friends and still have a good time.

I don't, because I feel angry for May about Finn wasting her time.

At the after-party at Stacey Green's house, I yell at Finn in front of everyone, telling him what a complete arsehole he really is. Teddy has to drag me away, and we leave the party early, him laughing hysterically the entire time. I'm not drinking, so I don't get sick on him this time, but in my room we do go further than we've ever gone before. Not all the way or anything, just . . . further. Not because I'm leaving soon or we don't have much time left or anything, but just because I want to.

It's strange when school is over, because suddenly all these people I saw every day are no longer a part of my world. I hear rumors, or see things on social media, about what people are doing. If they're going away or staying, if they were accepted into uni or turned eighteen and finally went clubbing in the city.

But I don't see them anymore.

I hear that Sophia and Finn break up. I hear Lucas is going to study some subject at a university I've never even heard of. I find out Emily Cooper is moving to London for a year. I hear a million different things, and everyone just keeps moving forward, the threads that held us together at school slowly fraying until I don't hear anything anymore.

May tried her best toward the end when exams were looming, but she's never done well in school, and her grades reflect it. She spends a tearful night at my house when she gets her results, and I think she feels lost and adrift, no ambitions, no goals, no dreams, nothing to guide her. It makes my heart ache because it's a dilemma I have no experience with, and there's no advice I can offer. There's always been a future laid out for me, set in stone by my parents so many years ago. For me the struggle was just about whether I wanted it or not.

But for May, the future is a terrifying place, not a world of excitement or possibilities. And because I don't know how to help, I just sit beside her and listen as she talks, as she tries to sort out her tangled thoughts and decide what she wants to do next.

She looks at different courses, at working for a year instead, or traveling, and in the end settles for a beauty subject she isn't even sure she wants to do.

But she tells me that doesn't matter. She can change her mind later if she has to, but for now, she just needs to do something, anything. And that will be enough.

I get accepted into my top university choice to study law. And when I defer, there's a part of me that wonders if I'll ever really come back to it, because now I've started dreaming again, dreaming of a different future beyond those two years of freedom I gave myself.

The ideas and plans are not quite there yet; they're still wispy like fog and I can't quite grasp them. But little by little they are taking form, an outline of possibilities. If I'm brave enough to choose them.

With school over, Teddy Taualai works full-time at a gas station near his house. He does the night shift, so it gets harder to see him, but I'm working, too, still at the cinema with Adalina, who decided to go back and finish her degree. I work until I can no longer stand the secret, and then finally, I tell my parents the truth.

It is everything I expected it to be and worse, because just like with Teddy and May, my silence hurts them in a way

I didn't foresee. And despite the distance that has grown between us and the lack of communication or openness, I can still feel their love for me, expressed in their anger and shock at my choice. In the end though, just like I always knew they would, they accept my decision.

But, in a way I *didn't* expect or even imagine, they listen to me.

We sit down and talk to one another in a way we haven't in years, and that alone gives me hope that one day we'll manage to repair things between us. It makes me look forward to what might happen after I return from my trip, and I wonder what we might rebuild. I decide I want to work hard at this, this tentative thing between my parents and me.

On his mum's birthday, I visit the graveyard with Teddy and his nana, bringing flowers and listening to the stories they both tell. The cemetery has red dirt and no grass, and big black ants crawl over the gravestones.

We stand in the shade of a towering eucalyptus, and I reach down and pick up a leaf off the ground, rolling it between my fingers as I listen to Teddy and his nana talk softly to the headstone. The smell of eucalyptus is strong and sharp, and when Teddy begins to cry, so do I. We stay for a long time, as the cars whiz by in an endless wave of traffic outside the gates.

Then, more than six months after I'd originally planned to, I finally say goodbye to the people I love, goodbye to my home, and goodbye to my small city beside the sea.

And I leave.

epilogue

US

I stare out the window at the night sky.

It's only small, my window, but moonlight shines through the thick layers of glass, sending dappled patterns of blue across the other passengers in the darkness of the plane. When I look closely, I can see tiny delicate snowflakes blooming on the glass outside. Extraordinary and completely unexpected. This is my first plane journey, and no one ever told me I'd see small miracles like that.

The woman sleeping beside me snorts and shifts in her dreams, and below us, so *so* far below, shimmers the ocean, all smooth surface reflecting the starlight and long blue clouds stretching out into the distance. Everyone else is sleeping, feet folded up and knees pressed against the backs of the seats in squishy economy, and even though it's the middle of the night and I should be sleeping, too, I cannot tear myself away. The world outside is magical, shiny and shimmering and blue. I've never seen anything like it, and I cannot bear to miss even a moment of this secret world.

Drawing my knees up against my chest, I pull the blanket the flight attendant gave me closer around my body, shivering as I take a sip from my water bottle. I can't help thinking about all the people at home, a warmth burning inside me because of their love, because they'll all be waiting when I've finished this adventure.

It's a good feeling. It makes me feel safe, like I know where my home is no matter how far away I've chosen to travel.

But I'll miss them, too. I'll miss my parents, despite the issues we've had, because I know how much they love me. And I'll even miss Julie and Harry.

And of course I'll miss May. Already I miss her so badly it scares me, maybe even more so because I know that I've left her adrift in the world by leaving, even though she assured me she'll be fine. She said being apart won't change our friendship, and I really want to believe her.

I glance around the silent plane as someone across the aisle coughs, shifting in their sleep. I'm nervous about my new life, but I'm excited, too. I'm excited to find out what will happen, to discover for myself what it's like to live in the world, to have adventures.

I smile and turn back to my tiny window, taking in the view of the night sky, the stars that spread across the blackness in a way you never see if you live in a city. They shine more brightly than they ever do at home, out here in the middle of the empty vast ocean.

The seats move again, and I turn as a figure leans in from the aisle in the darkness. Making a face at me, he clambers over the sleeping woman in the aisle seat and collapses into the seat beside mine. He moans, leaning to rest his heavy head on my shoulder. "Aliiiice, it won't stop moving. I feel siiiiick."

I peer out the window and shake my head. "It doesn't feel like we're moving at all, though." My voice is hushed, a whisper. "It's like we're floating."

He moans and buries his head closer into my back. "No, I can totally feel it moving." I smile and pat his hair as he moans again, glancing back through my window at the shimmering ocean outside. A shadow blooms on the surface, and I stretch my neck to peer farther down. A ship maybe? A tiny black dot all alone in the world.

I turn back. "Teddy, look, I think I saw a ship."

He barely raises his head, just groans again. I think about the airport just before we left. How my parents drove us, my mum holding me tightly and crying, telling me to stay safe. I think about how my dad took Teddy Taualai away to a coffee shop and they didn't come back for twenty minutes, and when they did, Teddy's face was pale and sweaty, and he seemed kind of ill. His nana was there, too, and she told me to take care of him and keep him safe, and I promised I would.

I glance back at him, absently stroking his hair as he moans again. "I hate flying. We should've taken a boat or something . . . I *hate* it."

"I don't," I answer, resting my cheek on top of his head. "I love it."

ACKNOWLEDGMENTS

First of all, thank *you* for reading this book. And thank you for sticking around to read my acknowledgments page. This story took a long time to get this far and I really hope it made you happy. When I was writing this novel I thought a lot about what it means to be brave and try our best, even when we don't know what we are doing. And most especially, I thought a lot about not giving up on dreams. Ever. If you are reading this, I hope you have dreams, too. And I hope you don't give up on them. I didn't. And now you are reading my book. Thank you so very much.

I want to thank my friends who have always supported me, Jess and Xzavier, Kirsty, Nicole, and Francesca. Clair and Monica. Lee. Mauro and Julie. Janine for the long and excellent story conversations. Ngaire and Teegan. D'Angelo. Thanks to the YA Circle at Dymocks (hi, everybody!) for introducing me to so many wonderful books. Thank you to my unbelievably excellent writing group, Adelaide's Novelist Circle: Helmine, Sonya, Susan, Joel, Steve, Debbie, Jen, Ros, and especially our group's founder, Sandy Vaile. I am so lucky to have found a group like this, thank you all for your time and thoughtful advice. And for teaching me EVERYTHING.

Thank you to the lovely authors I've met who have helped me, particularly Allayne Webster and Vikki Wakefield. And those whose feedback very early on encouraged me into thinking I could do this: Anna McFarlane and Jennifer Castles.

Thank you to the beautiful Art Gallery of South Australia for being one of my favorite places in the world, and thank you to the creators of the two art pieces that appear in this novel: Rayner Hoff (*The Kiss*) and Isaac Whitehead (*In the Sassafras Valley, Victoria*).

Thank you to Wakefield Press for choosing my book. Especially, thank you to my editor Margot. Seeing my story change with your time and help has been a truly amazing experience.

Thank you to Arts SA and Adelaide Writers' Week for short-listing this book in the 2018 Adelaide Festival Awards for Literature, which paved the way for it to be published.

Thank you to my cool family, Jools, Ima, and Ozi, and all the extended peeps both here in Oz and back in Ireland.

Finally, my dad. Thank you for all of it. Thank you for believing in me and helping with everything. And thank you for being my dad.

And for my mum who loved me and gave me everything, I'm lucky because I know how happy and proud she would be. Thank you for being my mum.

And to Gus, where everything begins and ends. I adore you. Without you my life would be very different (it would be stupid). Thank you for believing in me and always looking after me.

I love you.

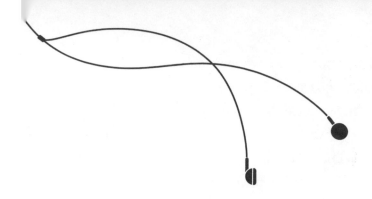

ABOUT THE AUTHOR

POPPY NWOSU grew up in central North Queensland, Australia. After studying music, she moved temporarily to Ireland. *Making Friends with Alice Dyson*, her debut novel, was short-listed for the Readings Young Adult Book Prize. She lives in Australia with her husband.